10/2018

PEOPLE
KILL
PEOPLE

ALSO BY ELLEN HOPKINS

PEOPLE

KILL

PEOPLE

ELLEN HOPKINS

Margaret K. McElderry Books

NEW YORK   LONDON   TORONTO   SYDNEY   NEW DELHI

MARGARET K. McELDERRY BOOKS I An imprint of Simon & Schuster Children's Publishing Division I 1230 Avenue of the Americas, New York, New York 10020 I This book is a work of fiction. Any references to historical events, real people, or real places are used fictitiously. Other names, characters, places, and events are products of the author's imagination, and any resemblance to actual events or places or persons, living or dead, is entirely coincidental. I Text copyright © 2018 by Ellen Hopkins I Jacket illustration by Greg Stadnyk I Jacket hand-lettering by Krista Vossen I Jacket photographs copyright © 2018 by Thinkstock I All rights reserved, including the right of reproduction in whole or in part in any form. I MARGARET K. McELDERRY BOOKS is a trademark of Simon & Schuster, Inc. I For information about special discounts for bulk purchases, please contact Simon & Schuster Special Sales at 1-866-506-1949 or business@simonandschuster.com. I The Simon & Schuster Speakers Bureau can bring authors to your live event. For more information or to book an event, contact the Simon & Schuster Speakers Bureau at 1-866-248-3049 or visit our website at www.simonspeakers.com. I Book design by Greg Stadnyk I Manufactured in the United States of America I First Edition I 10 9 8 7 6 5 4 3 2 1 I Library of Congress Cataloging-in-Publication Data I Names: Hopkins, Ellen, author. I Title: People kill people / Ellen Hopkins. I Description: First edition. I New York : Margaret K. McElderry Books, [2018] I Summary: Follows six teenagers as they are brought into close contact over the course of one tense week, in a town with political and personal tensions that build until one fires a fatal gunshot. I Identifiers: LCCN 2018013335 I ISBN 9781481442930 (hardback) I ISBN 9781481442954 (eBook) I Subjects: I CYAC: Novels in verse. I Interpersonal relations—Fiction. I Prejudices—Fiction. I Violence—Fiction. I Firearms—Fiction. I Classification: LCC PZ7.5.H67 Peo 2018 (print) I DDC [Fic]—dc23 LC record available at https://lccn.loc.gov/2018013335

This book is dedicated to the far too many victims of gun violence, and to the loved ones who grieve for them. Sending love and light, with a special nod to the young people taken too soon.
The future expected you. Now it mourns for you.

AUTHOR'S NOTE

I grew up with guns. My dad, who was both a hunter and an avid collector, taught me to respect firearms. I am, in fact, an excellent shot and at another time in my life enjoyed target shooting. Today, however, I don't own a gun and, as an animal lover, would only hunt if it was that or go hungry.

I respect the Second Amendment. But we must address the gun violence problem in the United States. Statistics show a steep rise in gun-related deaths and injuries since 2014. In 2017, as of November 6, more than 13,000 people had died as a result of non-suicide gun violence.* With an average 93 Americans killed by guns every day,** the year-end total would be around 18,000 non-suicide gun deaths, up 4,000 from 2016. (Suicides generally account for 62% of gun-related deaths,*** which would put the total figure at more than 47,000.) Mass shootings (three or more deaths per incident) also show a precipitous upward trend. Young people are often involved, both as victims and perpetrators.

While the outcome of stricter gun control continues to be debated, I felt it was important to try and understand why someone might be compelled to pull the trigger. This is what authors do: we ask why. Why are people prone to violence? Why do people seek revenge? Why do people hate or fear or despair? Why do people kill people? If we can understand the whys, perhaps we can begin to solve the problem.

The characters you'll meet in these pages have powerful life situations driving them in negative directions. Any one of them, in a precise moment in time, might decide to pick up a gun and fire it. If they seem familiar it's because they are, at least in some small way, inspired by stories that pop up in news feeds every day. They are fictional, but real.

Disclaimer: their views do not reflect my own.

---

*   Data from the Gun Violence Archive
**   Data from the U.S. Centers for Disease Control and Prevention (CDC)
***   Data from the CDC

Guns don't kill people.
People kill people.

YOU

Yes, you.
Come here.
Please? I need
to ask you something.

Have you ever felt the desire
to hurt someone?
I mean pummel them,
wound them, watch
them bleed?

Did you?
Would you?
Could you?

If I were the gambling type,
I'd put my money on "yes."

See, there's this thing inside
every one of you,
the collective human call
toward violence.
All it takes is one singular
moment to encourage
it into play

and the lamb
transforms
becomes
the lion.

TAKE IT ONE STEP FURTHER

Have you ever thought
about killing someone?
I mean, poisoning them,
bludgeoning them, grabbing
a well-honed knife
and carving them into pieces?

Chances are you haven't,
wouldn't, couldn't
follow through.

Contemplate.
What's required
to become the catalyst
for death?
A moral compass, sprung
and spinning haywire?
Antifreeze, flowing
through your veins?

Or, perhaps, nothing more
than circumstance?

In that instant when the lamb
unleashes its roar,
would you heed
the call or instead defer
to the quivering
voice of reason?

LIKE DAWN AND DUSK

Existence and demise
are inextricably linked
as per the Grand Scheme
either drafted by some
all-powerful architect,
or randomly designed.

Perhaps this is the true
knowledge of Eden—not
the mechanics of procreation,
but the promise that one's time
on earth is nothing more
than a journey toward
inevitable departure.

Surely the ancient ones
who bore witness to birth
in the wilds, and death
from claw or club or predation
by creatures too small
for the eye to identify,
were aware of nature's plot.

As their spines uncurled
and they drew upright to run,
discovered the value of flint,
the power of spear and arrow,
the lust for blood billowed
like a black-bellied cloud. Oh,
to wield a weapon mercilessly,
extinguish a beating heart.

THE MILLENNIA CREPT FORWARD

Dawn to dusk to dawn
to dusk, and humankind
shed its fur,
fashioned clothes,
deserted its caves
in favor of villages, cities.

But even as people
learned to plant,
harness sunlight
and rain to nurture
garden, fields,
their passion
for the hunt remained.

They killed
in the name of
survival,
protection,
vengeance.

They killed
in response to
lust,
jealousy,
despair.

They killed
for the thrill,
the simple pleasure
of witnessing bloodshed.

THINK

For one delicious moment
how they would have watched
in wide-eyed reverence
the advent of gunpowder,

marveled at the fire lance,
its relentless evolution

from crude spear-driven
flamethrower
into a fierce weapon
able to discharge one thousand

flesh-ripping metal projectiles
in sixty lethal seconds.

Ponder their amazement
at a machine with the ability
to level entire villages, infant
to ancient, in mere minutes.

They would've fallen on their knees
and lifted their arms in worship.

Now you understand the talent
of a firearm. But perhaps
you're unaware of the force
fueling its seductiveness.

YOU KNOW HOW

Sometimes you hear a whisper
fall over your shoulder,
but then you turn to search

for the source, find nothing
but landscape behind you?

So then you tell yourself
it was just a case of hyperactive
imagination, convince

yourself that sentiments
don't materialize out of thin air.

But the truth, at least as I like
to tell it, is that the voices
who speak to you from inside

your head have taken up
permanent residence there.

Some shout warnings, prodding
you to take cover, flee,
or brandish a weapon.

Others murmur, haunting
you with poetry.

Like mine.

YOU SEE, LIKE A GOD

I am nothing
without you.

Nothing but energy
in need of a vessel
capable of action,
and an intellect
able to form and follow
through with a plan.

Often, you will ignore
my pleas, feign deafness.
Ah, but I am relentless.
I know you can hear me
and sooner or later
you'll heed my call.

Unarmed,
we are formidable.
High tide
chewing into the sand.

Oh, but weapon in hand,
we are inexorable.
A tsunami battering
the breakwater.

BECAUSE WHAT IF

A few of those rumblings
inside your brain
aren't make-believe at all?

What if they could be the inspired
ramblings of an alien
creature, not flesh and bone,

but rather the embodiment
of a raging primordial power
dwelling within your synapses?

What if it's *my* murmuring you hear?
I am the voice of Violence.
You know me. You do.

I've made my presence clear
though you may pretend otherwise.
We need each other, you and I.

We're conjoined. Consider, if you will,
the notion that a similar symbiosis
is in play when it comes

to the oft-embraced theory
of daily communion
between man and a higher power.

PLEASE ALLOW ME

To introduce you to a partner
of mine. No, more than that.
A friend.

Meet Ruger LC9s Pro,
9 for short.

Light.
Compact.
9 millimeter.
Striker-fired.

> No hammer required,
> nor external safety.

Effortless.
Efficient.
> Nothing to slow you down.

Six inches in length,
weighs just over a pound.
Easy to hide.
Easy to hold.

> Even a child
> can cradle it in tiny hands.

Its magazine carries eight rounds,
more than enough ammo
to stop someone dead
in their tracks

if you've got decent aim.

Practice makes perfect.

Want to know a secret?
This piece doesn't even require
a magazine locked
into place.

All you need
is a single bullet,
chambered.
Hibernating.

Awaiting release.

If you don't understand
all those details,
not to worry.
In essence,
it's rapid-fire.
Simple to use.

A sexy little plaything.

At the ready.
Hold steady.
Draw a bead,
give a gentle squeeze.

And you will know power.

OUR MUTUAL HISTORY BEGINS

Quietly enough, with a series
of neighborhood break-ins,
the kind that rarely
even make the news.

9 was purchased,
brand spanking new
from Tombstone Tactical,
a totally legal,
federally licensed
Arizona gun store.
Protection was Zane's plan.

Now, it's possible I floated
a spore of mistrust
on the Sonoran Desert breeze.
Zane was ripe for convincing.

You see, Zane and Renee,
his loving wife
of forty-six years,
lost their only child
in the Persian Gulf War.
With fewer than four hundred
Americans killed in Desert
Storm, the odds of that were slim.

But Zane didn't accuse Fate.
No, he laid the blame
square on the *goddamn Iraqis*.
They sent his boy home in a coffin.

IN THE ENSUING YEARS

Zane mentally catalogued
every terrorist attack,
every crime attributed
to Middle Eastern monsters.

As he aged, edging further
and further away from mental
acuity, his neighborhood
closed in around him,
becoming ever more diverse,
and with the growth
came an inevitable uptick
in petty crimes.

I wormed inside
his brain, growled,

> *Punks moving in.*
> *Forewarned*
> *should be*
> *forearmed.*

The emphasis was on
the "armed," and Zane
understood completely.

As he got into his car
for the trip to the gun
shop, I urged him to,

> *Look. Practically right*
> *next door. Jihadists.*

He stewed for the entire
drive. I rose up
and reminded him,
>Who knows what those
>people are up to?
>Stay wary. Don't be
>taken by surprise.

As Zane wandered
the store, fondling
firearms, I spoke
for them by proxy.
>Touch me.
>Own me.
>Hold me, feel
>the weight of me.
>I will comfort you.

When he first hefted 9,
and the dealer explained
its myriad advantages,
I prodded,
>Feel that twitch
>below your navel,
>where everything's
>been silent for years?

He felt it.
He liked it.

ON HIS WAY HOME

Zane had to drive past
his new neighbors' house
and he cruised slowly,
observing. Gathering
information. Facts.

He could tell they were
young because of the baby
stroller parked by the front
door. Or maybe that was
just a red herring.
A suicide bomber disguise.

A chill sweat trickled
down his face from his brow.
He reached over and patted
the box containing 9,
and he felt a whole lot better.

Once he parked his car,
Zane hurried inside to load
his newfound best friend,
and was doing just that
at the kitchen table
when Renee ambled in.

                    Her eyes widened to
                    the approximate size
                    of small saucers.
                    "What are you doing?"

"What's it look like?
I'm loading my gun.
No damn punks gonna
come along and take me
and you by surprise."

       "Zane, dear, do you really
       think . . . ," Renee protested.

Guns made her nervous,
and her husband had shown
troubling signs of instability
since his retirement,
almost ten years back.

       "Now you listen here, old woman . . ."

His favored term of endearment.
He seemed to have forgotten
he was older than she.

       "You know those people, the ones
       who moved in down the block?
       I've been keeping an eye on them."

He lowered his voice, as if
those people could hear.

       "I think they're jihadists.
       Sure looks that way to me."

ZANE WAS NO DUMMY

He viewed Fox News whenever
he grew tired of game shows.
He watched lots of those.

His favorite was *Let's Make a Deal*,
even though the new version
couldn't touch the one on TV
when he was a kid. Good old Monty
Hall. "Behind door number three . . ."

Zane always picked door
number three because
three was his lucky number.

Reel the fool in. That was
Renee's thought and she gave
it the old country try.

> "I don't believe they're jihadists.
> I ran into the lady at the library, and—"

> "Terrorists *do* read books, you know.
> How else would they learn to build
> those incendiary devices?"

Zane loved the stuff he picked up
listening to his favorite pundits.

> "You missed my point completely,"
> answered Renee. "I meant the woman
> was kind. Articulate."

"Now you're saying Muslims
are uneducated? They force-feed
them schooling, so they're smart
enough to sneak into this country
and murder us infidels."

Renee wanted to say "Muslim"
wasn't a synonym for "terrorist,"
any more than "educated"
was for "smart."

But her husband was on a roll,
and she knew him well enough
to understand when his mind
was made up, and it sure
sounded like it was, she had
zero chance of swaying him.

Rather than try, which would
launch an argument. She simply
said, "Quite right, dear."

OFF THE HOOK

Zane drifted unencumbered
through
his pond of paranoia.

He maintained diligent watch
noting
license numbers and suspect

descriptions any time there was
movement
at the house down the block.

He jotted them down, patiently
awaiting
the action he suspected was imminent.

When all remained quiet, he would
return
to the comfort of his recliner and TV.

But he always kept vigilant because no
goddamn
punks were going to catch him unaware.

Every now and then, he would lift 9
from its favored
spot on the end table next to his chair,

slide his hand along the barrel, and
reassure himself
with a loving caress that all was well.

YES, HE KEPT

His loaded handgun
right there. Why not?
There were no children
in the house, and Renee
was wise enough to ignore
the weapon's presence.

Zane wanted his equalizer
within easy reach, in case
of attack. Unfortunately,
however, it wasn't punks
who surprised him.

Renee had gone to visit
her sister for the weekend
so Zane spent Friday night
tying one on and watching
cheap-thrill movies on HBO
until he fell asleep in his chair.

He had no clue that after
several delays Renee's flight
had been canceled.

It was well past midnight,
and rather than call and wake
the old man, Renee came on
home, pausing on the unlit
front step to wrestle
her keys from her purse.

ZANE WAS SNORING

In his recliner, dreaming
Monty Hall had picked him
out of the *Let's Make a Deal*
audience. He was dressed up
like a rooster, and when
Monty asked him to choose
a door, he shook his tail
feathers. "Number three!"

Before the pert blond up
onstage uncovered his prize,
she had to open the other
doors-to-riches first.

Behind number one:
a new dishwasher.
Renee might like that, but
this was his round to play.

Behind number two: a pony.
Zane could almost smell
the new car waiting for him
behind that third door.

Even in sleep, he started
to drip anticipatory sweat.

The studio noise crescendoed
as Monty offered him five hundred
dollars to give up the prize
behind door number three.

JUST BEFORE

He heard the sirens,
a thought crossed Zane's
admittedly skewered brain.
I know because I put it there.

End it all right now, right here.

I almost convinced him.
What was life, without Renee?
Fast food, beer, and TV viewing
from the depths of his recliner?

You will die all alone.

One bullet left, he lifted
9 all the way to his right temple,
placed the gun against the soft
pulsing there, and I cheered.

Do it now! They're almost here.

But he heaved a giant sob.
"No. Can't. They'll think it was
murder-suicide. Planned."
He didn't want them to believe

she might have deserved it.

"No!" yelled Zane. "I want
the car!" The audience
started to chant, *Car, car, car.*
and the blond reached
out, ready to reveal . . .

Meanwhile, on the front
step, Renee fumbled
her key into the lock . . .

On *Let's Make a Deal*,
door number three opened
and out jumped . . .

"Punks!" Zane startled
awake. "Goddamn ISIS
punks! What did you do
with my car?"

The front door began to
swing open. To be fair,
it could've been punks.

TRUTHFULLY

In that instant,
fear drawn up
from the belly
like water from a well,
it didn't matter
who was rattling the lock.

Zane's hand closed around
9, his finger found
the trigger, and just as Renee
stepped across the threshold,
no safety to get in the way,
Zane squeezed.

Once would've been enough,
but he emptied
the magazine,
eight bullets fired
in rapid sequence,
and damn, it felt great.

To me.
To him.
At least,
until he saw
who lay bleeding out
on the floor.

TOO LATE

Zane understood
the seductiveness of power.

Too late
he realized total control
is a myth.

Too late
to help Renee, he punched
911 on the phone and stuttered,

"H-hurry! I th-think I k-killed
my w-w-w-wife."

He didn't notice
her lungs expel
their final exhalation.

Didn't see the shadow
slip from her shell and dissipate,
the tarried release of soul.

He never got the chance
to say goodbye
or tell her he was sorry.

By the time responders
arrived at the scene,
Renee had arrived in the afterlife.

THERE WAS SOME DISCUSSION

Among those who came
to investigate. Was there,
perhaps, more to the story
than just a terrible accident?

But Zane was legit shaken,
and his only previous run-ins
with the law were traffic violations.

Family and friends were unaware
of any marital problems,
and neighbors rarely heard
raised voices.

Renee's planned flight
had, indeed, been canceled,
and there was no record
of a phone call warning Zane

that she'd be home early.
He was cleared to go on
with his life, and 9 was released
back into his custody.

But after Renee's funeral,
Zane didn't much care about punks
anymore, so he listed the gun
in the classifieds, sold it cheap.

No questions asked.

NO QUERIES

About qualifications:
Age
Residence
Knowledge of weapons
History of domestic violence
or mental illness

No queries
about affiliations:

        Church
        School
        Clubs
        Political party
        White separatist organizations

No queries
about details:

        Registration
        Concealed carry permit
        Safe storage options
        The advisability
        of a trigger lock

No queries
about motive:

        Target practice
        Competition
        Self-defense
        Revenge
        Suicide

THE ONLY THING

Zane cared about
was making back
a decent percentage
of his four-hundred-fifty-dollar
original purchase price
for a handgun fired
exactly eight times.

Cash offers only.

The first person who
came along was pretty
young, but looked
old enough to qualify
as an actual adult,
and the explanation
for wanting a gun—
staying safe from bad
guys—seemed legit.

Zane never mentioned
Renee. Or punks.

Anyway, the kid had three
crisp hundred-dollar bills,
which proved close
enough for Zane,
who handed 9 over,
ammo included, then
made a beeline down

the road to Plaza Liquors
and Fine Wines, hands-down
the best liquor store in Tucson.

Zane figured he might
as well drink himself
into a premature grave.
He'd emptied his house
of all that really mattered,
carved up his heart,
hollowed out whatever
piece of a person
harbors one's soul.

His plan was to sit there
in his chair, pickling his liver
until the Grim Reaper
showed up at the door.
He never gave another
thought to the person
who carried his ex-equalizer
clear across Tucson sprawl
to a decent little tract house
in a usually quiet neighborhood.

That's how my dear friend
9 wound up here.

FIVE FLAGS

Have flown over Tucson.
Old Glory.
The State of Arizona.
The Confederate.
Spain's.
And Mexico's.

The city's rich, fierce history
has made this desert
way station an inviting place
to spend a fair amount of time.

The first visitors
were Paleo-Indians,
who wandered through
millennia ago, stopping
to farm the fertile floodplain
of the Santa Cruz River.

By the time the Spaniards
put down roots here,
this was Apache territory.
I sprouted roots, too.
Neither mission nor fortress
was immune to attack.
Oh, the bloodshed!

Eventually, Spain cut Mexico
loose and this stretch
of sand became part of the state
of Sonora, only to be captured

by the Mormon Battalion
during the Mexican-American
War. They returned possession
as they continued marching west,
but not without casualties.
They kept me busy.

With the Gadsden Purchase
much of Arizona belonged to the US,
and Tucson became the western capital
of the Confederate Arizona Territory.
Hurray for the Civil War,
and the California Column
that drove those Southern boys out.

Now conflict is primal and vicious
and gory. Completely human,
and as people left homes
in the East to settle
the West, they packed up
their bloodlust,
brought it with them.

As a stagecoach and railroad stop,
Tucson was ripe for robbery,
murder, and Indian attacks.
Legend has it Wyatt and Virgil
Earp avenged their brother
Morgan's killing right there
on the train tracks.

Shoot-outs, duels, and armed
insurrections. You can see why
I've always felt right at home here.

THE CITY TODAY

Doesn't try to escape its heritage.
In fact, it displays it proudly.
It isn't far to the Mexico border,
and the population is almost evenly
split between whites and Latinos.

Some neighborhoods are called
barrios, and downtown is the Presidio.
You don't have to be Mexican
to shop at one of their many mercados
(markets), you just have to like the food.

The state of Arizona clings proudly
to its Wild West reputation,
but Tucson and Pima County
share a more modern outlook,
bucking the statewide trend.

Still, the area has drawn the attention
of the white nationalist movement,
which has infiltrated successfully,
building a philosophical crusade
at odds with the prevailing will.

And, regardless of any facade
of civilization, slumbering
within the fallow flesh of every
human heart is a seed of savagery.
All it takes to sprout is circumstance.

SO, JUST FOR KICKS

Let's play a game.
We'll call it Arizona Roulette.
Nice ring, don't you think?
And you get to participate.

The rules are simple.
I'll introduce you to the players
whose skins you will slip into.
You didn't believe I'd let you
off easily, did you? Oh, not at all.
This will be an interactive experience.

All are connected, through love
or hate, work or school, by family
or friendship or marriage.
Each possesses an incentive
to pick up a gun, pull the trigger.

They're my kind of people,
to a one willing—even eager—
to answer my rap on the glass
and crack open
the windows to their souls,
allow me inside to take up
residence in their parlors.

It's a waiting game.
Simply a matter of time
until my incessant whispering
becomes impossible to ignore.

So, walk in their shoes.
Trace their threads
through the narrative
weave, then you decide
who will be the one
to succumb to my call.

See, I've got this theory.
Given the right circumstances,
any person could kill someone.

Even you.

SPOTLIGHT: **RAND**

Rand Bingham is a responsible guy.
He was just barely sixteen, and
Cami only fifteen, when they found
themselves in a family way.
Rand did right by the girl.

He married her,
because that's what a reliable
kind of guy should do,
and because, yeah, he loved her.

That strong moral sense
didn't come from Rand's mom,
a bitter alcoholic who found out
about the impending nuptials
when her invitation arrived in the mail.
It was sent at Cami's insistence.

Rand's old-school dad sat him down,
helped him map out a plan.

> "Lead guitar is not a viable future
> for a young family. Beyond music,
> what can you see yourself doing?"

Rand had given it some thought.
"I'm considering law enforcement."

It's been in the back of his mind
for quite some time.

He wants to be a cop.
He wants to take out bad guys.
He wants to settle a very old score.

But Arizona's got standards,
and you have to be twenty-one
to graduate the police academy.

So until he's old enough,
he's getting a leg up on
his education, taking classes
part-time at Pima Community College,
studying criminal justice.

Plus, he's working construction,
putting in as many hours
as are reasonable for
a student, husband, and father.

So, yeah, he's absolutely responsible.
But he's only nineteen.
And once in a while he just wants
to feel like a teenager again.

Fade In:
SLIP INTO RAND'S SKIN

It's Friday evening, capping off a very long week. Scratch that. An excruciatingly long week. Sometimes you feel forty, but you're not even half that. Sometimes you think that, at nineteen, you've put in more working hours than someone twice your age, for very little return. With luck, things will get better once you're cruising in your patrol car, hunting bad guys.

I summon your attention. Hear my voice.

> *Patience, my friend.*
> *Your effort will be rewarded*
> *when you take down*
> *the bastard who shredded*
> *your childhood*
> *with a single perverted act.*

"Hey, baby. I'm home," you call as your feet cross the threshold.

"Take off your shoes!" Cami yells from the back bedroom.

Routine. You unlace your boots, step out, and leave them by the front door, where the heavy-duty mat can catch the sand and sawdust clinging to your soles and pant legs. Even that small gesture makes you feel ten pounds lighter.

Cami wanders out from Waylon's room, carrying the toddler, who sports red eyes and snot-encrusted nostrils. When the boy sees you, his hands telescope out, palms up, little fingers wagging in invitation. "Daddy!"

Even if you thought you had a choice, you wouldn't say no, but you idolize your son, so it's a slam dunk. Your shoulders are weary, and your arms ache from swinging a hammer half the day. But you open them anyway, fold Waylon into them, ignoring the crustiness. This kid is the best thing in your life.

Your boy pouts a kiss against your lips, puffing a vague scent of onions. "You been feeding the kid McD's again?"

Cami shrugs and weathers your glare. "We had playgroup there today. It was just a cheeseburger."

"That crap is garbage. Ground-up rat meat and fake cheese. Don't suppose he ate fries, too?"

"Fries!" agrees Waylon. "Yum."

The tension falls away, dissolved in your son's enthusiasm, and you sigh. "You're gonna turn the boy into a regular porker. Besides, he's sick. I bet your friends didn't appreciate you jump-starting an epidemic."

Cami rolls her eyes. "All the kids had the bug. We were boosting their immune systems. Anyway, why are you so pissed? Hard day?"

Go ahead. Tell her
every single day

is a fucking hard day,
and she doesn't make them
any easier.

Nah. You kind of want to get laid tonight. At least, if you can find the energy. You put Waylon down on the floor in front of his Little People farm, and the boy picks up the Guernsey, gleefully repeating, "Moo says the cow."

With his attention focused on the barnyard, you sidle over to Cami, coax her tight little body against your bulk. Your chin brushes her champagne-colored hair, and the scent that rises is cinnamon apple.

"Sorry, babe," you whisper into its silk. "I love you."

She turns her face up to look into your eyes, grins. "You just want to get laid." But she rises up onto her tiptoes, licks her delicate lips before kissing you.

The gesture moves quickly from "sweet" to "boner-worthy," and as your tongues collide, you lift her off the floor. Another time, you'd carry her into your bedroom. But Waylon interrupts. "Rooster says cocka-doodle-doo-doo!"

Cami's glittering laugh joins your unscripted guffaw. It was almost as if he purposely crafted the innuendo, though of course that's impossible. He's one smart kid, but he hasn't reached stand-up comic status yet.

Finally, your sexy woman wiggles out of your embrace. "Go get cleaned up and I'll feed Waylon."

"You're not going to feed *me*?" you sniff.

Cami shoots you a *seriously?* look. "You forgot, didn't you? We're supposed to go to the Rock tonight. It's Grace's birthday, remember?"

Grace is your stepsister, and as no-DNA-in-common family goes, you're close. She's the younger sibling you always yearned for as a kid, and you're more than a little protective of her. But all you want to do right now is eat in front of the TV, then play a few games of Sniper Elite on the Xbox.

"You don't think we could back out of it, do you?"

Cami's eyes narrow into dark topaz slits. "Only if you want to hurt her feelings and make me mad. I've been stuck playing 'mama' all week. I want to shake my butt to some decent music."

She puts her arms in the air, rotates her hips in spectacular fashion, reminding you of why you fell so hard for her. The first time you saw Cami, you decided she was the perfect girl, one you wanted to hang on to forever. Caught up in the daily tedium, it's easy to forget those feelings.

It's really not fair, is it?
You should be chilling
with your friends.

Kicking back, enjoying life.
Instead you're stuck here,
forced into staid adulthood,
and it's all her fault.

Waylon whoops, "Mama dancin', Daddy." The boy jumps to his feet and joins in, singing along to an imaginary Beyoncé track, melting your heart like gum on August asphalt.

But that begs the question, "Who's gonna watch the kid tonight?" Grace usually babysits on the admittedly few evenings you manage to invest a few bucks in recreation.

Cami quits her gyrations. "My sister."

Your muscles clench into hard knobs. "Seriously? That's not such a great idea, is it? I mean . . ."

Cami knows what you mean. "It's only for a few hours, and Noelle's solid. Her new meds kicked in great and she's been seizure-free for weeks. She's even applying to colleges."

"It's just . . . that one time . . ."

Was scary as hell. Noelle and you were sitting around, playing a car-racing game. All was well, or so it seemed, until her Camaro shifted into overdrive.

One minute Noelle was happily cheering on her stock car, the next she was jerking around on the floor, looking one hundred percent like a live toad tossed into a hot frying pan.

Her eyes kept blinking, blinking, as if she was trying to understand exactly what she was seeing, and she mumbled incomprehensible gibberish as spit-foam frothed from the corners of her mouth.

You had no idea what to do, other than let the damn seizure run its course. It only took a few minutes, and as her muscles quit twitching, she kept asking, "What's that smell? What's that awful smell?" Even then, just after the main event, she wasn't what you'd call "there."

She kept reaching out, trying to pet the "kitty-kitty," only there was no cat, and when you tried to explain that, she insisted, "The gray tabby, right there, sucking its tail." That was scarier than the twitching.

Later, Cami explained that they'd had a gray cat when they were kids. A big fixed male, who satisfied his angst by giving oral to his tail. You haven't look the same way at cats since then. Little Waylon better not ever ask for a kitten. A puppy, maybe. One day. Every boy needs a good dog.

Tonight, you have no real choice when it comes to a babysitter, and at least Noelle works for cheap. "Fine. But I can't dance on an empty stomach. Just so you know, I'm starving." It's true, and happens too often, going straight from an early morning class to work, no time to make lunch before you leave home, nor stop for a bite in between.

Cami paints on her prettiest smile, meaning sarcasm to come. "We could always stop by McDonald's on the way. Only no fries for you."

"No fries for Daddy!" agrees Waylon. "Only fries for me!" And he launches into an off-key version of some Miranda Lambert ballad, crooning into an imaginary microphone. God, your boy is amazing, better than might be expected from parents so young.

Cami's taste in music is eclectic, and that's a good thing, but if your son is to listen to metal, you'll have to play it. Maybe one day the kid will have his own band, so you might as well teach him the good stuff. You aren't exactly an expert, but you've played guitar since you were little.

It started with *Guitar Hero*, and when you begged to learn how to play the real deal, your dad signed you up for lessons. Your mom only laughed into her Tanqueray. "Don't be stupid. You're about as musically inclined as a chimpanzee." She was, and remains, a bitch.

I'll show her! That's what you thought, and repeated it over and over in your head, like a mantra. Though you were not a natural talent, through hours and hours of practice, determination made you better than competent. "You could play lead in a band," your teacher vowed. "Just steer clear of drugs. Drugs always take the best ones down."

No drugs. No alcohol. Not even tobacco. Most of your friends moved into that space and called you a loser, but you had goals and stayed focused on your music, and believed what your teacher told you. Until the talent show.

Playing in your room was one thing; in front of a crowd, even a small one, was something else. Unfortunately, your mom was in the audience when you walked out on that stage, picked up your guitar, took a long look at all those expectant eyes . . . and froze. When people started to laugh, her familiar chime rose above the rest and her words echoed in your head . . . *musically inclined as a chimpanzee.*

You will never forget it.
And never forgive your mother.

Your thirst to play lead withered completely. That guitar languished in its stand, collecting dust, until you finally sold it to help pay for Cami's maternity clothes.

Every once in a while, though, you wonder whether, if the law enforcement thing doesn't work out, music might be an option. You're older now, and less inclined to care what other people, including your mother, think. Cami would probably divorce you, but music might provide options there as well.

A few weeks back, while Christmas shopping, you almost bought Waylon a guitar. One of those cheap kids' models with plastic strings in place of nylon. The flirty saleslady asked how old the child was and when you said two, she pointed out even that size guitar was probably way too big for a toddler's hands. Then she smiled in a totally come-on way and asked, "So, does Daddy play?"

You were so busy being flattered that the double entendre almost slipped past. You caught it just about the time you opened your mouth and managed to sputter, "A little."

"Thought so," she said. "You look like the type." She touched the back of your hand with her own cool palm. "Maybe you should splurge on yourself. I think you deserve it." She was cute, tempting, and you realized how easy it would be to get away with a fling.

But then you glanced at that damn little guitar, and the thought skittered across your mind like a spider that one temptation could lead to another and everything you've achieved in the past couple of years could all go down the drain. You might even lose your kid.

And as you turned away, went back to the shelves to pick out Little People and Hot Wheels sets, you wondered just when you'd turned into an actual adult.

A couple of days later, when Gram's regular Christmas check arrived, you used it and some socked-away savings to buy Cami the new phone she'd been craving. Then you bought yourself a pawnshop guitar, because Santa would never bring something like that, nor like the other gift for yourself you'd been hoarding cash for. The instrument of vengeance.

And oh how famished
you are for revenge.

"Hey." Cami yanks you out of your reverie. "You stink. Go take a shower. Noelle will be here any time. And don't worry. There's leftover sloppy joes, so you won't starve."

She's not a gourmet cook, nor a very good housekeeper. Those things weren't part of the deal, but you do hold out hope for improvement.

"Okay, fine." You take two steps, turn back toward your wife. "Hey. What would you think about me joining up with a band?"

Cami's face wrinkles in consternation, and you get a glimpse of what she'll look like in a dozen or so years. Hopefully she won't put on weight, too. "A band? When would you even have time?"

"I don't mean tonight. I mean maybe in the future. It's always been a dream of mi—"

"You're not serious, right?"

Before you can say *damn right I am*, her cell phone rings. And when she answers it, turning her back on you and drawing away to talk, irritation erupts like a rash. Prickles.

> *Don't let her get away with that.*

"Who is it?"

"Hang on," Cami says into her phone before rotating toward you again. "Shannon," she tells you. "You don't know her." Now she points down the hall, an overt dismissal.

Still itchy, off you trudge to the bathroom. You have no idea who Shannon is, and you remind yourself to ask. It sure seems like Cami's getting a lot of random phone calls lately.

You let your dirty clothes fall to the floor, no plans to put them in the hamper. Cami can do it whenever. That's her job. Once the water is steaming hot, you step under the cascade and close your eyes.

The heat accomplishes small miracles, unknotting taut shoulders and boosting your mood. You even attempt a mediocre rendition of Disturbed's *The Sound of Silence* cover, cringing at the way the high notes bounce off the mildewed tile. Waylon might one day become the next David Draiman, but for sure his father never will. Fate can be cruel.

Then again, assuming all goes as planned, you'll enjoy police work. Something that requires using one's brain, not just his brawn. It's a career most people respect. You've even heard there are cop groupies, not that you're exactly in the market at the moment, but you never know what tomorrow might bring.

Fate is not only cruel, it's unpredictable.

But it's within your power
to manipulate fate.

Fade Out

FATE IS UNRELIABLE

Better to take a tight grip
on your future, manipulate
it to the best of your ability,
not that it's possible
to completely eliminate
some arbitrary interference.

You might think my existence
is all about grasping control,
but humans are a capricious
lot, given to acting on whims.
That's just fine by me.

I thrive on randomness.

     Thrill to curiosity.

        Celebrate rage.

           Relish jealousy.

Above all, I worship
the most awful, awe-inspiring
human shortcoming there is.

Revenge.

REVENGE IS SENSUOUS

It feels like a hug of ozone,
a thick, electric crackle
teasing the lift of every tiny hair
decorating your skin.

                                Sizzling.

Sounds like fun-house laughter.
The sinister chuckling
of the deviant clown
behind a hall of mirrors.

                                Pulse-quickening.

Tastes like icicles.
A rigid flavorless drip
of nothing, painful against
the sheath of your tongue.

                                Numbing.

Smells like waste.
Piss and vomit and spilled
blood, draining into summer
sand. Oozing. Staining.

                                Suffocating.

Looks like a bull's-eye.
Crosshairs trained
against a target,
a threat brought to bear.

                                Chilling.

SPOTLIGHT: **SILAS**

Silas Wells is an admirable guy,
that is if you admire serpents.
Cool.
Calculating.
Treacherous.

He looks—and acts—older
than his eighteen years, infused
with a meanness that goes
way beyond "tough." So why
are people drawn to him?

He likes being a leader.
Captain of the football team
suits him well, and he earned
the distinction. Truthfully,
if it wasn't for football,
he would've quit school already.

Well, that, and the fact
that his dad would literally kick
his ass if he didn't graduate.
"You can't get anywhere
without a diploma, boy, and
I'm not footing your bills forever."

Silas has no clue how
his father managed to graduate—
not like he talks about stuff
like that—but he did, and college,
too. Border Patrol has strict

qualification requirements,
and Agent Quentin Wells has worked
out of Nogales for, like, forever.

Silas will not follow in those
footsteps. He does not possess
the patience to build the necessary
skills. But that doesn't mean
he and his buddies can't manage
a little freelance border patrolling
every once in a while.

Ironically, his dad would not be
supportive. His job might necessitate
rounding up illegals,
but he doesn't resort to violence.
Not that I haven't worked
very hard to convince him.

Silas's mom would be livid
if she knew about his "hunting
parties," or about any of the stuff
he does as a devoted member of
the Traditionalist Youth Network.
But his mom is a social worker,
and so, a bleeding-heart
liberal. White nationalism?
Definitely not her cup of hate.

But it is yours.

Fade In:
SLIP INTO SILAS'S SKIN

Shitkickers. You dig 'em, especially once they get real good and broken-in, like this goddamn fine pair of Doc Martens Dad gave you last year for your birthday. You've kicked some definite shit with those steel toes, too.

> *You like how it feels*
> *when your foot connects*
> *with flesh, when it yields*
> *and splits and bleeds.*

> *You love the sound*
> *of bone and cartilage crunching.*

> *Cracking.*

> *Splintering.*

Football can provide a similar rush but games have rules, not that you don't detour around them. So, okay, you've had a fair number of penalties called against you each season, enough for Coach to make you run a few extra laps in practice. Some things are worth supreme effort.

The sport was an anomaly, really. Though you've enjoyed certain perks, like cheerleader worship, you're more the online gaming type. It was probably good that your dad immersed you in Pop Warner, which pushed you to participate in high school football, or you'd probably be a big slug. Exercise is good for a boy, and you don't mind it at all. It's just that winning is easier when you don't have to rely on a team to help you do it.

Anyway, football is over for the year, and not only that, but also for the rest of your life. You're a senior, and once you've got your diploma, you'll never set foot on a campus again, unless it's to crash a party or maybe deliver a pizza. You'll have to do something to earn a living. Working in a convenience store isn't exactly lucrative.

All dressed down in faded jeans and a Cardinals jersey, almost ready to head off for some Friday night good times, you check your phone, find a couple of messages. The first is from your dad: *YOU STILL COMING TOMORROW? PIZZA OR TACOS?*

You take a moment to text him back: *I'LL BE THERE. IF ZIA'S COOKING, TACOS.*

Your dad is shacking up with a Mexican. Her food is good, great in fact, but the idea of doing a brown-skinned bitch sickens you. That might be the way things are, but it's not how they should be. Unnatural, that's what it is. And God forbid the two of them ever make half-breed babies. You'd never live *that* down. Maybe you should have *the talk* with your dad, remind him to always use a condom.

The day he walked out on your mom and you in favor of Zia is seared into your psyche. You were in the sixth grade, and between classwork, homework, and your first real crush, you hadn't exactly been paying attention to his increased absences. He worked, sometimes late, he went out after to relax. That's what dads do. But not all dads fall out of love with their wives and in love with a coworker.

It was a Saturday, and you'd ridden your bike over past Delaney's house, hoping just to catch a glimpse of her. When that didn't happen, you pedaled home, and as was your habit, came through the door quietly. Sometimes you'd overhear interesting parental dialogues or arguments, and that afternoon was no exception. But it wasn't a conversation you ever expected to eavesdrop on.

"I . . . I don't know what to say, Quen." Your mom's voice quivered, and that was rare. She was gravely wounded.

"I am so goddamn sorry. I never meant to hurt you. I'll take care of you and Silas. Don't you worry about that."

Even at eleven, you had a very bad feeling that a vital change was blowing your way.

"I can take care of myself, thank you. But you *will* provide for your son." That part was iron. What came next was rusty tin. "I just can't believe this. Thirteen years means nothing?"

"Not nothing. Believe it or not, I still lo—"

"Shut up! Shut up! Don't you dare say it. Get. Out."

He did, and there was nothing you could do to make him stay. You tried. You begged him. His only response was you'd understand one day. He moved straight into Zia's little place in Nogales, and he's been there ever since. He tore your family in two. For a Mexican.

He assumes you've forgiven him, and on some small level, you have. But the residual resentment is barely beneath your skin. Time may scab over the wounds, but they're easily picked open. You drop by their place every now and then, mostly because your dad's guilt sometimes results in gifts. A fishing pole. A hunting rifle. Your pickup truck. The best is cash.

Speaking of cash, the second message on your phone is from your pal Josh, reminding you to bring ten bucks to help cover the cost of the keg. Okay, you've definitely stiffed your friends a time or two, so the not-so-subtle nudge is called for. Only problem is, you're broke, wallet drained dry. Pockets emptied of all but lint and air and, maybe, a toothpick, used or new.

That part-time QuikTrip gig pays minimum wage and you splurged your last check on a little weed, hoping to lower a certain redhead's inhibitions, finally finesse your way into her pants.

Try, try again, tonight.

It was close the previous Friday, but last minute she shut you down. To say you were disappointed would be a major understatement. You've been working on Ashlyn for weeks. That girl is the kind of smokin' you have to be careful not to burn your fingers on.

But she could never even approach "Grace." You exhale her name into the silence, and it hovers there like a dragonfly. Grace has red hair, too, but it's long, flowing far below her narrow waist, a thick mane of rust-colored waves. You remember her smile, how once in a while she aimed it straight at you.

The passing thought sparks a white-hot ignition of rage. Your mom says some people were "born angry," and you agree because you happen to be one of them. Anger smolders steadily in your gut, awaiting a puff of the bellows.

It's true, and you know it. You don't even try to fight it anymore. The burn grew worse after Grace pushed you away. She should've gone out with you again. Everyone deserves a second chance. That was a mistake on her part, but eventually she'll realize it was a major lapse of judgment.

> *Grace should be yours,*
> *only yours.*
> *There are ways*
> *to make that happen.*

"Chill, dude," you counsel yourself, shaking it off. The evening is young and you've got plans involving beer and weed and a different girl. As for the brewski cash, you know where you can borrow it, not that you've ever reimbursed your mom's "rainy day" jug.

Your mom probably doesn't even realize that, now you're eighteen, you can tap into your savings account without her permission. She calls it your college fund. College, right. What a joke. College is for loser know-it-all rich pricks who think they're superior to regular guys like you. They'll get theirs one day, though.

Since that transformative birthday three months ago, the one that magically turned you into an adult, you've made a few savings withdrawals. A few "major" purchases have been necessary.

You lace your boots, grab your wallet and phone, slip the contraband into your backpack before you open your bedroom door and take a long listen beyond it. No music, which means your mom can't be home yet.

First thing she always does is turn on the radio, dial it to some god-awful pop music station. It makes her happy, but you can't stand to listen to that crap. It's even worse than rap, which is nothing more than programming for impressionable minds. Metal, that's okay, but you prefer the lyric-free synthesized drive of fashwave. SoundCloud, YouTube, and BlackSun Radio are your go-to music sources.

But tonight, you hear no Taylor Swift, no Adele, or Bruno stinking Mars, and no Mom's slightly askew singing-along. She must've gone out after work. Still, better safe than sorry.

"Mom?" you call down the empty hallway. "You here?"

With no response but the tick of the antique clock in the den, you wander into your mother's tidy room, help yourself to twenty bucks in change—quarters only, though it all spends the same.

You suddenly recall a time you took a sandwich bag filled with smaller coins into a convenience store. When you tried to pay for three cans of Red Bull, counting slowly to be sure it was correct, the clerk made the mistake of getting all pissy. "Hurry it up! Can't you see there are people behind you?"

There were only three or four, and the bitch behind the register was wearing a scarf around her head. That and her dark olive skin told you more than you wanted to know. "Fuck off back to Sharia-land, bitch."

You threw a handful of change on the counter, picked up your caffeine supply, and exited quickly. You might have heard a gasp at your back, but you're relatively certain there was applause, too. Not like you're the only Muslim-hating dude in Tucson.

Tonight you take only quarters. No need to get Josh all riled up. Playing the good son, you leave a note so your mom doesn't fret: *Going out. Home late. Don't worry. Love you.* A surprising thought strikes you. You really mean it. She pisses you off, tries to tell you what to do, when you're so beyond parental influence. But all moms do stuff like that, right?

She's kind. Caring. Rarely does she put you down, even when she catches you doing stupid shit, and such infractions have been numerous, especially the older you've grown.

Your mom loves her job, really cares about the kids whose lives she tries to improve. Okay, that actually makes you more than a little jealous. Sometimes you think she'd rather mother them than her own son. Plus, you can't stand her boyfriend.

Imagine if your TradYouth pals ferreted out the truth: Len is Jewish. Okay, the dude's flush and, near as you can tell, he's good to your mom. Too good. Sometimes when she comes in after they go out, she's all blushing and messy, which is too sick to think about. They've been together for a while— long enough to be talking marriage, a damn decent reason to escape this house as soon as possible.

You don't want to be around if she becomes his wife. You don't trust yourself. A Jew could not be your family. A Jew cannot be your mom.

Heaven help her
if she goes full-on Jew
for that man.
As for him, hell
will open its jaws
and swallow him whole.

It pisses you off that it's come to this—that some random man can break up what's left of your family. The thought makes your gut churn hot, like magma. Once that rift is complete, you'll have no one close. Not even a real friend. You might term the TradYouth guys you hang out with "buddies," but you can't rightly call them friends.

The TYN is your community, a place to belong and celebrate whiteness. You proudly display your mother's Germanic genes in your angular face and frost-blond hair. Only your eyes, which skew slightly green rather than glacier blue, indicate the less-than-completely Aryan heritage of your father. Still, you're white, and that's what matters.

Your first hint that America was turning too brown was back in fifth grade, when a bunch of Mexicans ganged up on you and made you empty your pockets, not that there was much in them.

All they did was push you around, bouncing you back and forth between them. Not a single fist came flying. But that feeling of helplessness as you faced impending pain at the hands of a mob triggered an abiding thirst for control.

Gathering with like-minded individuals is one way to maintain that, and tonight's meet-up officially starts at nine. Your watch informs you it's five after seven. Plenty of time to grab a bite and head out on a scouting mission. You're not looking to hassle Mexicans tonight. No, you've got something different in mind.

You hop up into Lolita, the '72 Chevy pickup your gramps willed to your father, who gave it to you since Dad drives a sweet little Mustang when not using a government four-by. Lolita's bumpers are a little dinged up, and her upholstery wears a permanent perfume of cheap cigarettes. But the bitch's paint is cherry, her V-8 chortles happily, and she can outrun most newer models. You'd never trade her in.

She's a forever reminder of Gramps, your namesake, who taught you to hunt and fish, showing you secret watering holes brimming with worm-hungry trout. All your very best childhood memories are right there under the wide-open sky with Gramps, threading bait and hooking whoppers.

The memory almost makes you smile. But fuck that. Gramps is gone. Dad is gone. Mom will be gone soon. Worst of all, your Grace is gone, too, at least she believes she is.

That's where you're headed, over past her house, after a food stop at Chick-fil-A. You're keeping an eye on Grace, watching who comes and goes. Sometimes you follow her, to be sure she's okay. That draws another snort. She broke up with you exactly because she thinks *you're* not okay.

You pull through the drive-in window, order a Spicy Deluxe Sandwich, waffle fries, a large Coke. Fuel before fun, that's your motto. Grace's house isn't far; the food is still hot when you steer Lolita against the curb across the street from the handsome stucco building.

There's Grace's car, angled carelessly across the driveway. "Why can't you park the damn thing straight?" The complaint is a low mutter. "You need to go back to driver's ed."

There is movement at a lit window. You spy a pair of silhouettes. One definitely belongs to Grace. The other is taller. Broader. Masculine. And now the guy, whoever he is, reaches out a hand, touches Grace's face, an invitation.

They're kissing.

That is not all right.

Not all right.

Not all right.

> *You will destroy*
> *the person who dares*
> *defile your beautiful Grace.*

Whoever it is, he'd better stop or things could go wrong. For the anonymous (as yet) guy. For her. You pound your fists against the dash as the question surfaces: What, exactly, will you do about it?

They move away from the window, toward the front door. You realize you might be seen, and reach toward the keys. But first you need to identify the interloper. It takes only a few moments to see who he is.

Not that freak. First of all, he's Latino. Worse, dig down under that russet skin, there's something really ugly buried there.

You should tell Grace. Problem is, she won't believe you. In fact, she won't even talk to you.

> *You're stronger than she is.*
> *Make her listen.*

Fade Out

WHAT TO DO

When a favored possession
disappears, only to turn up
in someone else's hands?

                              Confrontation

might be the shortest
distance between rage
and satisfaction, but haste

                              often

leads to serious lapses
of judgment. No, unhurried,
painstaking strategizing

                              will

yield preferable results
when the last thing you want
is for your best-laid plans to

                              backfire.

SOME PLANS

Burst into clear view,
fully formed, with very
little brain work, as if
the subconscious had
filed away the logistics,
unsummoned, all along.

Others are years
in the making, each
tiny detail vetted,
every possible outcome
contemplated, the less-than-
savory ones eliminated.

Every once in a while,
circumstances dictate
action sans any strategy
at all, the necessity
of action detonating
like a mushroom cloud.

SPOTLIGHT: **DANIEL**

Sometimes circumstance is a cruel
dictator, and for Daniel Livingston,
that is most certainly true.

His mother, Alma, immigrated
from Honduras through Guatemala
and Mexico after Hurricane Mitch
laid waste to her country, leaving
millions homeless and hopeless.

At nineteen, her journey north
was arduous, but worth the reward
at the far end—temporary protected
status in the United States, authorized
by President Clinton in the typhoon's
wake. Alma would be allowed to work
in the US legally for eighteen months.

She found a job with a housekeeping
service and one of her clients
was a handsome corporate attorney
who, despite being married, swept
Alma off her feet and into his bed.
She knew less about birth control
than she did about the English
language, which he patiently taught her.

In addition to passion, Alma and Bradley
did share something akin to love.
He set her up in a decent apartment,
and they decorated the nursery together.
When Daniel made his appearance
in the world, Bradley Livingston allowed
his surname on the boy's birth certificate.

With another family elsewhere,
Bradley could only play part-time father,
but he was a generous parent when
his schedule permitted, and Daniel grew
up in an affectionate, if unconventional,
home. Until his mother, who'd failed
to update her green card status,
was caught in an immigration raid.

Facing deportation, she begged Bradley,
"Please. You must take your son."
Both the young boy and the man argued
against it, but Alma refused to drag her child
into Central American unrest. Bradley,
being an honorable man, had to confess
his dishonorableness to his wife,
Shailene, who pretended forgiveness.
At least, until Bradley died.

She blamed you, Daniel, for everything.

Fade In:

SLIP INTO DANIEL'S SKIN

You write the poem in your head:

She is a rainbow.

A whisper of prismatic light
promising the broken storm
has run its course.

                    Auspicious.

She is an early blush
of violets against a lingering
patch of shadowed snow.

                    Unexpected.

She is a dance of summer
leaves in a tepid rush
of sunset breeze.

                    Delicious.

She is a masterpiece,
sculpted by angels.
Even her name is beautiful.

                    Grace.

You are a poet, and Grace is poetry in exquisite motion. It seems
impossible that you belong to her. You think of it that way, not

that she, instead, is yours. Possessing her would be wrong, like caging a butterfly.

You want to be hers. Need to be hers. She is the one real hint of love you've experienced since your mami was rounded up, locked up, and ultimately sent back to Honduras, eight years ago.

All you have of your mother now are a few photographs and letters that have come, along with the years, farther and farther apart. You can barely recall her face. But, oh, how you remember those afternoons, tarrying in the kitchen where she bustled to and fro, humming as she prepared baleadas with homemade tortillas or sopa de frijoles—spicy delicious black bean soup. Your mouth waters suddenly. And so do your eyes.

As always, the memory of your mami throws you off balance, and to right yourself again, you coax Grace deeper into the fold of your arms. She tilts her cheek against your chest, and you rest your chin atop the crown of her head. "I love you, birthday girl."

Her mouth tips upward, lips tracing the stubble along your jaw, a surprisingly sensuous gesture. "I double-heart you, too. But you need a shave."

That draws a grin. "You telling me you're really not into the rugged he-man type?"

More like the couch-surfing type, where razors can be hard to come by. This, of course, she's aware of. What she isn't privy to is the truth of why.

"You could borrow my stepdad's shaver. Not like he'd know."

Her folks are on a ski trip, despite it being her eighteenth birthday. It's the Presidents' Day long weekend, giving them two whole days on the slopes. Grace was invited along, but she had other plans. Plans that include you. You're a lucky guy.

"You've already fed me, let me wash my clothes and use your shower. I don't want to take advantage of you."

She pouts, feigning hurt. "And here I thought that's exactly what you had in mind." Now she smiles. "Shave. Then we can go."

You feel strange in her parents' bedroom, which seems ridiculously large, compared to most of the dives you've been crashing in. It takes a half-dozen strides to cross the room to the master bath, which is jaw-dropping. On one long wall a huge vanity sports double sinks with copper waterfall faucets. The two sides have obvious gender leans. On the right, a row of perfumed lotions flanks a lighted makeup mirror. On the left are a nailbrush, a bottle of Brut cologne, and an electric razor on a stand.

You pick up the Norelco, examine the rotating heads, which appear spotless. When your eyes draw even with those belonging to the guy in the mirror, it's a stranger staring back at you. Dark disks underline your eyes and your perceived stubble approaches beard length. Grace was right. You can definitely use a shave. Also an entire night or two in a decent bed, which just so happens to be in the weekend's plans. And then there are smaller details.

Funny, how when all you believe you're in need of is a place to sleep and a toilet that flushes you lose track of the minutiae— details like chin debris or fingernails that could really use clipping.

Thank God you can mostly stay clean using the locker room showers at school. Homeless or not, you're determined not only to graduate, but to maintain a GPA that will net a scholarship to a decent college. You will be somebody the world must reckon with.

Meanwhile, to keep your beautiful Grace happy, you power on the shaver, lift it to your face, run it purposefully over your upper lip and the hollows of your cheeks.

Splinters of hair fall into the sink, and as the contours of your face reappear, it's no longer a stranger you see in the mirror. It's an apparition. "Holy shit."

"What is it?" Grace wanders in, checking on your progress.

"I look like my dad." Except for your complexion, which is two shades darker. But, comparing features, the kinship is obvious.

> Your dad abandoned you
> when he died,
> left you to the wolves.

"Does that surprise you?" She nudges against you from behind, circles your waist with slender arms, peeks around you to ascertain what you've found in the mirror.

"Not sure why, but it does." You wish it was a good surprise, but it makes you heartsick and hungry for belonging. If it wasn't for Grace . . . You tap the shaver against the sink, dislodging fibers of skin and whisker, chase the residue down the drain with hot water. "There. Is that better?"

You turn and Grace lifts one hand to explore the newly shorn landscape. Her index finger circles your lips and you suck it into your mouth. "Tastes like chicken," you mutter around it.

"You like chicken, don't you?"

"Love it. And you."

"And I adore you, Daniel."

Now your lips meet, and the kiss transports you into the realm of serious heat almost immediately. Lord, this girl is everything. If you didn't have somewhere to be . . .

But you do. Pressed together, heartbeat to heartbeat, your bodies insist you shouldn't stop, and you'd prefer to listen to the demand. Grace, however, takes a step back. "Later, okay?" Her voice is husky. "I told Cami we'd meet them at eight."

"Okay," you agree reluctantly. You'd never push her beyond her self-imposed limits. Luckily, she tends toward generosity, not to mention curiosity, so patience comes relatively easily. Anyway, you'll have three nights in her bed. That's a whole lot of heaven.

It's a warmish evening for February in Tucson, maybe fifty-five degrees, no jacket required when you step outside. As you start toward Grace's car, you scan your surroundings, as you've trained yourself to do ever since you got jumped. A glint of metal catches your eye. There, lurking beneath the streetlight. Good thing you were diligent tonight.

"Look, but don't be obvious," you say, without pointing or otherwise giving away that you know you're being observed. "That truck across the street. It's familiar, isn't it?"

Grace glances in the general direction of Lolita, leering against the curb. "Silas. Jesus. Is he watching me?"

"I'd say that's obvious." A combination of anger and anxiety prickles. You can't be certain what's on Silas's mind, but it can't be anything good. The guy is a conniving dick, not to mention a skinhead.

You know because not long after you chose life on the street seven months ago the dude teamed up with your half brother, Tim, who's also immersed in white supremacist bullshit. The two beat you like you see in movies, coldcocking you till you went down, then kicking you into oblivion. You swam back up into consciousness in a bleach-smelling hospital bed, which proved fortuitous for a couple of reasons.

One, when you healed up, you found a job working in the hospital cafeteria, even though you haven't earned a diploma yet. The nurses all put in a collective good word. And, two, that's how you and Grace got together. She'd witnessed Silas and Tim's vicious assault, and it was the last straw.

Grace brought you flowers, and you ended up talking for hours. You confided much, discovered many things in common, including the pain of losing a father without warning—yours to a sudden heart attack, Grace's in a road rage incident, the same one that left her best friend with a head trauma resulting in epileptic seizures.

But Silas didn't know any of that. He was lying low, expecting the cops to come knocking and bring him in for questioning on an assault-and-battery allegation. You never even pressed charges, though, afraid of retaliation. By Silas.

By Tim. Most of all, by Shailene, who has both the will and financial resources to bury you in a heaping pile of lies.

Fear and you are not strangers. You've been semi-constant companions for as long as you can recall. But you'd believed you'd put some distance between the two of you ever since you ran away from home and Shailene's fury. Grace knows some of that tale, but there are parts you can barely confess to yourself.

Like the fact that once your dad was gone, Shailene's resentment of your very existence blossomed into out-and-out wrath. The few times she actually talked to you, contempt branded her words. She made you eat in the kitchen, rather than joining Tim and her at the table. And often she locked you in your second-floor bedroom for hours at a time. More than once you were forced to relieve yourself out the window.

With no money of your own, and no place to go, you put up with her mistreatment for as long as you could, but eventually decided life on the streets would be better than living like an indentured servant. You were seventeen when you finally escaped out the very same window you used to piss from. As far as you've been able to tell, Shailene was happy to enough to see you go.

The only time you saw Tim after that was when he and his racist buddy pulped you, so it's more than a little disconcerting to discover Silas parked across the street.

"I had no idea he knew about us," you tell Grace. You and she go to different schools, so it's not like you walk around campus together.

"Pretty sure he didn't, at least until now. He would've said something. Maybe I should go say something to him!"

> Encourage her to confront him.
> Think of the fun
> we could have.

She takes a step in that direction, but you stop her with a tentative hand. "Stalkers thrive on attention. Don't let him ruin your day."

Grace chooses to avoid confrontation, but is obvious as she removes her phone from her purse and snaps a pic of Lolita, parked in front of her neighbor's house. The gesture encourages the ignition of a 302 engine and the swift departure of a '72 Ford pickup ahead of your own exodus, something you're extremely grateful for. It sucks being a wuss, but it's preferable to a hospital stay. You hope Grace sees things the same way.

It's her car, but she lets you drive, and you're glad your father had the chance to teach you before he died. If only you could afford a vehicle of your own! The insurance alone would kill one of your paychecks, which are reserved for food and your phone, neither of which you can do without. So for now you'll make do with public transportation. And Grace.

You drive cautiously, but then, caution is your middle name. It's Friday night kicking off a long weekend and Tucson is ready to party. Traffic snarls the streets, and people crowd the sidewalks. "Looks like the whole city has somewhere to go tonight."

Grace nods. "Makes me a little nervous. You never know who might get pissed over nothing and . . ."

The rest vanishes, unvoiced. But you know she'd finish with . . . *pull a gun and shoot*. "Where did it happen?" The words slip out, unbidden. You've only talked about her father's death in general terms, more detailed memory difficult for her to resurrect. "I mean, if you want to tell me about it. You don't—"

"It's okay. My shrink says it's good to talk about it. You should know anyway. Dad . . ." She chokes on the word, but continues,

"He'd just picked Noelle and me up from the mall. We'd been Christmas shopping and had our picture taken with Santa . . ." She pauses again to collect herself.

"Noelle and I were in the backseat, laughing about that silly pic. It fell onto the floor and Noelle undid her seat belt so she could retrieve it. I remember that clearly, but then things get sketchy. Dad yelled and hit the brakes hard. I didn't notice the guy behind us swerve beside us. Didn't see the gun. But I'll never forget the sound of bullets ripping through glass, the squeal of metal as we crashed. Blood sprayed everywhere, and bits of bone and flesh and hair. It was . . ."

It sounds like a scene from a horror movie, only not scripted.

Horror flicks are the best.
Smash 'em. Slash 'em.
Revel in the blood.

"I'm sorry, Grace, really I am. You okay?"

"Fine," she snaps. "But let me just tell you this. That guy was high when he went off, and he had a long history of domestic violence. He should never in a million years have had a gun. But Arizona doesn't really care. Even someone like him can legally own a gun, as long as he's not on probation. And he can carry it without a license. Can you believe it?"

You can. You've researched Arizona gun laws, in fact. But Grace doesn't have to know about that, and shouldn't. Nor should she know that you have had access to a very large collection of firearms.

It only takes one, Silas.
It only takes one.

Fade Out

ONE GIRL

At a time is more
than enough for a certain
type of guy.

One person

        to electrify
        to seduce
        to shelter
        to control.

One person

        to have
        to hold.

One weapon

at a time is generally
enough to accomplish
the task at hand.

One weapon

        to caress
        to possess.

One weapon
with which

        to dominate
        to defend
        to manipulate
        to pursue.

THE THING ABOUT YOUNG HUNTERS

Is that taste for venison—
or thirst for blood—is almost
always stirred up by their parents.

God bless 'em.

Putting meat on the table
is one thing, killing for sport
something else completely.

A primitive demand.

Upon initial consideration,
it might seem that men
are more prone to thrill at the stalk.

Delight in the pursuit.

But it isn't unheard of for women
to take pleasure in dropping a target.
Extinguishing a heartbeat.

I am equal opportunity.

Figure in adolescence,
the burgeoning need to conquer
an enemy, lay claim to the kingdom.

Bottomless possibility.

SPOTLIGHT: **NOELLE**

Before the accident
that killed her best friend's
father and tossed her
around in that Kia Sportage
like a 110-pound
flesh-and-blood crash dummy,
Noelle Whittington had big dreams.

She wanted to be a concert pianist.
She wanted to be a cartoonist.
Most of all, she wanted
to be a computer animator.
She figured she could do all three.
Ambition was a God-given blessing.

Everyone looked up to her
as a leader, and that included
her older sister, Cami, who tended
to act before thinking things
through, and often came to Noelle
for advice on how to deal
with the outcomes.

A brain injury changed all that.
Noelle knows she's lucky to be alive.
Everyone keeps telling her
that's the case, and sometimes
she feels fortunate. But then
the blackness descends, an obsidian
drape, curtaining any sense
of hope or plans for a future.

Fade In:
SLIP INTO NOELLE'S SKIN

It's a short drive to Cami and Rand's, and you are grateful for that because it keeps conversation to a minimum. Your mom is okay, but she's the nervous sort, and having a damaged daughter exacerbates the anxiety she and you have in common, along with largely absent communication skills. You try to talk, you do, but every conversation seems to devolve into a bout of anxious twitter.

> *What's the point of living like this, Noelle?*
> *There's a simple way out.*
> *All you have to do is find*
> *the courage to take it.*

Your mom turns down a short avenue that dead-ends in a wide circle surrounded by aging tract homes. Not the best neighborhood, but not the worst, either. A couple blocks over, the houses are almost identical. However, the people living inside them are much more representative of Tucson's diversity.

This street is noticeably white, and one yard actually sports a sign with sloppy lettering that reads: ILLEGAL MEANS ILLEGAL. TOSS 'EM BACK. "Undocumented!" you shout into the quiet space between you and your mom. "People can't be illegal." What *should* be illegal is hate. For them. For you. For anyone different.

"Calm down, honey. It's not important."

It's a lame attempt to lower your stress level, and while you love her for it, you hate being dismissed. "No, Mom." You force your voice steady. "It definitely *is* important."

"Since when did you become political?"

"This isn't about politics. It's about human beings. How can it be illegal to be one?"

"I think you're missing—"

"No! I'm not. Maybe *you're* missing *my* point."

"Okay. Okay. Let's drop it." The conversation has devolved. Cue the anxious twitter. "So . . . How are you feeling?"

"Never better." That's a total fabrication, of course, but whatever if it makes your mom more comfortable about your state of mind. After all, you are babysitting her only grandson tonight. Her worry isn't inappropriate, but you can't allow that to keep you from living.

"Because I won't be that far away if you need me," she puffs. "First hint of an aura, you call me and I'll dial 911. Then I'll be right here, lickety-split." She uses her nana's favorite saying. Lickety-split. You have no idea what that even means, but it sounds kind of dirty.

"I haven't seized in weeks, Mom. But anyway, your phone number is in my favorites and I'll keep mine on me at all times." Just like you've promised a thousand times before, and that is not even an exaggeration.

It would be great if you could drive yourself places, but your parents are terrified that you'll have a seizure behind the wheel, and truthfully, you're more than a little terrified of that, too. Just riding in a car results in an apprehensive outbreak of nerves. Currently, your palms are sweating, and you're chuffing shallow breaths. Your meds are struggling to keep things in check.

Once upon a time, people joked about how independent you were, always telling your parents to stop hovering and let you try things for yourself. Now a life without a caretaker seems entirely out of reach.

You can't even trust yourself to live alone.
What's the point of continuing?

Your mother pulls up in front of a gray duplex that sits much too close to the beige fourplex next door. "Thanks, Mom. I'm not sure how late they'll be, but Cami will bring me home." Unless she finds a way to get buzzed, in which case you will call Lyft and make your sister pay for the ride. "Have fun tonight." Bowling. Rank. But you're happy your mom's getting out. She spends way too much time worrying about you.

Music blares on the far side of the front door, so it's not surprising that your knock goes unanswered. You circle around to the kitchen door and, since it's unlocked, push straight through, hard enough so it swings loudly into the wall. Cami, who's standing at the sink, jumps. "Holy crap! Did you ever hear of knocking? Scared the shit out of me."

"I did knock, but your music's too loud." It's also obnoxious, not that you say so. Must be Rand's. You've never quite forgiven him for taking your sister away.

"Yeah, I told Rand he's gonna make Waylon go deaf, but he just thinks I'm crazy. Hey, maybe I am, actually."

You want to say no, Cami's rock solid, and always has been. But sisters don't talk to sisters like that, and if you did you'd have to admit that you're the crazy one.

Upsetting thought. Shove it away. Do your best to ignore the noise emanating from the other room and try to invent a bit of conversation. "So you're going out with Grace tonight? Tell her happy birthday for me. I wish I could go, too."

There's no way could you take a chance on strobe lights and a dance floor in motion. But even if you could, Grace never even bothered to invite you, and you feel mortally wounded. Before the accident, you and she were best friends. More than that, at least on your end. But that was in middle school, and confessing it to her was unthinkable. You could barely admit it to yourself.

After the accident Cami and Grace spent lots of time together at the hospital, waiting for you to emerge from your coma. During that time, sure she'd lose you too, Grace began to construct a door between the two of you. Later, she slammed it shut, and Cami became a conduit. You get it, but understanding and embracing it around the hurt are very different things. "Tell her to call me sometime, okay?"

Cami will tell her, and Grace will promise to get in touch. She might even drop by, but she won't stay long. You're a forever reminder of what life was before Grace's father was murdered.

As often happens whenever you think about that, a sudden impulse strikes. You wander over to the refrigerator, stick your head inside, then withdraw it again, disappointed. Or maybe you're blind, because your nose tells you there's something delectable nearby. "I'm hungry. What did you have for dinner? Anything left over . . . What?"

Cami levels a disapproving glare at you. "Didn't Mom feed you tonight?"

"Sure, but she only made a salad. Grazing isn't exactly filling." You know your sister is worried about the weight you've gained, but you couldn't care less.

"Are you trying to tell me all you had was lettuce? Because Mom and Dad—"

"It wasn't just lettuce," you snap. "There were carrots and broccoli and peas and a microscopic chicken breast. Hardly enough for a growing girl like me." You shoot that evil-eyed gaze that tells her she'd really better just drop it.

"Okay, okay. It's all good, *little* sister." The adjective is purposeful.

> *Her middle name should be*
> *Condescension. She's always been*
> *like that—pretending older sibling*
> *concern when it's control she's after.*
> *Sometimes you hate her.*

At the moment, you're literally seething with anger. It seeps from your pores not quite visibly, and yet noticeably, at least to you. "Look. I get you care about me, yada yada. But walk in my shoes—"

"No thank you, Ms. Obnoxious Cliché. Too much baggage there."

She means poundage, but you pretend ignorance of the fact. "Talk about clichéd. Don't worry about me, okay? I'm good with me just the way I am." But in fact, you aren't.

Cami winces, but offers, "Try the freezer. There should be Lean Pockets in there."

Her implication is crystal clear, but implications be damned! You head on over to the counter, help yourself to the small bowl of sloppy joes that remains, and carry it to the table. "Mmmm. Delicious," you say through slurps of lukewarm leftovers. Cami's refusal to reply reflects her disapproval, but you don't care. You gave up trying to impress your sister forever ago.

A volley of laughter blasts through the door to the living room, immediately preceding Rand, who comes sprinting into the kitchen. Behind him is Waylon, who's sporting a Nerf gun. "Hands up, bad guy!"

Rand turns toward the boy slowly, raising his arms as he does. "Who's gonna make me, little man?"

He lunges toward Waylon, who responds by shooting him in the gut with a Nerf dart. "Me! I stop the bad guy! I good guy. Bang, bang! You dead, Daddy!"

Rand falls to the floor, clutching his stomach, and Cami laughs, but you blanch. Even if the game is all in fun, why would Rand choose to play it with you watching? You don't want to be a wimp. Say something, *say something*.

Instead, you retreat to the other room.

You're silent as Cami finishes the dishes, goes into the bedroom to collect her things. Silent as Rand tells Waylon to be a good boy and they'll play Cops in the morning. Silent as Cami turns on the TV, tunes it to Cartoon Network, where a blue cat named Gumball is getting into some kind of trouble.

"Waylon's got the sniffles," Cami informs you. "I gave him a big shot of cold medicine right before you got here, so he'll probably crash out early."

The word "shot" makes you cringe. Bad Freudian slip. "Good to know," you tell Cami, before turning to Waylon. "Let's put on your jammies before we watch TV. That okay, buddy?"

Waylon agrees it is, and when you go into his bedroom, Cami and Rand sneak out, avoiding teary goodbyes. The boy chooses his favorite pajamas, with trains and planes and cars.

Back on the sofa, Waylon wiggles into your lap, lays his head back against your chest, rasping despite whatever elixir Cami gave him earlier. Its fake cherry scent lingers whenever he exhales. The child zooms in on the silly program, but you zone out. Watching too much TV pinches a place inside your head. It's not just the color, sound, and motion, but also electromagnetic waves, which sometimes trigger seizures. One second you're right there, the next you emerge from whatever rabbit hole you have dropped into, Alice exiting Wonderland without realizing she ever left home.

Neither can you spend an excessive amount of time in front of a computer or on your cell phone. For you, technology is a double-edged sword. Luckily, Cami's TV screen is relatively small and far enough across the room to keep headaches at bay. Nothing like your dad's sixty-five-inch monstrosity.

Lost in thought, not to mention a well-worn copy of the *National*

Enquirer, forty minutes pass before you notice the soft chuffing of Waylon's snores. Careful to disturb his sleep as little as possible, you scoot off the couch and carry him to bed, tucking him into the covers' deep pleats. He stirs, but settles back into slumber.

Watching him, inhaling the scent of shampoo and soap, disquieting questions skitter across your mind. *Will I ever have kids? Will anyone ever love me? Enough to take a chance on marrying me and starting a family?* It's a long shot at best. Your own sister barely trusts you to babysit. Your once best friend leaves you off her invitation list. Even your parents maintain distance, worried, perhaps, they'll lose you. They are right to worry; sometimes the desire to leave this world is overpowering.

> *You're a burden to everyone.*
> *There's an easy way to fix that.*

You kiss the little boy's forehead, mommy-like, tiptoe out of the room, leaving the door cracked in case he awakens. As you back quietly away, your foot crunches a plastic Guernsey cow, and you stifle a curse.

The toys scattered across the living room floor are not only dangerous to bare feet, but they irritate your anxiety, which goes hand in hand with your OCD, both of which you had in abundance even before your epilepsy. You're a mental mess. You take the time to pick up the Little People farm, tucking the animals inside the barn before moving it against the wall.

Then you retrieve a half-dozen Nerf bullets, placing them in the small toy box, and when you pick up the pretend weapon, you can't believe how real it looks. You study it for several long seconds.

The gold-colored barrel is stamped with these words: DESERT EAGLE PISTOL. ISRAEL MILITARY INDUSTRIES LTD. It disgusts you that a toy company would go to such trouble over something designed to shoot foam darts. Maybe they partnered with the NRA. Probably not beyond the scope, so to speak, of the National Rifle Association to invest in toys designed to get little kids hooked on "bang-banging bad guys." Only, in real life, it's usually bad guys doing the bang-banging.

You can't understand why Rand's so devoted to law enforcement as a career. Cami, you know, would be happy enough if he kept working construction, thus avoiding gun-wielding creeps. Seems like playing it safe would be preferable to taking a chance on leaving his kid fatherless.

Fatherless, like Grace. Her stepdad is okay, but you know she misses her real dad, who was, like, the coolest parent ever. Sucks so bad some doped-up loser ended his life prematurely. Sucks so bad the same doped-up loser stole your vision for the future. So many things you wanted to do, so much you wanted to accomplish! Now, when you open your sketchbook, blank pages stare back at you. Now, when you sit at your piano, your fingers become confused. Now, considering your limited options, you just want to eat.

The kitchen beckons. You answer the call. There's cereal in the cupboard, so you pour a big bowl of Frosted Flakes, douse it with whole milk. Sugar, carbs, and plenty of fat. Your kind of diet. And to think, once you worried about your weight. Not anymore. Let your parents and sister stress over your excess flab.

Food craving quieted, you check on Waylon, who's snuffling in his sleep, then return to the couch and tabloid hysteria until your bullshit meter can't take one more word. Rest is essential to seizure-free existence, so you cozy into the comfort of sofa cushions, close your eyes.

The free fall into sleep is always troubling because that dizzying rush also defines the onslaught of an aura—the hard-to-define foreboding that convulsion is imminent. But tonight it is simply a soft descent into the Cradle of Morpheus. Rocking. Rocking.

And here you are again. You've found yourself in this dream, or some variation of it, many times.

You're moving.
You know that,
but can't determine how.

Auto, probably.
Bus, perhaps.
Or maybe Sun Link,
the Tucson streetcar.
The mode

of transport
doesn't matter.

What does
is the pinkie-sized
black circle that materializes
at the window.
It's not so big, just large
enough for a small projectile
to exit through.

You stare.
Why is it familiar?
Words float
into view:
Desert Eagle Pistol.
Fake.
Of course.
But why . . .

Glass
shatters
loud
so loud!

Nerf bullets don't break glass.

But something does.
Something whizzes past
your face.

Close.
Too close.
Hits the far window.

Motion.
Shouting.
Wailing.
A single scream
No!

The metal
squeal
of brakes.
Impact.
You're loose.
Thrown effortlessly.
In the air.
On the floor. Or roof.
Upside down? Not?

Hot.
Stink of rubber
hovering above the abiding
gunpowder scent.

In front of you,
explosion,
a skull shatters.

Burst

of heat.
Rip
of skin.
Crack
of bone.

Time stops,
suspends you
in that moment.

Someone calls your name.
Noelle?
Noelle?

You look into the horror
filled eyes of the person
beside you.

See yourself reflected
there and what
you see
is a face
in pieces.

You've had this dream before, know how it's supposed to end—
with a somersault. A cartwheel, bumper over bumper.

With the girl you love holding your hand, coaxing, "Please don't
die." And now she screams, "Daddy! Oh, my God. Daddy!"

With her heart-wrenching sobs fading into the low buzz of traffic, of voices outside, a hum of distant sirens, swelling into chorus.

With a carousel of lights, red-blue, red-blue, and splashes of pain radiating from the top of your head, all the way down your spine.

But this is where you're supposed to check out for a while, wake later, swaddled in white.

Tonight's ending, though, is new. Now the gun appears again, ISRAEL MILITARY INDUSTRIES, LTD engraved, but not in plastic. As the short barrel turns, points toward the pulse in your temple, determined to silence it, you understand flight is impossible.

> *The hand directing the weapon*
> *is uniquely your own.*

Fade Out

JUST A NIGHTMARE

Revolving in an indeterminate
number of loops. The details
vary, but never before has
the dream suggested suicide.

The problem with a damaged
brain is you never know where
a notion might come from,
let alone what it might accomplish.

Some ideas pass all the way
through, indigestible, like meat
turned bad or milk left out to sour.
Be thankful for the purge.

Other thoughts lodge in the craw,
hard candies to choke on, sweet
at first taste, but insoluble.
Things go real wrong real fast.

One second, you're here, all
in a single piece, and then *blam!*
Nothing else to worry about.
Except maybe for your next of kin.

GIVEN THAT

It is, perhaps, best to keep
firearms a healthy distance
away from someone straddling

the razor's edge

between pill-induced balance
and teetering into the abyss.
It's a long fall, and easy enough

to be tempted

by the illusion of a safety net.
Frontal lobe sleight of hand.
Because all it takes is one

magic moment,

one little shove of desperation
or sheer exhaustion, and in that
instant, a bullet becomes the answer.

It's a lie, of course.

A sham solution to the maze,
valid detours remaining,
and yet the dead end seems

the preferable turn.

SPOTLIGHT: **CAMI**

Camilla Bingham is a study
in contrasts. Take, for instance,
her exotic complexion.

Chalk it up to genetics.
Her heritage is a buffet.
Basque.
French.
Native American.
German.

The results are stunning.
Gold eyes, marbled green.
Espresso hair.
Skin tinted
the approximate color
of bleached parchment.

Cami's a devoted mom.
Trips to the park
with Waylon are regular,
and weekly playgroups
are sacrosanct.
She devours parenting
magazines and manuals, distills
information into "doable"
and "no way" categories.
But playing such a serious
full-time role is more
than a little tedious.

Housework? Stupid.
Stuff just gets dirty again.
Cooking? Cami is so not a foodie,
and the boys will eat anything,
so why develop culinary skills?

On Rand.
She loves him, of course.
But she can't wait
for him to finish school,
and kind of wishes he'd stick
to construction instead
of doing the cop thing.

Not like the pay
will be so much better,
and other than the chance
of him falling off a ladder,
framing houses is a lot safer
than chasing down crooks.

And, boy oh boy,
would he be pissed
if he discovered how
she's making a few extra bucks.
But he won't.
Unless she gets busted
or has to defend herself.

She's probably safe tonight.

Fade In:

SLIP INTO CAMI'S SKIN

Holy hell, it's great to be out, shopping for fun with friends. You don't get to go clubbing often. Money's tight. And even if it wasn't, the people you used to hang out with currently live very different lives.

Married life does have benefits, like you know whom you're sleeping with every night, which is good and bad. Good, because you don't have to work so hard at being impressive. No worries about daily makeup or shaved-to-baby-smooth legs. Bad, because there are a whole lot of men in the world, and you've only seen this one small island of it. Who knows what kind of guy could be just around the bend? And while you love little Waylon with every ounce of your being, parenting is damn tough, especially when you'd rather party.

It would be nice if you had more friends who shared your mind-set. Most of your old ones have gone on to college or settled into full-time jobs. Not one is a housewife/mother combination. You like the playgroup moms well enough, but they're not exactly your type. The only things you have in common are your kids and the activities you entertain them with.

> *Nobody understands what you need, Cami.*
> *No one really cares.*
> *You wish you had more support.*
> *But you're not even sure*
> *Rand's got your back.*

You can barely consider tomorrow. Decades from now might not ever even come to pass. But even if they manage to, you don't want to think about having saggy boobs and time-etched skin and scraggly hair. You are a live-in-the-moment kind of girl, and that's exactly how you want to be.

In this moment, you lean across the front seat, kiss Rand, who's just parked the Civic—the great, safe family car that neither of you wanted, but it was the best you could afford.

"Love you, baby." You underline the promise with a longer, deeper kiss, one to make him believe his effort to take you out tonight will be justly rewarded at its end. That's so much fun that you go a little farther, dipping your tongue lightly into his ear before dropping your lips to his neck, where you lock them in place and suck gently at first, then a little harder. Hard enough to raise a telltale bruise.

"Stop already." He steers your hand into his lap, where it's happy to admire the impressive bulge behind his button fly. "I won't be able to walk, let alone dance. Jesus, what you do to me!"

"Hey. Jesus didn't do that. I did, and don't you forget it."

Hedging his bets, he invites, "Want to do more?"

The offer is tempting. Parking-lot sex might be a kick, with or without people walking by. "Let me text Grace. See where she is." It takes only a couple of seconds to get a reply. "They're almost here. So tuck it back in and chill."

You'll have to follow your own advice. Not the tucking-it-in part. The chilling part. Well, at least you've got a new goal. They say the only way to keep married sex interesting is experimentation. You'll have to play researcher soon.

Rand tucks it in, exits the car, circles around to your side, and opens the passenger door. He offers a hand, helps you out, pulls you close, and you remember again how you took one look at him and decided to try him on for size. He isn't the perfect guy (is there any such thing?), but he's borderline. At least in the Tucson corner of the planet.

As you wait for Grace and Daniel, there's plenty of parking-lot action to entertain you. The club allows minors, but only in one fenced-off section, so the over-twenty-one set can get blotto. A few stumble to their cars, most of the way to shit-faced already.

You poke Rand, point to a guy bent over beside his beater car, heaving. "He got an early start. It's barely eight o'clock."

When it comes to obvious drunks, your patience is in short supply. They remind you of Rand's mother, Pam, whose best friend in the world is named Gin. Start to finish, she's a total embarrassment, especially at family gatherings, which is why you prefer to avoid them.

Thank God Rand doesn't seem to have the same driving need for liquor, or any other substance, for that matter. Not even weed. Okay, you *are* a little sorry about that. Things would be so much easier. Marijuana has been your favored coping mechanism for a very long time.

You started smoking in eighth grade, courtesy of your then best friend's big brother. At first he acted all generous. "Have another toke. Plenty more where that came from." You were young enough, naive enough, that you barely noticed the way his eyes crept over your body.

Once your growing taste for a decent buzz became obvious, there came his demand for oral. You were a total blow job novice, but he taught you everything you needed to know. The first time, you almost puked. The nausea was as much about how you felt about yourself as about the actual act. Despite your disgust, however, you kept coming back for more.

You were a sophomore when he ran off and joined the army, and by then weed was a regular habit. In high school, you fell right in with the stoner crowd, where you felt welcome and, strangely, successful.

For your entire childhood, you could never measure up to Noelle, who excelled at everything without even trying, and she was the younger sister. Honor roll? Noelle. Blue ribbons for art? Noelle. Spelling bee trophies? Noelle.

After the accident, she struggled. It's hard to admit, but the truth is, you took a fair amount of pleasure in that. But still, necessarily, everyone's attention laser focused on her. Everyone but your weed-loving friends. You learned how to deal to cover your overhead and, good sense or good fortune, or a combination of the two, you've managed to avoid unfavorable attention.

Fortunately, your current supplier does not expect sex in exchange for the dope he provides. All he wants is payment on time. As long as you don't overindulge, you're always able to make a fair profit on what you move. Getting buzzed is cool, but the end game is saving enough to dress Waylon in firsthand clothes, keep the cable bill current, and maybe put together a future trip to Disneyland. By car. Cheap motel. You're a realist.

Rand will want to know where the money came from, but you'll figure out what to tell him when the time comes. Until that becomes a necessity, you keep everything on the down low—as low as you can manage, especially because sometimes you have to bring Waylon along on your runs. On one hand, he's good cover. On the other . . .

Nope. Won't happen. You're way too careful. Only deal to people you know well. In fact, there's one now. But he picked up smoke yesterday, so he can't be looking for you. And besides, he wouldn't know you're here.

He pulls over across the street from the parking lot, just as Grace's car, with Daniel at the wheel, turns in to find a spot nearby. Silas must have been following them. But Grace told him off months ago. Better file him away as a stalker.

Truth be told, Silas is a creepster, and the alt-right crowd he runs with is downright . . . disturbing, with their crazy white power bullshit. You wouldn't think someone so young would get caught up in that crap, but he's chest-deep, and a couple of his buddies, too.

Yeah, you're taking a chance, selling to that crew, but your customer base is limited. Not like the playgroup moms sit around toking dope. Nope, you need dudes like Silas. So you play the game, and play it smart, offering bottom-line pricing on excellent weed. No reason to mess with that. At least, you hope not.

But seeing him here, under these circumstances, weirds you out. If Silas *is* following Grace, whatever he has on his mind can't be good. You want to believe his goal isn't mayhem, but how can you be certain? He beat the crap out of Daniel, for no other reason than he hates the color of his skin.

Now, with Daniel and Grace together, both of them could be in danger. This is a tough line to straddle. You nudge Rand. "Check it out. I think your sister has a stalker." That was a mistake, and you realize it immediately.

Rand takes one look at Silas's truck, balls up his fists. "If he bothers Grace, I will kill that son of a bitch. I should've already dealt with the—"

"Stop!" You clamp a hand over Rand's ample bicep, tug backward. "Tonight won't be much fun if you wind up in jail." Or if Silas suffers a bout of temporary insanity, forgets the value of bargain-basement weed purchasing, and outs you to your obviously enraged husband.

Grace and Daniel spot you, and by the time they join you, Silas has dematerialized, leaving nothing behind but a belch of Ford smoke. You should probably say something.

Rand beats you to it. "What's up with Silas? He's not threatening you, is he, Grace?"

"He was across from the house earlier," she admits. "Why?"

"Because he was just parked over there." You point toward the approximate spot. "And he got there right as you pulled into the lot."

"What?" Grace scans the street with worried eyes. "He followed us?"

Daniel stiffens, on obvious edge. "That dude is a serious sicko."

"If he bothers you, I'll kick his ass. I wish I would've done that already." Rand's hand alights on Grace's shoulder.

The simple gesture stirs something in you. Something unsettling. Perhaps tinted green. Something hard to ignore. You choose the sensible approach, which is to bury that something for now.

"No ass kicking tonight," you declare. "Tonight we celebrate Grace's birthday. Tonight we dance!"

You extend your arm and are mortified when Rand ignores the hand you offer him, instead slips an arm around Grace's shoulders. "Happy birthday."

Rand kisses Grace easily on the cheek, proceeds to escort her toward the entrance. When he leans over to whisper into her ear, icy tendrils of jealousy snake through your veins, grasp your heart, squeeze tight.

It's an odd sensation because you aren't ordinarily the jealous type, and consider Grace a decent friend.

Maybe she's not so decent.

But it's hard not to be at least a little envious of someone who everyone else undisguisedly loves.

Maybe even worships.

You've never witnessed Grace invite flirtation from Rand, but sometimes his interest seems more than brotherly.

Maybe even more than stepbrotherly.

They didn't live in the same house very long. Grace was thirteen when her father was killed, not quite fifteen when her mother married Rand's dad. That's how you met Rand, in fact, at a family barbecue Grace invited you and Noelle to.

The two girls tried to maintain their friendship for quite a while, and that day they were still pretending like it was working. As they chattered and giggled about everything and nothing, your and Rand's eyes kept connecting across the patio, then across the table. And as the hamburgers and potato salad were passed, divvied up, and consumed, Rand's knees closed in on yours, closer, closer, until they were touching. You didn't pull away.

Instant attraction, that's what it was, the kind that begins in the pit of your belly, a flutter of nerves like breeze-worried leaves. Your fingers touched and your heart hiccuped faster, and you fleetingly wondered what, if anything, would come next. But then you knew something would because you were damn sure going to make it happen. Rand felt the same way, his smile told you so, and you found a way to sneak a kiss poisoned with lust and promise.

He asked you out the next day, and your second kiss was fireworks. Neither of you tried to fight the heat. Neither of you thought twice about it leading to sex, and a couple of times unprotected sex because he forgot the condoms. But when that resulted in your pregnancy, a lot of thought was required.

You confided in Grace first, hoping to borrow a few dollars for an abortion. "Have you told Rand?" she asked.

"If I can scrape together the money, I won't need to."

She shook her head. "He has the right to know, don't you think?"

Mulling it over, you had to agree. But the last thing you expected was for him to suggest a wedding. "A kid deserves two parents. I'll work my butt off for both of you. We'll be okay."

That didn't worry you, and neither did the way other people, including your family, might look at you, knowing there was a wriggly thing living inside of you. No, the biggest question to cross your mind was: *Do I love him enough?*

But then he bought you a ring, and it was beautiful. And so were the wedding gowns on that TV show you binge-watched. Your parents couldn't say yes to one of those, but the affordable one Grace and you found at an outlet made you feel like a princess. Walking down the aisle of Grace's church was a fairy-tale dream come true. For once, all eyes were on you.

Rand has kept his promise to work his butt off for you and Waylon, who amazes you every day. And love, you've found, continues to linger long after the fireworks have fizzled.

Which brings you right back to your husband acting a little overfriendly with his stepsister, your best friend. For some reason Daniel doesn't seem bothered by Rand's protectiveness, if that's what it is.

> *Protectiveness? It's called flirting.*
> *You can play that game, too,*
> *and you can play it better.*

Clearly, Daniel's crazy about Grace. Every time he looks at her, his eyes downright glitter with adoration. Probably not healthy to love someone like that. Especially someone so different. Daniel and you aren't exactly close, but you're aware of the fact that, unlike his girlfriend, who lives in a lovely house with supportive parents, he has no permanent home or family to speak of.

Grace has confided as much and besides, you're acquainted with Daniel's half brother, Tim, who's a racist jerk just like Silas. You tread lightly around him and, in fact, have taken to carrying a weapon in your bag, along with the weed you sell to that crowd. Daniel, however, seems decent enough, despite his challenging circumstances.

You fall in beside Daniel, hook his elbow with yours—hey, what's good for the gander is fair game for the goose. "You worried about Silas?"

He exhales a huge sigh. "It's hard not to be, although this is the first time I've noticed him prowling around Grace. Hope it doesn't become a habit."

You want to add, *Or isn't one already.* Instead, you say, "You really like her a lot, huh?"

Cue the eye glitter. "No, man. I worship her. She's amazing."

> *Amazing. Everyone thinks so.*
> *Might be fun to knock her down*
> *a couple of pegs.*

"Grace *is* amazing. But everyone has faults, not to mention a ghost or two stashed somewhere." Everyone, you're pretty sure, is possessed.

> *Perhaps it's time for an exorcism.*

Fade Out

CLOSETED APPARITIONS

Fuel desperation,
and so are valuable
assets in the game
of spinning chambers.

One spook is all it takes.

You might not believe
a person still wading
through adolescence
could harbor such
malevolent intent.

One slight is all it takes.

Age is barely even
a consideration when
haunted by the desire
for revenge or need
of self-preservation.

One fragile moment is all it takes.

Fewer years simply
equate to shallower
perspective, exacerbating
youthful impulsivity.

One bullet is all it takes.

HOLD YOUR BREATH

But keep your eyes
wide open.
Anticipation is integral
to the thrill.

Approaching the summit
comes a mad rush
toward the apex,
assumptions crumbling

as the widening
view reveals
unforeseen
territory.

Was this how
explorers felt,
cresting
the precipice

to discover
on the far side
of the peak
the Promised Land?

YOU'VE MET ALMOST

The whole cast, excepting
bit players. Only Ashlyn to go.
She and I are well acquainted.
In fact, we're very old friends.

Her story is one of neglect
and abuse at the hands
of her father, who's currently
serving twenty-five years
to life for stabbing her
mother to death, an event
she unfortunately witnessed.

The first decade of her life
was a series of escalating
rage-fueled acts. Early on
she learned to duck and run.
Having friends was impossible.

You'd think at least one kid
might show a little compassion
for a classmate who sometimes
came to school wearing bruises
and muttering fabricated
excuses about their source.

Think again.

Ashlyn's escape was books.
And while tripping off into
fantasy worlds offered respite
from personal upheaval,

she was particularly drawn
to nonfiction tomes
about history.
Tales of survival
in the face of war
or natural disasters
bolstered her confidence
that she, too, might somehow
make it through. She did.

But her mom did not.

Then came five years living
with her paternal grandmother,
whose own death
precipitated the handoff
to her father's brother, Frank,

and his wife, Louise.

It was Uncle Frank's nephew
who introduced Ashlyn
to the nationalist movement
she embraces. And why not?
The Traditionalist Youth
Network not only accepts her,
but promises to protect her,
if only to maintain white purity.

Finally, a place where she belongs.

Fade In:
SLIP INTO ASHLYN'S SKIN

The party fired up at nine, but you are one of those people who always arrives late. Not because you're unaware of the time. You want to make a statement. You will address life on your terms. At least, that's the case when you're able to sneak out of the hellhole you're supposed to call home.

> *Think of it, Ashlyn!*
> *A solid home, with people*
> *who really love you,*
> *unlike the posers*
> *you live with now.*
> *Users. Abusers. Liars.*
> *One day soon you'll exact revenge.*

Aunt Lou only agreed to take you in because of the remuneration the state provides for your care. And Uncle Frank? Well, he has other reasons for keeping you around.

Another year, you'll be out on your own. At the moment, you're thinking about a military career, and have tentative plans to join up. You've been drilling with the Junior Reserve Officers' Training Corps. JROTC has taught you a lot about leadership and marksmanship, both of which suit your interest and talents.

The big question is whether or not to join ROTC and go on to college before committing to the service. You'd go in as an officer, so it makes sense if you make a firm decision to sign a few years of your life away. You like the idea of freedom, so you're torn. But good, bad, or indifferent, once you turn eighteen, your decisions will be all yours to make.

Right now you decide to go on inside, knowing all heads will turn at your entrance. As you're one of the few girls here, the guys will seek your company, and that makes you powerful. You've hungered for even a small sense of power for your entire life. Strange to have found it here, with *these* people. You just have to know how to play the game because, make a mistake around this gang, things could go real wrong, real fast.

All heads indeed turn when you slink through the door, slender hips and legs sheathed in skintight denim. You're one of those fortunate young women rewarded by genetics with generous breasts, and yet other girls envy you more because of your ability to wear skinny jeans and look spectacular in them.

The jeans are almost always secondhand, but nobody has to know that, even if they might guess it. What counts is how you wear them, at least to the guys, who are unabashedly impressed tonight. The fact that your swagger is manufactured around a crumbled-to-dust ego seems totally lost on them.

Of course, their *woot*s and whistles might be slightly emboldened by too-eager consumption of cheap beer and accessible weed, and likely other substances not so readily shared. Official TYN guidelines discourage this. But these guys don't play by rules. Anyone's rules.

At seventeen you might have a narrow perspective built by relatively limited experience, but you have well-honed intuition, and put both viewpoint and instinct into play now. You wander over to the keg, half fill a plastic cup. Instinct informs you predators are on the prowl, and familiarity with this crowd reminds you that there's value in keeping your head straight.

Don't forget to maintain at least one eye on your drink, lest somebody spike it.

You pretend to sip brew while scanning the room. Not much use coming to a party if you hang out by yourself, though that's truly how you're most comfortable. Knots of guys, maybe fifteen in all, overfill the small living room, which opens to the equally diminutive kitchen.

You enjoy thinking in big words, though you rarely speak them. Better to let people believe their own vocabularies are superior. Feigning a lack of intellect is smart, and another facet of acing the game.

> There's no point in playing
> if you don't play to win.
> Take every advantage.
> Lie. Cheat. Steal.
> Lash out.

From time to time a guy peels off and disappears down a short hallway, into a back room. Bedroom, probably. There's heated conversation in there, muted by a door, but you can't ferret out what they're saying. That piques your interest, but you haven't been invited, so you stay put.

You could say hi to the three girls who hover against the far wall. But you've tried that before, only to be rebuffed. You understand their derision is rooted in envy, which is one part hilarious (jealous of *you*?), two parts devastating.

Instead, you thread your way across the room to greet your cousin, Tim. Second cousin by marriage, or something like that, which is fortunate. The gene pool on that side of the family is almost too weak to fulfill the promise of a superior race.

Regardless, they are relatives of a sort, and without Tim you probably would never even have heard of the Traditional Youth Network. It's not like they advertise in the local newspapers, though they do maintain a Facebook page, and the national organization has a website. All that's required is to do an Internet search.

"Hey, cuz." You have to work pretty damn hard to ignore the obvious interest in his eyes. Incest with an in-law is not on your to-accomplish list, however.

"What's up?" he asks, somehow missing that what's up for him is what's up for you. "Awesome thrash, yeah?"

You should just agree, but tonight your mouth gets the best of you. "Yeah, I guess. Except, how is this different than any other party?" Disregarding the gender ratio, and like you've been to so many parties.

Tim grins. "What do you want? Live waterboarding?"

"Well, no, but . . ." Truth be told, you're not sure what you want. Organization? A call to action? With nothing specific in mind, you amend, "Actually, that might be entertaining, as long as I could pick the person to torture."

It's better to sound tough. Act tough. One major problem with this group is the guys are charged with "protecting" their women. Deeper context: own their females. Control them. Maintain the integrity of the tribe.

"Oh, really?" Tim perks right up. "Who did you have in mind?"

The list is extensive, but if you try real hard you can narrow it down to a few pertinent people. Easiest to consider chronologically. Farthest back, perhaps, should go straight to the top of your tally.

That would be your father. Damian. He was never Dad, never Daddy. Thinking back on him now, he was the Wicked Wizard. Any time you and your mom found some small measure of peace he'd make it vanish, and while some critics want to believe there should be love between child and parent regardless, that's bullshit. Good times together? You'd define those as Damian, crashed into oblivion before he could deliver some kind of blow—verbal, physical.

Fatal.

The night your mom died will forever remain an indelible stain on your psyche, the kind of blot that gestates nightmares. Your childhood, if you can call it that, was framed by Damian's violent outbursts. Sometimes they were directed toward you, and always your mother stepped in, willing to suffer his fury if it spared you.

Throughout those ten years of spiraling abuse, you witnessed her subtle manipulations, designed to divert his rage. Often that meant submitting to him, like a mare to a stallion. More than once it happened within your direct line of sight. That was your sex education. You knew the mechanics by age six.

Such diversion was not always successful, however. Whatever frustrations Damian suffered at work were amplified by a stop at his favorite bar, where he'd down as much alcohol as the cash in his pocket would cover. If you were lucky, he was flush and would come through the door, head straight for the couch, turn on a game, and watch it through vodka-hazed eyes until he tipped over into sleep. But luck wasn't always on your side.

When he got home that evening, you were watching your mom chop vegetables for a big pot of homemade soup. The beef bones were already simmering, and the kitchen smelled a whole lot like what you imagined heaven might. You had just picked up the book you were reading when Damian barreled in, already pissed and drenched in scotch-scented sweat.

He crossed the room in three long strides, closed one iron hand around your face. "How many times have I told you not to leave your fucking bike in the driveway?" His grip tightened.

Oh, no. You'd parked it there to help your mom unload groceries and forgotten to move it.

"I—I—I . . . I'm sorry. I meant to—"

His backhand caught your mouth hard enough to rattle your teeth. "Shut up, you damn brat. No lame excuses. Ever."

Your mom turned away from the stove, knife in hand. "Damian! Let her be!"

His eyes flared wrath, fueled by insanity, and his hand fell away from your face as he turned toward your mom. Noting the weapon in her hand, he taunted, "Or what? You gonna cut me, whore?"

"Ashlyn . . . ," she warned. "Go on."

But Damian would have none of that. "Don't you dare move a muscle."

You knew better than to defy him, and didn't so much as twitch as he swept across the linoleum.

Your mother attempted persuasion, she did. "Hey, baby, take it easy. How about you let Ashlyn put her bike away, while we—"

It wasn't a backhand that felled her. It was a fist. In the moment her spine thudded against the floor, she raised the knife. In your memory, it wasn't self-defense. It was supplication. But that isn't how Damian took it. "I don't think so, bitch."

He was a lion. She was a wounded gazelle, and no match for his power. The first time he plunged that knife into her chest, you were frozen in place. But as he raised it again, your mom managed a last plea. "Run, Ashlyn, run."

You ran.

Past your mom's twitching form and pooling blood.

Past Damian, who kept right on carving her into pieces.

Out the door, into the purpling light, and up the street.

You ran without looking back, sure he'd come after you, waving a blood-crusted knife. You ran until drawing breath felt like inhaling slivers of glass. And when exhaustion finally halted your legs, you found yourself in an unfamiliar part of town. At another time, that might have made you afraid. But you'd just become immune to fear.

Beneath a bruised sky, you sat cross-legged on the sidewalk and wept. By the time a sympathetic passerby called 911, your tear supply was spent.

The pain of losing your mom was as sharp as the blade that

took her life. It has dulled in the years since, but still throbs faintly. The worst part now is the two images of her that appear when you let yourself remember: Damian fucking her and Damian killing her.

"Hello? Where did you go?" Tim coaxes you out of that time and place, pulls you back into the present.

What were you talking about again? Oh, yeah. Candidates for enhanced interrogation procedures. "My PE teacher seems to enjoy torturing me. Wouldn't mind returning the favor. Besides, she's a spic." The word is distasteful, but you use it deliberately. You have to fit in.

"Who is?"

The words drop over your shoulder, into your ear, initiating an anxious rush. When you turn, you have to take a step back so as not to go chest-to-chest with Silas. "Jeez, dude, sneaking up on a person like that could get you hurt."

Silas grins. "Oh, really? You think you could hurt me?"

Cocksure, that's what he is, and somehow you find that at once repellent and attractive, mostly the latter. He's tall. Buff. Silver blond. Gorgeous, really. Which is how he almost—too damn close to success—convinced you to have sex the last time you met up.

Not that you're abstinent. Sex has proven to be a useful tool. And beyond that, you like it. But only on your terms. Any time there's any sense of coercion, you're finished with the seduction game.

"Yeah, well, you never know what kind of protection I might have concealed somewhere."

Tim, who is now sure it won't be him getting lucky with you, snorts. "She's got a point. I'll let you two discuss self-defense. I've got something else in mind." He wanders over to the gaggle of girls, insinuates himself between a couple of them, and soon has them cackling like poultry.

"Sorry if I interrupted something," says Silas, who isn't sorry at all.

"Nothing but small talk. Well, not really small. We were discussing waterboarding and possible 'volunteers.'" The last word you put in air quotes. "Thus the reference to my PE teacher."

"Ah. The spic. I get it now."

Silas reaches out, dares to rub the back of your head where it's shaved beneath the longer swath of coppery tresses you've left on the top and sides. "You should grow it out," he suggests. "Nothing prettier than long red hair."

You push his hand away. "I like it this way. It's comfortable and besides, it's me." It's a statement, like your piercings and tattoo. You'd have more ink than the flying monkey sprawled across your shoulder blades, but tats are expensive and money is scarce. The monkey was bartered, sex as commodity.

There have been times when you needed something expensive that you straight-out traded sex for cash. Better than giving it away for free, like too many ridiculous girls, looking for love. You're not even sure you'd trade it for love. That scenario, as yet, has not presented itself.

Silas shrugs. "Suit yourself. I happen to like feminine girls. Lots of guys do."

"To each his own. It's not my job to make you happy. You don't own me. Nobody does, or ever will."

He reacts by nearly choking on a huge guffaw. The result is a giant cough, complete with spit spray.

He's fucking maddening. "What's so goddamn funny?"

"We are all owned, lamb chop. If not by parents or spouses, by the United States of America. I work a half-assed minimum-wage job. Can barely pay for gas and insurance to transport myself to school. But the government wants to tax me to cover wetbacks on welfare. I call that ownership."

Disregarding the "lamb chop" thing, he might be right. "Which is why we rise up and fight tyranny!"

This time his laugh is a low chuckle. "Where did you hear that? The movies?"

Such contempt is intolerable.
Put him in his place.

"Who says I heard it somewhere? Don't you think women are capable of independent thought?"

He looks like he's chewing on that. At least, he pauses before answering. "Well, sure. Obviously, they're capable of melodrama, too. Look. The point isn't 'rising up against tyranny.' It's embracing white identity. Safeguarding our race by keeping it pure. Discouraging others who want to overrun us, yes. Making bold statements sometimes, sure. But nothing like armed insurrection."

"So you mean you wouldn't pick up a gun if government goons came after you?"

"I never said anything like that. I'd have no problem at all defending myself or my home and family." He strokes your cheek with the back of his hand. "Or you."

Somehow you believe that. It's both kind of sweet and a whole lot frustrating. "Well, thanks, but I can take care of myself."

He looks you straight in the eye and you can't help but notice his eyes look like marbles—milky blue, with swirls of green around the irises. Striking, really. The tug toward him strengthens.

"I'm sure you don't need my protection," he says. "But the offer is there just the same. Now, how about we step outside and smoke?"

You know you shouldn't. You know what he wants. And yet, you say okay. You follow him to the keg, where he refills your cup and pours one of his own, after emptying his pockets of a whole lot of quarters, which he adds to the contribution jar.

He gives you your beer, takes hold of your spare hand, and leads you out into the cooling evening, where the two of you sit on a sad patch of browned sod. At least it's soft. He lights a joint, already rolled; you pass it back and forth. It's decent weed and between that and the beer, which you drink to fight the dope-inspired dry mouth, a warm fog writhes inside your skull and words thicken on your tongue.

Still contemplating action that does not involve actual torture, you suggest, "We should organize a rally or something."

"You haven't heard? There's a pro-immigration rally in Tucson on Monday. We're organizing a protest. It's all over the Internet."

"I haven't been online much." Fact is you don't have a computer, and your aunt Lou wasn't about to spring for a Wi-Fi-capable phone. If it weren't for school, you'd be totally disconnected from the wider world. "When and where?"

"We're meeting at nine o'clock at U of A. But we're not encouraging girls to come. Things could turn violent."

"Like I care? I told you, I can protect myself." You've made damn sure of that. "I'm coming, okay?" At last, some action.

"If you're sure."

"I'm positive." You scoot into his lap, allow him a sloppy, beery kiss, one he returns wholeheartedly. A small corner of your brain reminds you that he's played you, and remarkably well. But the reverse is also true. This will be sex as reward.

Violence as aphrodisiac.
You are totally turned on right now.

Fade Out

FOR A RARE FEW

The mere suggestion
of violence serves
as intoxicant.
Aphrodisiac.

Wish more people
felt that way.

Get down.
Get high.
Get off.

That doesn't always
mean gunplay, of course.
But when it does, oh!
Every facet
is heightened.

Blow 'em away.
Blow your mind.
Blow your wad.

SOME SECRETS TAKE TIME TO UNCOVER

No one gives everything away right away.
No one tells the truth always. Deception
is programmed into human DNA.

It's an ancestral survival technique,
integral to the species' continued existence.
Even that can't save everyone

from a premature demise.

The finish line lies dead straight ahead,
not yet within clear view. And so
I offer you this clue. I am more

than narrator.

I am instigator, and before my time
with you is over, I will have won.
Someone or two people you've met

within the shallows of these pages will fire.
Someone or two, fewer or more,
will fall victim to the whim of a bullet.

Fade In:
SLIP BACK INTO RAND'S SKIN

You wake to the raucous crowing of the goddamn alarm. All you want is to turn over and go back to sleep, and you would except you're supposed to be at work in less than an hour. It's going to be a long, butt-kicking Saturday. Last night went late, later than you're accustomed to. It was awesome. It was awful.

> *It was so representative*
> *of your life, Rand.*
> *Shake it up now.*
> *Before you fade*
> *into white space.*

Truthfully, you've never been much of a partyer. "Too serious," that's what people have called you since you were a little kid. That's probably true, but when evil shit happens to a child, somberness tends to be the result.

Going out dancing might be Cami's idea of a great Friday night, but for you it's about as much fun as a root canal, at least usually. You have to admit, though, you enjoyed the music if not, as the world's worst dancer, the activity. If you're ever going to try that band thing, you should probably learn how to do it better.

Regardless, you enjoyed getting out of the house for a few hours, and spending time with Grace and Daniel, who you took aside at one point. "You'd better be good to my sister. She means a lot to me."

"Yeah, well, no worries," he answered. "She means everything to me."

Warning, danger level yellow. High atop a pedestal is a precarious place to be lifted.

On the surface, Grace is all self-possessed, but her spirit is fragile. Whether that was true before the accident you can't say, but you recognized it the first time your lives connected. That gave you something vital in common and forged an abiding bond. When she hurts, so do you.

Grace came into your life during one of those dark, despairing episodes you sometimes wander into. She was your lifeline out of the cesspool. The love you feel for her is innocent enough, but apparently it seemed like something else to Cami last night. And that led to one of the awful parts of the evening—a huge blowup between the two girls.

Looking back, you can see Cami was spoiling for the fight when she walked through the door with Daniel. You and Grace had already located an open table, convinced another group to give up a spare chair, which you occupied. Cami strutted straight up to you, grabbed your hand, and pulled you out onto the dance floor, without so much as a single word.

"Showing off" would be an understatement when it came to the way she shimmied and twisted, and it was all you could do to fake keeping up. You weren't the only guy there who admired her maneuvers.

She's an attention whore.
Better keep her in line.

"Everything okay?" you shouted into her ear.

"Perfect!" she yelled back.

But when Grace and Daniel joined you in front of the band, Cami made it clear she was the only girl to be looked at. Grace watched the obvious challenge with increasing consternation. She is so not the type to play juvenile games. Too bad you can't say that about your wife. In fact, observing the pair of them, Cami's immaturity was striking.

Still, despite the tension, the four of you acted as if you were just two couples celebrating a birthday. It worked out fine while the music was blaring, too loud for conversation. But when the band took a break, things went south when the subject of the Pulse gay nightclub massacre came up.

Cami made the mistake of saying, "Too bad people weren't armed."

Grace's eyes flashed incredulity. "You mean with *guns*?"

"Well, yeah. What else would I mean? Hammers?"

You couldn't believe she'd go there, advocating for *more* guns in a public place, knowing how Grace feels about the fact that they even exist. But Cami doubled down. "Of course. What if some lunatic came barging in here, shooting up the place? I'd hope lots of people could return fire."

Grace lost it, started yelling about cross fire and collateral damage and drunken assholes' aim. Cami could barely play defense, but honestly you were damn surprised she'd even try. Finally, Grace excused herself for a trip to the restroom and Daniel confided they'd discussed the details of her father's demise on the way over.

When Grace returned to the table, calm but still visibly upset, Cami apologized. Not that she meant a word; she just didn't want to stir things up again. The evening collapsed after that. Before you let Grace and Daniel leave, you insisted on scanning the parking lot, to make sure that punk Silas wasn't outside. But there was no sign of him.

You thought that would be that, but then on the way home Cami lit into you. "Why didn't you stand up for me?"

"Whoa, now, wait—"

"No! You should be on *my* side, not hers."

"I wasn't on anybody's side. I didn't feel the need to get involved in a catfight."

"Catfight? You thought that's what it was?"

There was no way to win, so you backed all the way off. "Sorry, baby. You were right, of course."

"Next time, say so!"

> *Next time grow a pair.*
> *Tell her she's full of it.*

She was silent the rest of the way home. And you didn't get laid. Not last night. Not this morning.

Cami is already up, and so is Waylon. As you slip into clean work clothes, you listen to your son, who's in the living room, warbling along to a favorite cartoon theme song.

You noogie him gently as you pass by, on your way to the kitchen. "Morning, slugger."

"Don't bug me, Daddy." Still, he offers a snotty kiss.

You take a chance on his germs. "Have a good day, okay?"

"Yep."

"Love you, buddy."

He ignores that, returns to cartoons, and you go into the next room, praying for coffee and your wife's forgiveness for . . . whatever. Apparently she's not totally pissed. There's a fresh-brewed pot of java waiting.

"I suppose you're looking for breakfast." The tone of her voice informs you she's cooled off. All the way to dry ice.

You want to hug her, but are afraid to touch her, in case you get burned. "If you don't mind. I have to leave in fifteen minutes, though. Did you make me a lunch?"

She rolls her eyes. "I make you lunch every morning, don't I?"

That is a straight-up lie.
Call her out.

Instead, you back off. "So you're not mad at me?"

"I didn't say that."

"Try to forgive me before tonight, please?"

She actually cracks a smile. But she says, "Don't bet on it."

You go over to the stove, chance scooting your arms around her waist. At first she tenses, but then you lift her hair, draw your lips softly across the back of her neck, and she shivers in just the right way.

"Oatmeal?" you ask, noting the bubbling mess in the saucepan.

"Sorry. Waylon wanted to help. Breaking eggs is his favorite thing, and he managed to break every last one," she says, bumping you backward. "Pour yourself some coffee and sit. Fifteen minutes isn't very long."

It takes ten to finish your protein-free breakfast, and as you carry your bowl to the sink, you tell Cami, "I promise to always take your side in the future."

"You'd better."

You brush your teeth and put on your work boots, kiss Waylon goodbye. "See you later," you call to Cami, who does not respond.

As you head out the door you hear her in the kitchen. "Not a problem. Around two."

> *That girl is on her phone again.*
> *She's always on her damn phone,*
> *talking to who knows who.*

No time for queries now, but you fret the entire drive. You can't tolerate Cami sneaking around, and though she always seems to have legit excuses, you're intuiting deception. Then again, you haven't been totally honest with her, either.

You told her you'd always take her side. But you're not sure that's true. As per last night's argument, you have to agree with Grace. Not that you have a problem with private gun ownership or concealed carry options, at least for those capable of real responsibility. People like you, who have a valid reason to want one. But alcohol and bullets can be a deadly combination, and hopefully not one you'll have to deal with often as a cop.

You reach the job site, park, and lift your tool belt from the box in back, thinking about the bastard who gave you a reason to want a gun. As far as you knew, he was still in prison. But a few weeks ago, you were on a different job at an apartment complex and there he was, crossing the street. Older, scruffier, but no question it was him. You'll never be able to scrub him from your memory.

When you got home, you investigated the sex offender registry, and sure enough, there he was. He was released last year, having served only eight years of the fifteen he'd been sentenced to for sexual misconduct with a minor. Not you, because you told no one, but another boy, abused by his scoutmaster.

You were nine when it happened to you. Your parents were divorced, your father still in the air force and stationed overseas. Your mother had plunged into alcoholism and revolving-door relationships with a series of shitty men, none of whom wanted to serve as your male role model, something you hungered for.

Scouting served a certain purpose, allowing you camaraderie and camping, an activity you'd never have experienced otherwise. Dean taught you the ropes, literally and figuratively, and allowed you a much-needed ear. He was a well-practiced predator, cozying up like he was your very best friend. Sadly, he was, which made you overripe for the picking.

He played the game for months before going all-in for the win on a weekend campout. It was just the two of you in the wilderness, which might have seemed strange to a parent who was looking, but your mother was happy to have you out of the house. As for you, you trusted Dean.

The prelude was seduction—an arm around your shoulder in front of the campfire while he told you stories—dark fairy tales that made you shudder. He held you tighter. "You're not afraid, are you?"

"No!" you lied.

"Not even a little?" he taunted.

You shook your head, but both of you knew that wasn't true. You were scared, but not for the proper reason. Yet. He rolled you into the danger zone quickly, however.

"Has anyone ever showed you how to feel good?"

"What do you mean?" You really didn't know.

"Has anyone ever touched you like this?"

He pulled you into his lap. One arm remained possessively in control, while his spare hand dropped to stroke the crotch of your jeans. That part didn't hurt and, in fact, you were surprised that your wiener responded positively. Still, you knew it was wrong, so wrong, and you tried to get away.

"Oh, no. Not yet."

The hand holding you gripped tighter while the other unzipped your pants and yanked them off in one swift, well-practiced motion. You struggled, but couldn't come near to matching his physical strength. He unbuttoned his own fly, freeing his sorry erection to worm its way between your butt cheeks. He slapped a hand over your mouth. "This might hurt a little if it's really your first time. Let's see if it is."

If there was one small saving grace, it was that he possessed a pencil dick. Still, when he drove it inside you, the pain was exquisite and you screamed into his filthy palm.

But your pleas carried no weight. The wind blew cinder-heavy ashes into your face, and he grunted like a hungry pig, over and over, until he was finished.

When he shriveled out of you, he let you go and you crawled away, bare knees and hands through the dirt. You would've run, except there was no place to go but farther into the wilds, and it grew colder and colder as the distance between you and the campfire lengthened. Once you evacuated what you could, washed with frigid stream water, you wandered back to camp, claimed your jeans, and crept into a sleeping bag.

"That wasn't so bad, was it?" Dean asked from within the warmth of the adjacent bag. "Here's the deal. If you tell anyone what happened, I will come after you," he vowed. "I will hurt your mother. Oh, and I'll kill your ugly dog, too."

Hurting your mother didn't bother you so much, but you loved Robo with all your heart. Losing him would have done you in, so you never said a word to anyone. Except Robo. That mutt carried your secret with him to his grave.

Your mom asked once why you gave up scouting after that weekend. You told her wood smoke and dirt clogged your lungs and made your eyes water. That wasn't exactly a lie. You still have a hard time going camping today, ten years later. But it's more about the shame that bloats every single cell whenever you remember that night. Shame, and rage.

Between you and the boy they sent Dean away for, there must have been others. It's doubtful prison quelled his disgusting appetite, so there will be more now he's out. Unless somebody stops him, and you're thinking that someone might have to be you.

No doubt about it.
That person is you.

"Hey, Rand! Is that your wife?" calls one of the crew.

Another guy whistles, and not show tunes. It's the whistle of the wolf.

Yanked out of your nightmarish reverie, you find you've been driving nails for over an hour with barely a thought to your work. You look around and, yes, Cami has just pulled in next to your pickup and exited the car, wearing short shorts and a halter top. Both expose a fair amount of skin.

You put down your nail gun, storm across the lot to meet her.

"What are you doing here?" All that bottled-up anger is evident in your voice.

Cami looks at you with puzzled eyes. "Um. You forgot your lunch?"

She offers it now, and you remember leaving it on the counter when you went to brush your teeth. Nice of her to deliver it, but still . . .

She's dressed like a slut.

"Why are you dressed like that?"

"Like what?" She glances down at herself, ascertaining what you're pissed about. "Because it's warm today?"

It *is* warm, and normally this wouldn't bother you, so what's going on inside your head?

"Sorry. It's just the guys are checking you out."

"Are they? Well, that's not such a bad thing, is it? Considering I'm yours, maybe you should be proud."

Attention slut.

You yank open the car door, demanding her departure, notice Waylon, asleep in his car seat, and some small measure of wrath falls away. "You should take him home. His nose is all runny."

"Fresh air is good for him, and I've got to buy groceries unless you want oatmeal for dinner."

"Had oatmeal for breakfast. You trying to kill me with fiber?" At least you're grinning.

"Totally up to you, but tell me now. Waylon and I can always get McD's." She's funny when she wants to be. "Otherwise, I'm thinking chicken chili."

Which happens to be one of your favorites. "Okay. Get groceries. I'll see you tonight."

You go ahead and kiss her long and hard and deep, reminding her—and the crew—that she does, indeed, belong to you. As she motors off, you realize how important that is. She brings meaning to your life, and so does your son.

"Yo, Bingham. Damn, dude, your woman is one hot bitch. You ever get bored, I'll take her."

You spin, anger rising again, look right, left. "Who said that?"

A couple of guys point toward Levon, who joined the crew just a week or so ago. He shrugs. "Guess I did."

That was a loogy in your face.
Don't let him get away with it.

You reach him in five long strides. He's ready for you, hands raised, so you go in low, take him out with a head butt to the gut. He goes down with a *whff*, lies chuffing on the ground. Half of you wants to apologize. The other, the beast half, stands gloating.

The beast is your better half.

Fade Out

HUMAN RESILIENCE

Is vastly overrated.
You can think you've tucked
something far, far away,
relegated it to a dark cupboard
inside your psyche, slammed
the door closed.

But you can never secure
the latch completely.

Childhood traumas
are especially persistent,
knock-knock-knocking,
ricocheting wall to wall to wall
until finally a crack appears,
leaking memories.

And with them, often,
the desire for reckoning.

Here, character counts,
reinforcing strength of will,
the lean toward good or evil
as much about programming
as instinct.

PROGRAMMING

Will supersede innate character,
if such a thing, in fact, exists.

Consider every infant enters
the world essentially a blank journal.

You might say the quality of the paper
will determine the ultimate value

of the chronicle, but who could argue
that the words to be imprinted there

matter more? If one scribbles
bullshit on vellum, it remains bullshit.

Take a child by nature gentle,
teach him to excise insect wings

and reward him for such behavior?
He'll run off in search of butterflies

with no regard except, perhaps,
pride at leaving his indelible stamp

on the natural realm. Dear ones,
instruct your youngsters well.

Fade In:

SLIP BACK INTO SILAS'S SKIN

Oh, what a day lies ahead for you, Silas. You got lucky with Ashlyn last night, or maybe it was more about figuring out the right approach. That girl might not be Grace, but she is something special in a whole different way, something you might read about or find in a movie. Violence, or at least the thought of it, turns her on.

> And that turns you on.
> It's a match forged in
> blood and brimstone.

At the very least her proclivity will challenge you to find creative ways to keep her coming back for more. "On hands and knees" optional. Either way, you'll have someone who belongs to you.

Ashlyn and you hung out at the meet-up, smoked weed, drank beer, and discussed the upcoming protest at Monday's pro-immigration rally. Including her seems like a really bad plan, but she's insisting on participating, whether or not you think she should.

The talk turned to recent demonstrations around the country, and how some of them have gone off the rails into violent protests. People have gotten hurt.

"You willing to risk that?" you asked.

"Of course. If I weren't, I wouldn't be here." She jutted her chin and clenched her jaw, a silent dare to defy her determination.

Strong woman.
Quite the challenge.
One you're more than equal to.
Don't ever let her forget
who's in charge.

"Come on," you urged, tugging her to her feet and toward Lolita. "I know a place."

It was a short drive out of town and into the desert, to a spot you've been dozens of times when you needed to clear your head, get high unimpeded, or mess around with a girl. Ashlyn did most of the talking, not that you paid much attention.

There were a few other cars out there, parked discreet distances from one another. You found your own location away from curious eyes, left the radio on. As you worked your feet out of your Docs, she asked, "You have a blanket?"

"Why? You cold?"

"No. I was just thinking it would be more comfortable back in the bed, except not on bare metal."

"So happens I carry a sleeping bag, in case I ever get stranded somewhere. It's behind the seat. But we're not totally alone out here."

"If someone wants to watch, let 'em."

You didn't mention the recent Gates Pass "lovers' lane" assaults carried out against couples like you, looking for some private make-out time. This wasn't Gates Pass, for one thing, and for another, you had the means to protect yourself. No damn punks ever going to take you down, at least not without a nasty fight.

After you spread the sleeping bag, Ashlyn and you stripped down to skin, and you found yourself grateful the air wasn't colder. February in Tucson usually brings chilly nights, but it didn't seem so bad, especially once she kicked things into high gear. In fact, by the end of the rodeo, you were sweating.

There is nothing shy about Ashlyn, nothing tentative. She knows what she likes, and exactly how to get you to comply. She showed you where to touch her, how to touch her, and wouldn't let you deviate. Yet she was willing to accommodate your demands, too.

"I want to make you feel great," she said, and oh brother, did she!

Your previous sexual encounters were clumsy, directed by instinct, not practice. Ashlyn took you way beyond fumbling, past the limitations of missionary, into the realm of weirdness. It took extreme force of will to hang on, but you managed, and you're anxious for an encore. Maybe even today.

Because when you mentioned the activities you had planned, she convinced you to let her come along. Now, your little hunting trips don't always net game, but they often do, and when you're successful things tend to get ugly. Not girl turf, at least not for regular girls. Ashlyn, however, is anything but regular.

This girl is fascinating. Maybe even dangerous. Her desire for violence is intoxicating, and you can't help but wonder how far she's willing to go. Today will test her resolve.

Tim, plus a spare guy, are your usual companions on these missions. Three is a good number. You want to play semi-fair, but still have the odds solidly in your favor. And you don't want a whole lot of witnesses, just in case something goes too far. That hasn't happened yet, but it could.

You've never invited female participation. Until now. Logistically, it's a challenge because after tacos at your dad's, you'll want Ashlyn for dessert, and a couple of guys would make that problematic. So you asked Tim and Court to drive separately and meet you at the turnoff to your favored scouting area.

You pick up Ashlyn at nine on the nose. She's waiting at the curb. "Right on time. I like that in a man."

You like that she calls you a man. "We're supposed to catch up with the others at nine thirty. Which means we'll have to haul balls."

"Or they'll just have to wait."

You do admire this girl's style.

The first part of the trip is a straight shot south down the interstate, quite suitable for ball hauling. Lolita hums happily at seventy-five miles an hour. You'd go faster, but don't need to invite trouble, and highway patrol is usually busy out here.

"Where are we going?" Ashlyn asks.

"Out into the Sonoran Desert, west of here. This do-gooder group set up a bunch of watering stations so the wetbacks wouldn't die of thirst crossing that stretch. A lot of 'em do croak out there, if their coyotes run off and leave 'em."

"Coyotes?"

"Not like the kind that howl. The guys they pay to show them the way out of Mexico and into Tucson or Phoenix. Lots of them are drug runners, too. Those dudes make bank."

"Why doesn't Border Patrol pick them up?"

"They do. But they can't be everywhere at once. And they made a deal not to trap the beans at the water stops. They want to catch them, but they don't much appreciate hauling corpses out of there. I, on the other hand, have not promised to stay away from those barrels. Sometimes we get lucky that way."

She digests that for a moment, and then asks, "Have you ever come across dead bodies?"

"No, but my dad has, lots of times. He says the hard ones are the women and children. What kind of bitch drags her kids into danger? Did you know out in that desert, when it gets superhot, between the animals and the elements a body can decompose into a skeleton in days?"

"Rad."

That's one way of looking at it, you suppose. "I hardly ever see anyone but bucks, though."

"What happens then?"

"You'll see. I wouldn't want to spoil the surprise."

You exit the highway, not even late. In fact, you have to wait several minutes for Tim and Court to arrive, bleary-eyed and smelling like weed. That wouldn't usually bother you, but you prefer to scout clearheaded.

"You guys want to ride with me? You'll have to sit in back." Not squashing four people into Lolita's cab, especially not putting one of those dudes leg-to-leg with Ashlyn.

"Nah," decides Tim, "we'll follow you. Just take it easy, okay? My piece-of-shit truck needs shocks."

Lolita is thirty years older than his little Chevy, and her shocks are in perfect condition because you maintain her like Gramps taught you. "No problem. We've got all day. Hey. Did you bring your drone?"

"Does a duck drop dung in the lake?"

"Not if you shoot it first." Old joke. "Okay, then. Let's hit the first water station and send 'er up."

Back in the truck, it's slow going down a rutted dirt track that dips through a huge stand of saguaro. It's been a wet winter, so there's actual green vegetation taking a chance on sprouting in the sand. The open windows admit the scent of damp desert, and it's one you relish. You'll probably always live here, or somewhere in the southwest, at least if the Mexicans don't overrun it.

Some conversation is called for, and something's been eating at you. "So, how'd you hear about TradYouth? It's not exactly girl-centric."

"I figured you knew," Ashlyn answers. "Tim invited me to a meet-up, mostly because I am a girl. He thinks more of us should be involved with the movement."

"Tim?" He's a worm. Surely she's never sunk that low.

"Yeah. He's my cousin. By marriage, so we're not actually related, but we do family stuff together sometimes."

"He's not, like, a kissing cousin, is he?" You're pretty sure not, but these things are good to know.

"Um, no. How whacked do you think I am?"

You can't help but chuckle. "Girl, you're scouting for wetbacks on a Saturday, sending up an eye-in-the-sky to spot them so we can kick the shit out of them if we find them. Most people would think that's pretty damn whacked."

"Ha-ha. Good point." She thinks a minute. "So why do you do it? Are *you* whacked?"

"I don't think so. There are a lot of people who talk a big game, but when it comes to action, they chicken out. I'm willing to act on the things I believe in."

"Like white power?"

"I prefer the word 'sovereignty.' It's more noble."

A raspy laugh escapes her. "Not sure how many would agree, but I get it. So what about you? Where did your sense of Caucasian nobility come from? Your parents?"

"Nah. My mom's a bleeding-heart liberal, all about equality for all. You'll meet my dad later. He's cool and everything, but he's shacking up with a Mexican. It's kind of an occupational hazard for a Border Patrol agent living in Nogales."

"So, then . . . ?"

"I first started thinking about it talking with some dudes on 4chan. I dropped in there to discuss gaming and music, but then wandered over to a page called 'Politically Incorrect.' I thought it would be jokes or something, but it's not. It's guys talking about all kinds of political stuff, including white power.

"But it was my JV football coach who convinced me. Considering the team was filled with spades, he wasn't the best person for that job."

Behind their backs, he called your black teammates "apes," and the Hispanics were "taco benders." Well, that was the nicest slur. If not for their talent, he wouldn't have played them except as a last resort, and he resented their abilities.

"So, your *coach* introduced you to the TYN?"

"His brother, actually. Todd's been a recruiter for a while, connected with the group at the university. He came to a few practices, started shooting the shit, and a lot of what he said made sense to me."

He asked if you'd ever been passed over in favor of a player of color. If you'd ever felt intimidated in the locker room or on the field, for no other reason than because you were white. If you'd ever been ganged up on by a group of blacks or Latinos. Yes, you answered, to all three questions, and that opened your eyes completely.

"White people have to stick together because before you know it, we're going to be the minority race in America," you finish. Great timing, because you've reached the nearest water barrel, marked with a blue flag.

> Here it comes, Silas.
> That first hint of thrill.
> You were made for this.

You stop Lolita, wait for Tim and Court to catch up, and while you do, you look for signs of recent activity. There are lots of footprints—there always are, unless you get here right after a rain, and still indelible impressions remain. Today, it's obvious people have been here. But who, or how recently, is a mystery.

The guys come chugging up. They park and get out of Tim's truck, then join you and Ashlyn. "Any sign of chickens?" asks Court.

"Nothing too fresh," you say. "Let's send up the drone."

It takes only a couple of minutes to let her take wing. She isn't the fanciest model, but she sure does the trick. Tim straps on the goggles that will let him see the video she records in real time. He works the controls, and the rest of you watch the drone bank and dive, scanning the landscape, at least until she's out of your line of sight.

"Can't see anything human moving," observes Tim.

"Jackrabbits. Quail. That's about it. Oh. On that stretch of barbed wire just north of here? Looks like someone went over and left a piece of their shirt. But no sign of the someone."

Disappointment jabs at your gut. You hate getting skunked. "Maybe look south? Maybe we can catch a thirsty one. They're not as much fun, but still . . ."

Tim does as you suggested, searching the rugged terrain toward the border. "Nope. Nothing. They must be high-footing it through the res today."

"The res?" queries Ashlyn.

"The Tohono O' Odham," you explain. "It's huge, and those Indians don't much care for illegals dying while cutting across it, though they won't let them put water stations out there because they don't want to attract 'em. The chiefs or elders or whatever they are say there are enough problems without drug runners polluting their settlements."

The whine of the returning drone draws your attention. "Her battery's getting low," says Tim.

"Well, if we can't do this the easy way, let's drive the water route, see if we get lucky," you suggest.

"And make things harder for the next ones who come along," adds Court, tipping the barrel so it empties, then righting it and hoisting the flag again. Eventually someone will refill what you spill, but in the meantime it's kind of a kick fooling the thirsty bastards.

You pile into your trucks, go barrel to barrel, repeating the routine. You half expect Ashlyn to comment, say something about possibly being the reason some Mexican or ten end up croaking in the desert, but she remains mostly silent. Unfortunately, that turns out to be the extent of your scouting mission. You hope for better luck next time, and there *will* be a next time.

It's afternoon when you part ways with the other guys. They head north, back to Tucson, while you turn south toward the Mexican border. "Ever been to Nogales?" you ask Ashlyn.

"Nope. My aunt and uncle aren't exactly the 'let's pile into the car and go explore' type, and I don't have my own transportation."

"Too bad. How long have you lived with them?"

"Almost four years. Seems longer."

"So, where are your parents?"

It's a straightforward question. She answers in kind. "My father is in prison for killing my mom."

"Shit. Sorry, man."

Go on. Ask her
for all the gory details.
You're salivating to hear them.

No. Not now. Maybe once you get to know her better.

"Yeah, well, it was a long time ago. He was a seriously fucked-up man. I survived. She didn't. End of story."

Now you really want to know more, and will plot a way to make that happen. First things first: you'll have to gain her trust, and that's your specialty. "Do you like to fish?"

Okay, that was a strange segue, and she snorts. "Fish?"

"Yeah. You know. Rods and reels and worms on hooks?"

"I've never even attempted it. Why?"

"There's great fishing up in those mountains. We should go camping sometime before it gets too hot. Maybe spring break?"

A memory steamrolls over you. You'd gone camping with your grandfather at Patagonia Lake. It was an off-season weekend, much like this one, only not a holiday. They stock the lake with rainbows during the winter months, before the water gets too warm, and you caught your limit, which was cause enough for celebration.

But as Gramps lit the campfire to cook your spectacular catch, your parents pulled into the campsite. Together. They were still together, and you believed they always would be. You were so excited to brag about your angling skills, you could hardly get the words out.

Your mom took over CKP (Camp Kitchen Patrol) duty as your dad and Gramps set up your parents' tent. By the time they finished, the fish was done, and that was the best trout you ever ate, and—

"Camping, like in a tent?" Ashlyn disturbs the lovely recollection.

"I don't own an RV, so tent, or in the back of the truck."

And that was where you slept that night, right there in the back of Lolita, which still belonged to Gramps. You wanted to sleep there because you loved looking at the stars, but were worried about snakes slithering into your sleeping bag.

You didn't know enough to worry about your parents breaking up. When it happened, not so long after that camping trip, you held on to the happiness of the weekend just as long as you could. But slowly, inevitably, it faded away.

"Closest I've come to camping was a few days Mom and I spent on the street before my father . . . She wanted me to be warm and clean, so she went back to him. He killed her a few weeks later."

What is it with you and girls? Last one's father was killed by some crazy fuck. This one's crazy-fuck father killed her mother. Death seems to be a theme here.

"Well, if you come camping with me, I promise it will be better than crashing on a sidewalk. Plus, I'm one hell of a campfire cook. And you haven't lived until you eat fish caught fresh less than an hour before you panfry it."

"Considering almost everything I eat comes frozen or in a can, I'll take your word for it."

For whatever reason, Ashlyn scoots closer to you, and you find yourself extremely grateful for the long single seat when her hip touches yours and her hand alights on your thigh. Whoever invented bucket seats was a total dipshit.

She rests her head on your shoulder, offering a captivating jumble of scents—some earthy shampoo, a hint of coffee, and a trace of girly sweat, which doesn't stink nearly as bad as a guy's.

Nogales is the largest border city in Arizona, but that doesn't make it very big at all. Most visitors pass through on the way into Mexico, which leaks culture and architecture back into the US. Once you exit the freeway, you take a few minutes to tour Ashlyn around the small downtown area, not that there's a whole lot to see except for a few shops selling touristy trinkets. Then you head on over to your dad's.

It being Saturday, he didn't work, so he's chilling when you pull up in front of the little house he shares with Zia. Ashlyn follows you up the short walk to the front door, and when you knock, Zia answers. She offers Ashlyn a warm smile, extends a hand. "You must be Grace. Come in, come in."

Zia's never met Grace, but she has heard you talk about her. This is awkward. Especially when Ashlyn looks at you with eyes flashing fireworks.

"Who's Grace?"

> *You don't have to answer to her.*
> *You don't have to answer to anyone.*

Fade Out

WHO CAN SAY

Exactly how or when
obsessions are sparked?
Sometimes they creep up,
grab hold and hang on,
chewing into you
bite by relentless bite,
like a dog worrying a bone.

Other times you're aware
of their approach
and with focused resolve
you can sidestep
the repercussions
of single-minded adulation
bordering on worship.

But when a fixation
springs into existence,
fully formed,
one has to wonder
if its creation
is simply happenstance,
or at the directive
of some otherworldly force.

THE UNIVERSE

Carries energies—
positive,
negative,
created by architecture
or random thrill.

Consider
each molecule,
and every atom therein,
is a microcosmic mirror
reflecting the vastness
beyond human vision,
and a vessel containing
nature's elemental forces.
They are living things,
and so, then, is a slab
of wood or piece of metal,
as well as flesh, blood, and bone.

Contemplate
for one curious minute
the theory that molecules
attract each other's energies
in continuous exchange.
Thus the weapon
absorbs the psyche
of the hand that holds it.

Fade In:

SLIP BACK INTO DANIEL'S SKIN

A narrow slant of sunlight draws you into the day. You sense it must be late morning because there is noise outside the window—a lawn mower's growl, a car's impatient honking, someone calling their dog inside. It takes you a minute to remember where you are, why you've been sleeping so soundly, afloat in the comfort of a soft mattress and sheets that smell like lavender. The rasp of Grace's breathing reminds you it's her bed you share.

> *You've never lived*
> *like this, Daniel, and never will.*
> *All you'll ever get are borrowed*
> *hours with Grace. It isn't fair.*

Not wanting to wake her, you lie very still, remembering the details of last night. What should have been a perfectly fun evening was marred by a couple of things. First, Silas. The guy is unpredictable, and you'd have vastly preferred he didn't find out about you and Grace, who he seems to still have a thing for.

You must be prepared, in case he decides to come after you again. Dropping your guard would be a mistake. Remember how it felt to go down under his fists, forced flat on your back by his boot-clad feet, and stomped on like a cockroach. Next time he tries, and he quite likely will, you'll have a weapon at the ready. Preferably one that allows no room for error.

Then there was the row between Grace and her supposed best friend. Cami is apparently a gun enthusiast, something Grace probably should've known. She does now, that's for sure, but whether that will affect their friendship is hard to tell. Truly, you wouldn't mind at all if a wedge has been driven between them. You'd just as soon Grace didn't share her time and affection with anyone but you.

At one point Grace left the table, claiming she needed to pee, but it was obvious she wanted to distance herself from the contentious dialogue. When she returned, Cami apologized, and the girls seemed to bury the ol' hatchet. But Grace was off after that, her usual good nature prickly instead.

On the drive home, you chanced asking, "What was up with your friend, anyway? She has to know how you feel about guns."

"Of course she does!" she snapped. "It was like the bitch was looking to ruin my birthday. I'll get her back. You watch."

You shot her an obvious sideways glance, and she understood the implied question.

"I don't wage war with battleships," she said. "I prefer submarines."

That brought you up short—not only the statement's intent, but also the flavor of her diction. It was the first time you witnessed that side of her, and it was tantalizing. She's more like you than you realized.

She stirs beside you now, as if your thoughts have invaded her dreams. "Daniel?" Sleep shadows her voice, and the net effect is to make you remember the best part of last night, which was the kind of lovemaking that makes people commit to stay together forever, knowing no other person could make you feel so totally complete.

Anxious for an encore, you draw your woman into your arms. "Morning." But when you try to kiss her, she pulls away.

"Later, okay? We should clean up first. Last night was nasty."

Stunned, you ask, "Nasty good or bad?"

"Good." Her fingers trace the front of your body, belly button (no lower, despite the insistent throbbing there) to neck. "But I feel kind of crusty. Crusty is not sexy."

You could argue that, but decide it's better to let her have her way. After all, you *do* want sex at some point today, and she is a firecracker you don't want to set off. "Okay then. A nice hot shower and . . . breakfast? We could go out, or I could cook for you."

Grace sits up, holding the covers over her nakedness, suddenly shy, like Eve, post-apple. "You cook? Do you shop, too? Not sure what's in the kitchen. A trip to the store might be necessary."

She slips out of bed, goes off toward the bathroom. Crusty or not, she's something to behold, all lean and tan and luscious. How did you ever get this lucky?

Keep dreaming.
It's temporary.
Like everything in your sphere.

Somewhere in the room, Grace's cell buzzes, signaling an incoming text. You want to know who it is, but before you find the courage to investigate, she returns, wrapped in a towel and hair dripping water.

"Someone messaged you," you say, standing to go take your own turn in the shower. You stop long enough to embrace her and inhale the fragrance of her freshly washed hair.

Two days in a row, allowed the luxury of soap and shampoo, seems like a regular vacation, not that you've enjoyed many of those in your lifetime, and none since your father died. One day when you're rich and famous, you'll take regular trips to amazing faraway places, with Grace on your arm.

As you lather, rinse, and dry off, you make a list in your head. Thailand. France. New Zealand. Tahiti. The one place you don't think you'll go is Honduras, or anywhere south of the border. Yeah, it might be nice to see your mom, but you don't know how you'd even find her. The last letter you got from her was three years ago. She could be dead, for all you know.

That's the only acceptable excuse.
Anything else is proof
that she never loved you at all.

And what a nightmare it could be, trying to return to the States, considering the color of your skin. Lots of horror stories in the news. It's bad enough here in Tucson. Arizona cops are notorious for pulling people over, then demanding to see their papers. Trying to clear customs? What a joke, even *with* the proper ID.

You don't possess papers, not even your birth certificate. If your dad had it, it's probably long gone, tossed into Shailene's shredder. You should probably remedy that. You can't even get a driver's license without it. But how? Don't you need papers to *get* papers?

No worries about slinging a towel around yourself, you return to Grace's room sporting your birthday suit. "All decrusted and raring to go," you declare. "Where are we off to? Back to bed?"

Grace, who is completely dressed, grins. "I was thinking about a different kind of exercise. Like maybe a bike ride."

"Bike ride?"

"You *can* ride one, can't you?"

"I could when I was, like, eight." And never much cared for the activity. Too many skinned knees and biffed chins. Maybe she and you aren't quite so alike after all.

"Then you still can. Bet you can't keep up with me!"

It's too early in the day for challenges. "Do I have to get dressed first?"

She rolls her eyes. "Pretty sure my dad wouldn't appreciate your naked heinie on his expensive seat."

You slip into some of the clothes you washed yesterday. Damn, you're spotless, which makes the idea of a sweaty bike ride totally unappealing. But you won't say no and track Grace into the kitchen, where her face is jammed into the refrigerator.

She extricates it. "There are eggs and veggies and cheese. Can you handle an omelet, chef?"

"I believe I can. Put everything on the counter and I'll be right back."

Paranoia is a regular visitor. You go into the living room and peek out the windows, ascertaining that there's no old Ford pickup parked on the street. Sucks that you have to be careful again. You'd pretty much decided he was done messing with you. And now you have to keep Grace safe.

Satisfied there's no one outside but the neighbors, you return to your chef duty.

"You okay?" Grace has already chopped a bell pepper and sliced an onion. And now she grabs hold of a frying pan.

"Of course. I was just making sure your friend Silas wasn't sitting outside with an assault rifle or something."

"Since you don't look too concerned, I'm guessing he wasn't. And he isn't my friend."

You break four eggs into a bowl, beat them with a fork, add salt, pepper, and a dash of cayenne. Just the way your mami used to make them. "I still don't get why you went out with the guy. You attracted to loutish Neanderthals or what?"

"Is there such a thing as non-loutish Neanderthals?" Grace is fabulous with comebacks. "And are you calling yourself a caveman? Because I'm attracted to you."

"Seriously, Grace. I mean, the dude's a skinhead." You add butter to the frying pan, toss in the veggies to sauté. They aren't the only things sizzling in the kitchen.

"Didn't you know? Skinheads are radical lays. I just couldn't help myself. He made me all hot and horny for his hard, Aryan six-pack."

It's a bad joke, and you want to laugh it off as that, but part of you wonders if there isn't a thread of truth there. Not only that, but now you want to know if she actually had sex with him, and if she did, if it approached what the two of you shared last night. But now is probably not the time to quiz her.

"Sorry. That was rude."

You reach for a spatula, drop it on the floor, bend to retrieve it in unison with Grace, and when your faces are three inches apart, her eyes pierce your eyes. That's exactly how it feels, like she's slicing into you. This girl has a temper.

"Look, Daniel. I didn't know Silas was a white-power prick when I first met him. I was vulnerable, he was good-looking and popular, so I felt flattered by his interest. And, believe it or not, he listened to me. It wasn't all about him, like some other guys."

There's something in her voice. Some hint of affection that makes you think sex came secondary to love.

> *No. That's impossible.*
> *No one could love* him.
> *You loathe him with every ounce*
> *of hatred you hold inside.*

There are only two people you despise more. Next thing you know Grace will make excuses for Tim and Shailene. Not that she knows everything. Oh, no, not even close.

The smell of softened onions and peppers reminds you to finish cooking the omelet, though you're not nearly as hungry as you were before this dialogue—which *you* started—entered the awkward zone.

When it's done, you carry plates to the table and Grace brings a couple of glasses of orange juice. The scene is so domestic it's almost upsetting. You could get used to living like this, but two more days of comfort, and then you'll be back out on the street.

And Grace will be here.

You look up from your plate. "Do you really think he's good-looking?"

"Would I go out with someone who wasn't?"

Mic drop.

Of course she wouldn't. But how could she think Silas qualified? The guy is nothing but a thick slab of meat.

She thinks he's better than you.

No. That can't be. But it will gnaw at you forever unless you know for sure.

"I'm just going to come straight out and ask. Is he more attractive than I am?"

She chews her mouthful of eggs and swallows, takes a sip of juice before answering. "Are you seriously jealous of Silas? Daniel, I broke up with him because I can't stomach violence, and he enjoys it. Any feelings I had for him died when I witnessed the pleasure he took in beating you unconscious." She reaches out, caresses your cheek. "Besides, I happen to love someone else."

You know she means you, so why is your first reaction: *Yeah, like who?* Daniel, my friend, you've got a problem. You know that's true when a sudden suspicion crosses your mind. "So, who texted you earlier?"

Her hand jerks back. "That's what you've got to say?"

This is not going well, and it's all your fault. "I'm blowing it, man, and I'm sorry. I'm a jealous person, mostly because I have so few things worth holding on to."

She nods understanding, but says, "Trust is important. Relationships can't survive without it. If I haven't earned your trust by now, I'm not sure I ever can."

This is starting to sound like an: *I love you, but . . .* Quick. Think! You can't lose this girl. Say something funny.

"Hey, I trust you. Enough to go on a bike ride with you, even though I'll never keep up."

That wasn't funny.

Still, she smiles. "Okay then. Oh, so you know, the text was from Noelle. She wants me to stop by later. She's got a birthday present for me. I'll do that, then afterward maybe we could grab a bite and see a movie."

"I, um, I'm kind of strapped after last night." Cover charges and soft drinks were about all you could afford.

"My treat."

Pretty much everything is her treat. She's liable to grow tired of that, but you can't exactly say no. "If you're sure."

"I'm positive. You ready to roll?"

She stands and clears the table, and you breathe a sigh of relief. So far, no breakup.

Grace's dad's eighteen-speed mountain bike is a lot more machine than the five-speed you had as a kid, but you get the hang of shifting without much problem and actually find yourself enjoying the cruise along the Tucson area's system of paved paths.

It's a nice Saturday, with perfect February-in-Arizona weather, so Grace and you aren't exactly alone on these favored trails. Hardcore cyclists in Lycra and fancy helmets share the thoroughfare with single riders and families, taking advantage of the holiday weekend.

You pass a couple of boys, maybe ten, standing off to one side, arguing. One of their bikes is on its kickstand; the other lies fallen over. Déjà vu hits, and hard.

Tim and you are almost the same age. He's a few months younger, but because of the circumstances of your childhoods, he was the one who always received the best gifts because your dad understood that Shailene wouldn't have it any other way. Your BMX bike was an inexpensive model, but his was a fancy Schwinn, which he received for his eleventh birthday. You hated them both.

And, while you were cautious with your cheapie, Tim was rough on his Cadillac, something your dad warned him about time and again. So it was easy enough to get away with bending his derailleur when no one was looking. The two of you went riding, you challenged him to a race, and off popped his chain, while he was going maybe fifteen miles an hour. For sure, both he and the bike were under pressure, and one ridiculous downshift sent him over the handlebars.

For once, it wasn't you suffering chin lesions and chewed knees. It was your fair-skinned "brother," who deserved all that and more.

That felt good, didn't it,
watching him howl in pain.

He wasn't hurt too badly, but he did get a trip to urgent care and a huge verbal takedown from the one thing you and he had in common—your father.

Tim suspected you had something to do with the accident, probably because of the huge grin you couldn't quite shake off your face. But when he tried to lay the blame on you, you denied, denied, denied. Shailene might have believed Tim. But your dad rested his faith in you, and that's all that mattered.

Then one day he was gone.

Everything about your life went downhill after your father's funeral. With Shailene in charge, you were pretty much at her mercy, something Tim rubbed in every chance he got. It became a game of will and backdoor revenge.

You'd get him.

He'd get back at you.

One very big lesson you learned from all that was to never assume all is well.

You still never do.

And you always hold a trump card.

Fade Out

ASSUMPTIONS

Often lead you astray,
coax you out of
the region
of probability

into the realm
of conjecture,
a place where you can
easily lose your way.

Wander there
too long, it's hard
to separate
fiction from non.

Best to gather facts,
consume
digest
perhaps regurgitate.

You only choke
on truth
when you don't expect
to swallow it.

A HARD TRUTH

While necessary
to comprehend
can be difficult
to grapple with,
especially if its bottom
line is something
you can't crawl under,
let alone rise above.

And when you're mired
real good, and sinking
in a thick tar soup
of inescapable facts,
sometimes you stop
looking for a way out,
just want to let go.
Even wish you could
push yourself
all the way under.

Ah, despair!
How I adore thee!

Fade In:
SLIP BACK INTO NOELLE'S SKIN

Today will be the best day you've had in a long while, Noelle, because today you'll get to spend time with Grace. You actually bought her birthday present in December, meaning to give it to her for Christmas. But she spent winter break with her family in Vail, and every time you tried to meet up with her after that, she was busy with other things.

> *She wanted nothing to do with you.*

You were afraid she wouldn't come by this time, afraid she'd find yet another excuse to stay away. Other than seeing her at church occasionally—something you make sure will happen— you don't remember the last time you met up with her. Must have been late November, when you were still in school.

God, how you wish you were back there, celebrating your senior year with prom and pep rallies. You tried to stay, but the increasing workload, coupled with testing, testing, testing, was exhausting and left you vulnerable to seizures. You've had a couple in classrooms, and one on the soccer field. Neither peers nor teachers were exactly sympathetic.

Now you do online learning. Low pressure. Self-directed. Boring as hell. Even that requires some modifications because you can't stay in front of a computer for too long. So you read printed text as much as possible, listen to lectures without the visual stimulation of the video seminars, and only tap into the virtual arena to check boxes on their programmed tests. Sometimes even that gives you the headaches that signify the approach of an "event," as your dad calls them.

At least you'll earn your diploma, and everyone says that's what matters. But college is a distant dream, one that won't materialize because the pressure would be debilitating. As for a career, your options are extremely limited. Ditch digger, maybe.

> *As if you could be trusted*
> *with a shovel.*

You command yourself to stop thinking, already. It's Saturday. No schoolwork today and you need to eat. With luck, your parents will already be finished and immersed in some activity. No oversight means buttered toast!

Unfortunately, however, no such luck. Your mom and dad are at the table, sipping coffee and drinking smoothies. Dad looks up from his newspaper. "Morning." He lifts his glass. "We left you some in the refrigerator. Banana-carrot-kale."

"No wonder it's such a disgusting color." Hopefully it will taste better than it looks. You'll just have to find something more substantial later.

"So how did everything go last night?" asks Mom.

When Cami dropped you off, they were both in bed, pretending not to be waiting up. But their TV was on, so you know they were awake and doubtless anxious. Your mom checked up on you four times over the course of the evening.

"A-OK, just like I told you every time you called last night."

You pour your liquid breakfast, plus a cup of coffee, which you sweeten with sugar and cream, silently daring your parents to say one goddamn word. They notice, but remain quiet, and you join them at the table, pretending to listen to their banter.

Meanwhile you think about last night, and the tiff you had with your sister. She and Rand got home a few minutes before midnight. You expected them later and asked Cami why they were so early.

"Grace and I had a little argument, and after that things weren't so much fun, so we called it a night."

When you asked what they had words about, you couldn't believe Cami's story. "You seriously told her everyone should be armed?"

She shrugged. "Why lie?"

"Why say anything? Cami, Grace's dad was murdered, and the same gun ruined me. How can you think guns make people safer?"

"I'm well aware that you two happen to be prejudiced against firearms. But that's on *you*, not on *me*. I think everyone should be prepared to defend themselves or their families. There are lots of crazy people in the world, you know."

Prejudiced? Maybe that's so, but not the way she thinks. Carrying a gun around to look important, intimidate, and maybe even use when you're pissed at a driver who's going too slowly in front of you is ridiculous, and so is Cami's neurotic lust for a weapon she'll never have a use for.

Your parents used to keep guns. In fact, your mother taught you and Cami to shoot, something she learned growing up in New Mexico. "Better to understand and respect firearms," was her philosophy. But after the accident, after your brain rewired itself, sometimes dropping you deep into pits of depression, they got rid of them.

But they don't know everything,
do they?

Honestly, in those times when you're sucked under, you've fantasized about putting a barrel into your mouth and pulling the trigger. The gun wouldn't have to be new or expensive. You could buy it used, and it would be worth every penny to be assured, if and when you made that decision, there'd be no turning back. Most girls, you've read, prefer other methods. Usually boys choose a bullet. But as long as you did it correctly, it would be quick. Painless. An escape from pain, in fact.

Regardless, the conversation does get you thinking. Maybe, now that a wedge has been driven between Grace and Cami, just maybe this is the time to initiate some sort of reconciliation between Grace and you.

Truthfully, had you stayed in school, it would've been harder for Grace to cut ties. How would that have looked? And Grace truly does care about how her reputation is shaded. "Dump your bestie because her brain is clearly not working the way it should" could possibly have put her in a hideously colored spotlight. Then again, people can be cruel.

"Don't you think?" It's your dad's question, but the reference is totally lost on you.

"Sorry. My mind was wandering. Think about what?"

He gives you a *you can't be serious* look. "We were talking about spring break. Maybe taking a little trip to Hawaii?"

"Hawaii?" Somehow you missed that.

"Yes," says your mom, "we've decided to do something special for your birthday this year, and since it happens to coincide with your vacation for once, this is the perfect opportunity."

"You can bring a friend if you want," adds your dad, completely missing the fact that your pal list is practically nonexistent.

Only one person comes to mind and she'll be here later. This could be the very thing to lure her back into your sphere. "You mean, you'll pay for everything?"

"Including the sunscreen," agrees Dad. "But it's BYOB."

"What does that mean?"

"Bring your own bikini."

You laugh, even though there's zero chance of you wearing a bikini. You'll have to go shopping for a suit that will fit your body. Maybe you and Grace can go shopping together and . . . And you haven't even asked her yet. She wouldn't say no to Hawaii, though, would she?

A sunburst of hope scatters endorphins throughout your brain. Spring break is two months away. If you start right now and stay focused, you could drop a few pounds so you don't have to wear a swim caftan. The last thing you'd want is for Grace to be embarrassed by your company.

"I think I'll take a walk."

In unison, your parents glance at you, then look at each other and smile. Apparently it's a plot, but that's okay. You know they're conspiring out of love.

"Do you want me to come with you?"

"It's just a walk, Mom. I'll be fine."

"Okay, but take your phone. Just in case."

One of the things that sucks about having epilepsy is how everyone worries about you all the time. Bad enough you have to worry about yourself. You've noticed the stress lines on your mom's face deepening, and there can be no other reason than fretting about you.

You down your smoothie, which doesn't taste bad despite its sickening hue, pour half your coffee down the drain, and head outside into the vibrant Arizona sunshine. It isn't very hot, maybe sixty-five. Still, despite the slow pace you set, you're sweating by the time you reach the corner. Huffing a little, too. Maybe this exercise thing was a dumb idea after all.

But now your thoughts turn to Grace and the wild notion that maybe she'll agree to travel to Hawaii with you. Spend a week in a steamy tropical paradise with you. Now, you'll be ecstatic if she agrees to go as your friend, but once you would've prayed for something closer to romance.

Grace is the only person in the world who knows for sure you're queer. You weren't certain yourself until a few years ago. You've always admired pretty girls, never thought twice about the way your eyes were drawn to the swing of their hips or curves at the dip of their necklines. In elementary school, unlike some of your classmates, you much preferred female company to that of roughneck boys.

But then middle school rolled around, and with burgeoning adolescence came feminine cattiness. It was all about competition, and mostly they competed for the attention of guys. The word "lesbian," if uttered at all, was hissed as an insult, along with the abbreviated "lez" or highly favored "dyke." You threw those words around a few times yourself.

You tried to fit in, tried flirting with boys. But on those rare occasions you were successful, somehow kissing them wasn't a huge turn-on, and their hungry fingers fumbling to unbutton your blouse or touch you *there* only made you feel dirty, rather than desired.

Thank God you had Grace for your best friend. She never judged. Never called you weird or a loser for failing with boys. In fact, the two of you laughed about it.

Grace, of course, was pretty much perfect from the day she was born, at least to an outside observer. She could have any guy—or girl, for that matter—she waggled her finger at, and she never rubbed that in, either. There are things about her most people would never suspect, a darker side. A secret side. For you, that only intensifies her magnetism.

It was around eighth grade that you began to suspect your love for her meant more than simple friendship. Back then, she felt the same way, or at least pretended to. You were so close, moving into the forbidden zone felt completely natural, an outpouring of the desire for complete connection.

You didn't dare out yourselves in public, but sleepovers took on new meaning. In the beginning it was just spooning, soaking in each other's body heat, the exhilarating scent of sun-basted female skin. Easy, then, to caress each other, every brush of fingers cloaked in innocence.

"Infatuation" isn't strong enough to cover the way you felt, because that word implies something temporary, and you're still smitten. But on Grace's end, the ardor eventually cooled. She was adamant no one else should ever find out, though you would have been happy to stroll down any street or corridor, holding her hand. The rending was subtle, a single thread unraveling a seam.

And then came the accident. It was the final blow. You suspect she turned completely off, seeing you in the hospital, face bloated like a corpse in the sun, hair shaved, accommodating the removal of a slice of your skull to alleviate the swelling in your brain. Yes, you were a beauty, okay.

That was also the time Grace went religious, seeking confirmation that death is only a pathway to the next life. After you were released from the hospital, you followed her there and honestly, though you're still not sure about heaven or God, you've found some solace within worship.

There, too, you discovered a cause. It surprised you, really. You've lived in Tucson your entire life, but never really understood the depth of the hatred some people here harbor for their south-of-the-border neighbors.

As a Latino immigrant, your pastor is leading a charge against such prejudice, organizing a pro-immigration rally on Monday.

You'll be there, standing elbow-to-elbow with others who believe in an easier path to citizenship. You've heard there will be thousands there, which is at once elating and petrifying. But you're determined to manage it.

Walking the approximate speed of that proverbial tortoise, you circle three long blocks in around forty minutes. Not bad, considering it's the lengthiest continuous distance you've managed for many months. The last real exercise you got was PE the first semester of your junior year.

You'd think a gym teacher would be at least somewhat familiar with epilepsy. But not Ms. Harrison, who had no desire to understand your disability. Meds or no, you can still have seizures, and that one was triggered by the onset of your period. Hormones again. You happened to be running across the field when you felt it coming, so you stopped and sat quickly rather than fall. A few of the girls gathered around you, along with Ms. Witch.

You entered the tunnel. When you finally emerged again, disoriented and woozy, lying in grass that smelled like an unlit cigar, she wasn't even there. Candace said she'd gone to get the nurse, but you never saw them. And after that, you decided to take the F.

Fortunately, there will be no more PE classes. But, as tired as you feel after forty easy minutes, you realize you should have cared more about taking care of yourself. To do this again tomorrow will require force of will, something you're in short supply of.

Might as well give up right now.
No matter how hard you try
you'll never be attractive.

Back in the house, you take a quick shower, then dress in a pretty shift, one that conceals a couple of bulges, pick up a book, and read until Grace arrives. She promised to be here by two, but shows over an hour late. That's okay. Not like you were going anywhere, and when you open the door, see her standing there, a huge wave of joy slams into you.

"Come in! God, it's so great to see you."

She returns your hug. "You, too. How have you been?"

"Good. I'm good. Let's go to my room."

You take her hand, lead her down the hall, marveling at how soft her skin is, smoothed by some lotion that smells like melon. Once you're through the door, you turn on some music. You want to jump straight to Hawaii, but decide to wait, hoping she'll hang out for a while. "Sit. Tell me what's up with you."

"Not much, really. School, yeah. That's going okay. Only three more months to graduation. Oh, I got accepted at U of A. Can't see the need to leave Arizona to get a teaching degree."

A thrill shoots through you. She'll still be close next year!

"Are you going to prom?"

"Nah. Too expensive, and Daniel doesn't have a lot of spare cash. I mean, my parents would probably cover it, but I think it would make Daniel feel bad. I've been to prom. It's not all that."

Daniel. Too bad his name had to come up, but of course it did. "How are you two doing?" Behind your back, you cross your fingers, willing her to say she wants to break up with him.

"We're solid. He's waiting for me at the mall, by the way, so I can't stay too, too long."

> *He means more to her than you do.*

But then, you already knew that. Anger crackles, hardwood in a fireplace.

"Waiting . . . ?"

"Yeah. He's been staying at my house for the past couple of days. Took the time off work and everything. My parents are gone until Monday, so he's keeping me company."

> *He's doing more than that, you know.*

Now the crackling intensifies.

"That's nice. At least he's off the streets." That was kind of obvious. Change the subject. "Cami says Silas is spying on you. Creepy, huh?"

"Totally. And I'm not sure what to do about it."

"Call the cops."

"And tell them what? He hasn't really done anything."

You state the obvious. "Yet."

"Correct. But, like Rand said last night, the police work after the fact, and it's not like Tucson cops don't have more important stuff to do than track down a guy over a 'maybe.' I couldn't even get a restraining order without him actually threatening me."

Good point. "Well, please be careful. If anything feels off—"

"Dial 911."

"Exactly." You let it drop, veer away from the subject, toward something more positive. "Oh, hey. Hang on."

You go over to your dresser, pick up the little package sitting atop it. It's wrapped in bright red foil, with a silver bow, but Grace won't necessarily realize that's symbolic of Christmas. And even if that thought crosses her mind, it's what's inside that counts, not when you bought it.

When you turn, she's waiting, and the smile on her face, pre-gifting, is priceless. You offer the present with a heartfelt "Happy birthday." If only you'd thought to get a cake.

Grace removes the paper carefully, opens the small box, revealing the sterling silver bracelet you shopped so diligently for. She studies the charms you chose with much consideration: a dragonfly, symbolizing freedom; a yin-yang symbol, for opposites attracting; and, of course, a heart.

"You can add more." Again, you state the obvious.

"Maybe one day. For now, these are perfect. Help me put it on?"

You do, and she rewards you with another hug, punctuated by a sweet kiss on the cheek. It meant nothing but friendship, you know, but still it makes you blush. "You like it?"

"I love it. Thank you."

She'll want to go soon, so you hurry. "Hey. For *my* birthday, my parents are taking me to Hawaii. They said I could bring a friend. Want to come with? Dad says they'll pay for everything except a new bikini."

Surprise—the pleasant kind—lights her eyes. "Seriously? Wow. That would be fun. I'll have to check with my parents, of course." But now she sobers. "You—you'll be okay on a plane for that long, right?"

"We wouldn't be going otherwise."

Looks like you'll have to go over the epilepsy primer with Grace. She should know how to help in case there's a problem. But, hey, whatever. You're pretty sure she just agreed to go.

She's got plenty of time to change her mind.

Fade Out

PROTECTING ONE'S HEART

Requires diligent introspection
and careful analysis
of every interaction
between you and the target
of your affection.
But even if you miss a vital signal,
few enough succumb
to a broken heart.

Protecting one's person
demands vigilant observation
and not only know-how,
but also a well-rehearsed
reaction to the approach
of perceived danger.
Refusing to walk in fear,
rather enjoying a steady tightrope
stroll above borderline paranoia.

Protecting one's child
commands ferocious resolve
in the face of overwhelming odds
and the willingness
to sacrifice your own skin
if that becomes requisite.
Forced into this unimaginable space,
would you step between
danger and your little one?
Or run?

IT'S SAID

Like metal to magnet
or stud dog to bitch in heat,
some people attract danger.

Do what they will,
slither off into the night,
disguise their trail, hell,

pretend "Christ" and finagle
their way onto a missionary
outreach to South America,

they'll trip over a shoelace or
wolves will sniff them out,
or headhunters will sacrifice

them on altars of "don't fuck
with me," imbibe their blood
in good faith ritual.

But there are also those
who court danger,
stand in its path, thumb

their noses, dare its approach,
believing themselves well
prepared to win the day.

Close your eyes to jeopardy,
it very well might circle,
take you out from behind.

Fade In:
SLIP BACK INTO CAMI'S SKIN

Another day, another dollar, as your grandpa used to say. At least, you really, really hope you can make a few bucks the semi-easy way. Waylon needs new shoes, and you're not about to put anything less than Nikes on the kid's feet. That boy is worth it.

> *He's worth a lot, Cami.*
> *But does he merit*
> *the confines of marriage?*
> *More and more, you feel*
> *like you're incarcerated.*

Too often lately, you think about where you'd be if you and Rand hadn't hooked up. Definitely not married. You've stay-at-home parented for, like, forever. It's getting old. Some girls are happy to do nothing but babysit, watch TV, and eat. You've got more ambition than that, but exactly how much do you possess?

School was never much your thing, but if you'd graduated, maybe you would have gone to college. It's even possible you would've liked it, but that prospect is dim now. You don't even have a GED.

PUP (Pre Unplanned Pregnancy), you had no clear career goals in mind. Not like your sister, who knew exactly what she wanted to do—and look where it got her. Exactly nowhere. See, that's the problem with keeping your eyes on the prize. Sometimes it's snatched away from you. Life ain't always fair.

You do feel sorry for Noelle, at least usually. She should have an art school acceptance letter by now. But she doesn't, and probably never will. All the big dreams she's had since she was young are on permanent hold. It would suck to have a malfunctioning brain.

Still, that's no reason for her to get snippy, especially not with you, her older sister. You did not appreciate her bullshit last night, or Grace's either. Thank God your brain seems to function correctly, unlike theirs.

"Where we goin', Mama?" Waylon asks from the backseat.

"I have to see some people, then I'll take you to the park. Sound good?"

"Yeah! I wanna slide."

That kid loves the slides, especially the big spiraling ones. You used to worry about that, but Rand talked you into letting him try. "He's a little man. He should act like one."

It's weird, really. On one hand, Rand thinks french fries will kill the child. On the other, he's not the slightest bit worried about sending Waylon up an extremely tall ladder for a long, fast, circular ride down a piece of hopefully substantial plastic. So far, so good, you have to admit. Not a single fall.

But it does make you wonder if good parenting is something you inherit, or something you learn. Your mom and dad are decent, and raised you with care and concern. There was no hint of abuse or neglect. In fact, if anything, they were on the overprotective side, at least when you were younger. Once adolescence hit, they kind of lost track of you, mostly because you were an excellent sneak. Then when Noelle was hurt, they necessarily directed all their attention toward her. That didn't bother you, and when, in the midst of her long recovery, you managed to get pregnant, they supported your decision to have the baby, although your mom did try to persuade you to postpone the wedding.

"No reason to hurry," she urged. "You can always make it legal once you're absolutely certain that's what you want."

Too bad you didn't listen.

But you didn't. Like tuning in to your mom and dad was ever a trait. Still, your kickback parenting philosophy reflects theirs. McDonald's every now and then isn't going to turn Waylon into a porker. Finger painting on otherwise neutral walls (rather in need of painting anyway)? Maybe the kid is an artiste in the making.

Rand's childhood was a shit show. Jeremy, his career air force dad, was strict but fair, at least according to Rand, who claims, "He never spanked me unless I had it coming." Which means, duh, he did get whacked a time or two.

After Jeremy and Pam split up, Rand didn't see his father much until he got older. And then when Jeremy remarried, he had new kids to play Daddy to. Rand's mom has always been all about herself and the bottle. Any abuse there was verbal, other than whatever punishments her man-of-the-moment might inflict, and you've got a feeling that happened more than once.

The offshoot is, nature or (lack of) nurture, Rand keeps cold fury boxed up inside like dry ice. Lift the lid, the frigid smoke roils and rises. Probably not the best trait for a cop, not that you'd voice that opinion out loud. You've never seen him direct it toward Waylon, but you've witnessed it pointed at others, like yesterday with Silas. And it has flashed your way.

The other night, after soothing Waylon to sleep, you discovered Rand hyperfocused on his computer. First you thought he must be viewing porn, something that doesn't bother you much because afterward sex is generally good. But when you asked, "What are you up to?" he slammed the lid of his laptop closed.

"Nothing. Not a goddamn thing."

His eyes, when he turned to look at you, swarmed with rage, not lust. And there was no sex at all when he came to bed. In fact, he curled up away from you. Whatever he'd seen on-screen had flung that box wide open, and the frozen steam that escaped burned, searing into his dreams.

He woke you with his nightmare-fed ramblings. "No! Stay away!"

You reached out to stroke him, try to calm him. He bolted out of sleep, into confusion, and came up swinging. Luckily, he only connected with air.

"Rand! Stop!" Your heart hammered.

Zombie-eyed, his head swiveled side to side, searching the room for something not present. "Where'd he go?"

"Who?"

The question went unanswered. Instead, Rand vowed, "I will kill him." The frost in his voice lifted goose bumps on your arms. He threw back the covers.

"Rand, there's no one here. It was just a bad dream. Go back to sleep." Tentatively, you coaxed him against his pillow, smoothed the blankets over him again.

Somehow, he settled back into slumber. You tried, but after several anxious minutes you clambered out of bed and crept to the bathroom for a nerve-induced pee. The entire episode was chilling, especially the calm, even way Rand declared he would murder someone.

That was not the by-product
of a nightmare.

"Mama, I hungry."

Waylon's plaintive plea reminds you that he didn't get breakfast. Rand left without his lunch this morning, and you wanted to deliver it to him so he wouldn't come home and wonder why you weren't there. You've got a pickup scheduled, and a couple of runs to make after, and don't want to worry about explanations. Better he doesn't even ask questions in the first place.

The dashboard clock confirms you've got plenty of time before Hector's expecting you. Like most big-time dealers, the dude is relatively confined to his dwelling anyway. "Okay, baby. Let's get some pancakes."

"Yay! Bacon, too."

Fortuitously, Denny's happens to be right over there. It's a bustling location, but a nice older lady, name-tagged Nadine, seats you right away. Waylon bounces up into the booth as she hands you a menu.

You build your own Grand Slam. Waylon can have the pancakes and bacon. You'll take the two eggs, scrambled. Pretty good eating for under seven dollars.

Waylon's blowing bubbles in his chocolate milk and you're about to check your phone when all of a sudden two guys plow through the door, wearing hoodies and masks and pointing handguns. "Everybody down!" yells the taller one, punctuating the order with a bullet, which hits the far wall.

People move. Drop. Sprawl on the floor. You jerk Waylon under the table, wrap him up tight in your arms.

"Gun go bang, Mama!"

"Shh. Stay quiet."

"Open the register!" orders one of the men.

A gun goes off again, followed by the sound of shattering glass. "Don't be a goddamn hero. Next time, you're dead."

Helpless beneath the scant shelter of a gum-encrusted table, you watch a pair of feet move past you. The man darts around the restaurant, collecting valuables. No! You've got to get your purse, but it's beyond your reach on the seat beneath the window. Too far. Too dangerous. And you don't dare let go of Waylon, who's snuffling against your chest.

The guy grabs hold of your bag instead. "Holy shit. This bitch is loaded."

Your stomach lurches, like you just jumped out of an airplane, unsure of the state of the parachute. You clench your teeth and hold on, forcing yourself to stay still when instinct insists you should run.

*You're the only thing
between Waylon and them.*

"Hurry, goddamn it!" yells the dude up front.

"I—I'm try—"

Another shot silences Nadine, and now the feet are running. "Why'd you do that?" one man shouts.

The answer trails them out the door. "She pissed me off."

Nobody moves for several long seconds. Once it's clear the men are really gone, there is motion. Still holding Waylon, you work your way out from under the table. Other people stand, assessing their persons, possessions, and neighbors.

"Oh, my God," says a woman near the front. "He shot her. Call 911."

You inhale.

Exhale.

Wheeze.

Rasp.

Stress sometimes triggers your asthma. Dazed, quaking, you retrieve your purse, now emptied of money. Luckily, your inhaler is there, at least. One quick draw quiets your air exchange, though your heart still feels like a kettledrum.

"Mama okay?"

"Yeah, baby. I'm okay."

Not so Nadine, who lies prone on the floor. A couple of people kneel beside her, trying to stanch the blood. That guy had no reason to shoot her.

The harsh cry of approaching sirens comes faster than expected, and a half-dozen cruisers whip into the parking lot. And now you're sucked into the vortex. Police. Rescue. More police. An ambulance. Another. Apparently "the hero" was also hit, though by a piece of glass, and the wound is superficial. Unlike that of Nadine, who at least is still breathing.

You sit panting softly, willing the race of your pulse to slow as you wait to give your statement. Waylon keeps repeating, "Cops, Mama. Look. Where the bad guys?"

"Gone," you tell him. "They're gone now."

He bounces on the booth seat, chattering, until a skinny policeman with a buzz cut and eyes like ice comes over and hands you a report to fill out. What can you say, except the guy who stole your cash was wearing pricey red-and-black athletic shoes? When he returns to collect it, you ask, "I don't guess I'll ever see that money again?"

The officer chuckles. "I wouldn't count on it."

"Can we go now?"

He scans what you wrote. "All he took from you was cash? No credit cards or other valuables?"

"No. That's it." As if you owned a credit card, and the only other thing of worth in your purse, other than your inhaler, is your cell phone. Too easy to trace that, is your guess.

"Okay, then. You may leave."

Waylon waves as you exit. "Bye-bye, cops! Bang-bang the bad guys!"

You'd like to bang-bang the bad guys.

That's what crosses your mind as you buckle Waylon into his car seat. That, and thank God those jerks didn't take your keys and steal the car.

"Where my pancakes, Mama?"

Oh, man. The poor kid still needs to eat. Your appetite has dissolved, but he has no clue what just happened. "That nice old lady got sick, so they closed the kitchen."

He's hungry, and you are fresh out of cash. You root around in the cup holders, locate enough change for a cheeseburger, drive through McDonald's, and spend every last cent. The cashier even spots you a nickel, mostly because your kid is in the backseat crying about starving to death.

A nickel is nothing. Getting Hector to spot you five hun worth of weed is a whole different thing, but you have to ask him. He's not the kind of guy who wants to be kept waiting. Surely he'll understand this was the random will of circumstance, not in any way your fault.

It's a ten-minute drive through a risky neighborhood, one you wouldn't want your car to break down in. As usual, when you cruise these streets, you're slightly uncomfortable having Waylon in the backseat. Stray bullets have been known to . . .

It strikes you again how very close you came to that very scenario today, only in Denny's of all goddamn places.

Too bad you didn't have your own gun along.

The weird thing is, as scared as you were under that table, it also gave you the tiniest thrill, like walking on the very edge of a cliff, knowing the sandstone beneath your outside foot could crumble. Stupid, for sure, especially because had you gone over the precipice, Waylon would've gone with you.

Which puts you right back in the moment. You remember the first time you drove through here, petrified, and not only about the neighborhood. You wanted to meet up with Hector, you did, but you were pretty damn certain he was a scary guy.

He didn't seem that way in high school, though he was older and you only knew him tangentially through his sister, Lara, who was a classmate. You happened to run into her at the park, where she was babysitting Hector's son. She asked if you wanted to smoke a little weed, and you said sure. It was the first time since before you got pregnant. Waylon had just turned two, and while he showed off his sliding ability to his new little buddy, Lara and you passed a joint.

That was enough to get you thinking about a way to supplement Rand's income, and one day you rode along when Lara was on the score. You kind of ducked down in the seat, and your friend laughed. "Don't worry. You're with me. Nobody in this hood is gonna mess with us. Hector takes care of his people."

That has proven to be the case, at least for the most part.

You pull up in front of an old cinder-block house, help a ketchup-faced Waylon out of the car. Holding him protectively, you stumble through the litter-strewn yard, trying not to trip. When you knock on the door, Hector's humongous Akita barks gruffly, announcing your presence. As you wait to be let inside, your apprehension grows.

"Get down, goddamn it," Hector yells from the far side of the threshold. "Melinda? Do something with this fucker, would you?"Another sixty or so seconds, the door opens. "You're late."

"Sorry. Not my fault. I'll tell you inside."

Admission is granted and you follow Hector into his small living room. That, at least, is neat, except for a few of his kids' toys. The two of you have that in common. Waylon wriggles out of your grasp and goes to investigate some Hot Wheels cars.

Might as well dive right in. "So, we went out to breakfast . . ."

As you relate the story, Hector watches you, suspicion building in his eyes. But two people shot at Denny's should be easy enough to confirm, something that must finally occur to him, because when you finish, he says, "What do you want from me?"

"Can you front the weed? Please?"

"Hey, I ain't no payday loan."

"I get it. I'd never ask if this didn't happen. But we've known each other a long time. . . ." True, almost a year, and you know him well enough not to ever try and cheat him. "I'll bring you the money ASAP. I've got people waiting on me, so it won't be a problem."

He keeps eyeing you like a jackal scoping out roadkill. Finally, he decides, "I want the money by Monday." He stands and goes over to the cabinet housing his stash, comes back with two ounces of very good green.

When you reach for them, his fingers close around your face, squeeze your cheeks just hard enough to let you know he means business, but not quite enough to loosen teeth. "Stiff me, you'll be sorry."

Your heart stutters fear, but that is momentary, and replaced by a hot shot of fury.

If he ever touches you again
you will make him very sorry.

Fade Out

THE HUMAN HEART

Is delicate.
Breakable.
Prone to trauma,
and thus an effortless
vehicle for vengeance.

With a river of pain coursing
through arteries
and slender vessels linked
between the most vital
organ and the source
of thought, emotion
quite often thwarts wisdom.

And, oh children,
a steel serpent lingering
within easy reach
remains ever ready
to strike
at will.

PROVIDE SUFFICIENT PAIN

Manipulation becomes a snap
of the fingers. Ask
any Guantanamo detainee.

Offer him an eager weapon,
he wouldn't think
twice about eliminating a guard.

But the desire to settle a score requires
neither simulated
drowning nor electric shock.

Sometimes it starts as nothing
more than a tiny itch,
best left alone or soothed with salve.

Because scratch it once, the prickling
will intensify until
the craving becomes insatiable.

Fade In:

SLIP BACK INTO ASHLYN'S SKIN

No one's ever accused you of having an overabundance of patience, and this evening seems determined to test it. First, after spending the day with Silas, trolling for wetbacks, you stop by his father's place. When you arrive, an actual Mexican warmly greets you, but she calls you by the wrong name.

> *What's awful about that, Ashlyn,*
> *is that it outs your boyfriend.*
> *His heart belongs to another girl.*
> *You're nothing but a piece of tail.*

One night of sex, even after a few weeks of demonstrated interest on Silas's part, doesn't exactly mean a dedicated relationship has formed. So why do you consider him worth hanging on to, and maybe even fighting to keep, especially after his admission that he has forgiven Grace for breaking up with him? Forgiven.

He's still talking about her now, every word weighted with undeniable affection, as you wait for Zia to call you to the table. "So, yeah, I mean, watching her dad get blown away was really rough on her."

"Hmm," you muse. "I wouldn't mind seeing my father get blown away."

That shuts his mouth for several long seconds. "Do you mean that?"

Floppy lips sink ocean liners, you dunce. You've said far too much. Now you've got only a couple of moves. You can divert. Or explain. Silas is waiting.

"Actually, yes, I do. A firing squad would be too good for him, in fact. Way too quick."

"Because he killed your mom."

"Yeah."

He starts to say something. Thinks better. But finally can't stop himself. "How did it happen? I mean, will you tell me?"

A long sigh escapes your mouth. You haven't talked about it in a long time and prefer to keep it bottled inside, so you offer the CliffsNotes version, omitting all but the basic details. Any outside observer might comment on your obviously subdued affect and monotone recital of facts. Emotionless reporting, as if you weren't really there. But you were.

He's sitting beside you on the small sofa, and he slides an arm around your shoulder, draws you in. "Jeez, man, that totally sucks. I'm sorry."

Auto-response: I'm sorry.
It pisses you off.

"Why? You didn't do it."

"Well, duh. I'm sorry because it hurt you, I guess."

Sympathy isn't something you asked for, and empathy is rare. Nonexistent in your life up to this point, in fact. The ice dam you've constructed around your heart softens just a little. "Thanks." One hoarse utterance is all you've got.

He rewards it with a gentle kiss. Probably a pity kiss, but you like it anyway. It almost feels like he cares about you, and as you sink deeper into it, resentment at Grace fades.

"Oye, chicos. Ven a cenar." Zia's chirp from the kitchen interrupts the pleasant moment.

You feel warmed, thawed by spicy tacos or this sudden insane blast of attraction to a guy you barely know. Up until last night, you weren't even sure you liked him. You definitely do, but you know that attachment to any living human being is simply the highway to heartbreak. Which is why for the past seven years you've avoided it.

"What did you do today?" asks Zia, who's clearing the table so she can end the meal with tres leches cake, also her own concoction. "From scratch" at Aunt Lou's means opening a can.

Silas doesn't hesitate. "We put up Tim's drone. It's pretty cool."

He and his dad do not exchange knowing glances, so you assume Mr. Wells is unaware of his son's hunting proclivities. Which totally makes sense, considering the company.

"What did you see?" Zia looks at you, so you're on.

"Oh, uh, lots of desert. Some rabbits and quail . . ." None of which sounds "pretty cool." Quick. Make something up. "And . . . I probably shouldn't admit this, but it happened to fly over a couple doing . . . you know . . ."

"Doesn't surprise me," says Mr. Wells. "We come across them all the time. It's kind of fun to give 'em a scare."

Silas is all in. "Scaring them with a badge is one thing. Imagine an eye-in-the-sky taking a low pass over!"

Everyone laughs. Score one for the well-seasoned liar.

After one of the most delicious desserts you've ever tasted, Mr. Wells asks, "Are you spending the night? We didn't expect an extra guest, but we can work something out."

"Didn't plan on it," answers Silas. "Ashlyn needs to get back before midnight."

"But thank you for the invitation," you add.

"Por supuesto," says Zia. "Nuestra casa es su casa. Oh. ¿Hablas español? Do you speak Spanish?"

"No." Nothing beyond "tacos," "salsa," and "tres leches," which, as you learned tonight, means "three milks."

"I said, of course. Our home is your home. And you are always welcome here."

Her English is almost as good as her Spanish. She's definitely been in this country for a while. Probably second generation, not that it's any of your business. One thing's for sure. It's hard not to like her. How would she feel if she knew how Silas spends his Saturdays? How would his father feel?

Are you worried about other people's feelings now?

Honestly, that has rarely been a concern, at least since your mom died. You chew on this notion for a long while on the way back to Tucson: very few people have ever cared about how you feel. Two, you reckon. And they're both (cremated) ashes, blowing in the wind.

The thing about a girl like Grace, who admittedly lost her father in a terrible way, is she had support to help her deal with that. A solid mother. Friends. No doubt, a great deal of therapy.

You have nothing.
No one.

Yes, you had your grandmother for a while. She gave you a couple of short satisfied years, but those could not assuage the omnipresent ache of losing your mother. While you lived with her, you tried hard to fit in at school, make friends, excel in the classroom. But your past kept creeping up to bite your ass. In the books you loved and the gossip you hated, history cast a wide shadow.

The result, as hard as it is to admit it, is having lost faith in the concept of love. Some girls in your position might search for it in any person pretending to offer it, and do anything to keep the small semblance they found. You, on the other hand, have no desire to hunt for it because you know you'd just get burned if you did. And if it happened into your life by accident, accepting the truth of it would be almost impossible.

Two huge questions keep dangling in front of you, like proverbial carrots in front of the donkey. One: Do you want love? And two: Are you able to give it? Either you're terrified of the emotion or you're a sociopath.

Not such a bad thing to be.

Silas could also match the description. You don't know him well enough yet to say for sure. A lot of people might believe just being involved with TradYouth qualifies a person as a psychiatric deviant. The jury's still out on that.

"Nickel for your thoughts. I'd offer a quarter, but I dumped them all in the keg offering plate."

"Probably not worth five cents, but I was thinking about love."

"Oh. What about it?"

You veer into the realm of the possible. "It seems like your dad and Zia are in love."

He tenses noticeably. "Yeah."

"Does it bother you?"

His face puffs crimson, and blood visibly throbs in his temples, but his voice remains level. "It makes me sick to my stomach."

"Have you told him?"

"Sure. He's still there. Not like my feelings matter. C'est la vie."

"You know French?"

"Only as it applies to fries. Oh, I know another one. Chérie."

He's actually funny. More depth here than you expected. It's too bad you can't read him better. Other than the obvious, you can't quite ferret out what he wants from you.

Nothing. Nothing but the obvious.

"You're still in love with Grace." The words shoot from your mouth, totally unintended.

"What? Wait? Where did that come from?"

"I don't know. Just the way you talked about her, like you dream about her every night."

One beat.

Two.

Three.

He's aiming to lie to you.

"Listen, Ash . . . Hey, I like that. I'm going to call you Ash, okay?"

You want to tell him no damn way, that nicknames are plain damn lazy, but he doesn't give you the chance.

"I fell in love with Grace just like you see in the movies: wrong guy connects with totally the wrong girl. It was cliff diving, a crazy huge rush that can't be described unless you've been there, shooting speed or cocaine. Not that I've done those. I haven't. Too easy to lose control.

"We aren't the same kind of people. I still worry about her, but she's out of my life. So, unlike the movies, there's no happy ending for Grace and me."

"No such thing as happy endings. Everyone winds up the same way."

"Dead, you mean? Guess you've got a point. Which is why you should live in the moment, right?"

He's angling for sex
before he takes you home.

Might as well indulge him, not to mention you. A need for physical union crackles inside. That, and a wicked desire to scrub Grace from his heart, make her not only inaccessible, but all the way gone. You don't even know this girl, but there's a good possibility that she could become an unpleasant obsession.

So when Silas pulls off the highway, you don't tell him to turn around. And when he parks Lolita in a quiet, unlit patch of desert, you open the window to admit the song of the night and a shimmer of moonlight. He turns toward you, but before he can say a word, you yank off your T-shirt, unclasp your bra, the act a silent demand.

He takes it more as invitation, but that's okay. Winning the game means things going your way. "Here or in back?" he asks.

"Not enough room in here for what I've got in mind."

He moves swiftly, indulging your request, and to a soundtrack of crickets and distant coyote yips, you do your very best to eradicate Grace from the night's memory.

Afterward, lying side by side on an old sleeping bag beneath a starscape, he says, "Girl, you are something." He props himself up on one arm, leans over to kiss you.

It's short, because you keep it that way. "We should probably go. Uncle Frank gets pissed when I'm home late."

"What about your aunt?"

"She couldn't care less. She hardly even knows I'm there, except when she has to feed me. Not that she does very often. The microwave is my personal chef. She's going to hate it when I turn eighteen and that foster-care money dries up."

As you straighten your clothes, you realize just how true those sentiments are. Better to be ignored than hyper-observed.

Uncle Frank, of course, is a different story. He watches you, though he's not as yet tried to push things beyond the realm of visual stimulation. You let him have his jollies, at least when Aunt Lou isn't around. Hey, what does it hurt if he watches you walk naked from the shower to your room, or sunbathe nude on the patio?

Should he ever try to push beyond your boundaries, you'll have a choice. Allow it, because it accomplishes something you need. Or defend yourself. You've got the means and the knowledge to thwart physical assault. And goddamn if you don't have the willpower, emphasis on the "power."

Thinking about power, the rally comes to mind. "So what's the plan for Monday, other than showing up?"

"It's not just TradYouth. There will be other groups gathering, too. Once we're all there—strength in numbers—we march."

"Peacefully?"

Silas shrugs. "Who knows? It will be a pretty big crowd. Us, the pro-immigration people, and a whole lot of law enforcement. It'll be tense. But we're there to make a huge statement."

"Which is?"

"That white America is taking this country back. We are telling the world in no uncertain terms that we're sick of being pushed aside in favor of random 'others.' To help people remember that America was founded as a white Christian nation, and make them understand that we plan to keep it that way."

His forcefulness makes you shiver. You break out in a rash of goose bumps. "I can't wait."

"You're a strange girl, know that?"

"I've been called worse. Anyway, I kind of own 'weird.'"

"Cool." He pushes you down, slips off your shirt, and settles his bulk gently over you. "Let's get weird."

You worm out from underneath him, coax him onto his back.

Weird is okay.
As long as you stay on top.

Fade Out

A COLLISION

Of opposition forces
is something special
to behold, when both sides
come armed with certainty
of God-ordained victory.

The clash is spectacular,
regardless of weaponry.
Soldiers drop beneath
the weight of clubs, bleed
from wounds inflicted
by knives or broken glass.

Windows shatter.
Barricades fall.
Mace and burning rubber
perfume the air.
And should bullets fly,
scatter art decorates
every viable surface.

Beyond the physical,
the real beauty lies
in human spirits
openly embracing hate.

STEREOTYPES

Are difficult to disintegrate.
People tend to embrace
long-standing definitions
of human identities.

Children should be seen
and not heard.

Women belong at the hearth
and in the kitchen.

Men carry the torches of war
into battle.

Evolution is a slow current,
erosion the faster element
of change, revolution
the quickest route of all
unless you advocate
nuclear options.

Revolutionaries are rare,
a breed apart from mundane
thinkers, and when they rise,
the world trembles
at their feet.

Fade In:
SLIP BACK INTO RAND'S SKIN

If there's one thing you can't stand, it's coming home after work to an unexpectedly empty house, like yesterday. Even worse is when a call to Cami's cell goes unanswered. Voice mail doesn't count, especially when there's no call back.

> *She has no right to ignore you, Rand,*
> *no right to make you worry*
> *about where she's spending time.*

When she finally came in, Waylon in tow, her excuse was flimsy. "I was running errands."

"You were running errands before lunch," you complained. "What kind of errands took you all day?"

"Well, there was a problem. . . ."

She went on to recite what seemed like an implausible story about an armed robbery at Denny's. But then you caught it on the news, and it was incomprehensible that your wife and son had actually been embroiled in it.

Waylon noticed the scene on TV. "Bad guys, Daddy. And guns going bang, and cops, too. We was under table."

Cami did the right thing, taking cover, but if you'd been there, those guys would've gone down, that's for sure. Yeah, the guy who tried to interfere got shot, but you're way too clever to take a bullet in an armed robbery. You have to be sneakier than the crooks. It's too bad about the old lady, who's fighting for her life in the hospital. The very idea that one of those jerks might've wasted Waylon or Cami makes you livid. If you wore a badge today, you'd prioritize tracking them down.

You'd prioritize taking them down,
taking them all the way out.

However, your family stayed safe and when you thought about it, even after Cami recovered from the shock, she had plenty of time to go to the grocery store like she promised. But there was no chicken chili, no fresh milk, no produce or paper towels. No groceries at all. So where did she go? When you asked, her explanation changed.

"I needed to chill, so we visited some friends."

"Friends? Like who?"

"You don't know them."

That refrain again.
It's becoming too familiar.
How many people does she know
that you don't?

"Waylon plays with their kids," she added.

"Kids," agreed your little boy. "Hot Wheels. An' McD's."

When you gave her the *what the hell* look, she whined, "He was hungry, and it was all I could afford after they stole my money. Our money."

"They robbed *you*? How much did they get?"

She hesitated, and her face creased, as if she either couldn't recall or couldn't concoct a decent lie.

"You don't remember?"

"No. I do. You're not going to like this."

"Okay, I won't like it. How much?"

"Two hundred dollars."

It was like she'd slugged you. A third of your paycheck. She shouldn't have been carrying so much cash.

As if reading your mind, she explained, "I was going to pay the cable bill and go to the grocery store. I'm sorry. Wait. No, I'm not. It wasn't my fault, you know."

"Obviously." You totally realize that, but that much money doesn't come easily, and you'll never see it again. "I don't get paid until next Friday. Are we okay?"

She nodded. "We'll get by. We might have to eat peanut butter most of the week, but we won't starve."

"PB and J!" Waylon was agreeable.

You didn't get chicken chili for dinner, but you weren't stuck with peanut butter. Cami managed to scrabble together grilled cheese sandwiches and tomato soup, which happen to be favorites of yours, so all was pretty much forgiven.

Truthfully, you've remained mostly in the dark when it comes to banking and bills. Cami's good at it, and it would just be another chore you don't need. But you don't really like being this blind to your finances, so maybe you should pay better attention.

As for surviving until Friday, you can always bum a little cash from your dad. You value autonomy and hate when you have to ask, but it's become necessary a few times over the last couple of years, and he's always been generous. He doesn't even try to make you feel like less of a man.

That matters. Which is why you couldn't let the thing with Levon go at work yesterday. Only a pussy would've backed away. The old "boys will be boys" idiom does not apply when it's your woman some dude's slobbering over. Any reaction other than the one you chose would've made the whole crew lose every ounce of respect for you.

You learned to fight at age ten, not long after the camping trip.

It wasn't that you were small, at least not short. You were always one of the tallest boys in your classrooms. But your mom fed you garbage. Worse than McDonald's. Thank God she acquiesced to your dad's demand that you get hot lunch at school (an expense he personally paid for) or you might have withered completely away.

As the gawkly loner with the drunk mom, the bullies picked on you relentlessly until one day you decided you'd had enough. You were outside on the playground when a big, buff kid called you "fag." And when the others started laughing, you went off. Came at him, swinging. You connected a few times, but your feeble strength against his ample meat, the blows were meaningless. His, however, were anything but.

>*He kicked your spindly ass.*

Yes, but as he pummeled you black and blue, you stepped outside of your body, observing his moves and programming them into your memory banks. He was cool in his delivery, and that impressed you the most. Later, after the school nurse stanched the blood and the vice principal suspended the victor for three days, you would meditate on the nuances of hand-to-hand battle. The next time a fistfight necessitated itself, you fared better. The time after that, you won.

>*What a rush that was, dropping him!*
>*And the hard-won respect*
>*in the other kids' eyes*
>*made a bruise or two worthwhile.*

It's Sunday, and while others go to church or watch basketball, you'll spend a good part of the day working. Most of the guys relax on Sunday, but you always ask for extra hours, and since tomorrow is a holiday, not to mention the fact that your bank account is two hundred dollars lighter than it should be, it's especially important this weekend.

You've stirred early, just a thin trickle of light announcing that it's morning. And while you consider yesterday's events, you notice Cami twisting and hissing within her dreams, distressed at whatever is chasing her there. So you coax her into your arms and wake her with a kiss. "Morning."

"What time is it?" she whispers.

"A little after six."

"Why are you awake already?"

The drowsy husk of her voice is sexy as hell and coupled with the heat of her skin, she is a total turn-on. And, for probably the millionth time, you think how incredibly lucky you are that she's all yours. "So I can get laid before work?"

"Oh," she sighs. "That."

Sometimes she says no, which is why you framed your request as a question. But that is rare, and today she's more than willing. She's ready, as if whatever was stalking her in dreamland was as much man as monster. Can't fault her for that, and for that reason or another, her lovemaking this morning is a tango—hot, slick, complicated moves requiring dexterity and skill.

After all this time together, she still surprises you. Usually that's good, but sometimes it bothers you. Like when she wants to be in control. You're the stud; she's the filly. This morning, however, she just wanted to please. "You been taking lessons or what?"

"Lessons?" she asks.

"Yeah. Like, sex lessons. You keep getting better and better."

Cami grins. "No lessons. Just lots of practice." Noting your consternated expression, she quickly adds, "With you, Rand. How do you think I know what you like?"

Good point, although she couldn't have known how much you'd like the unique position she pretzeled herself into this morning. "We have done it a time or five hundred, huh?"

"At least." She runs her hand down the length of your torso, and you might take that as an invitation to be accepted, but the alarm blares.

And today, you're on a mission.

You toss back the covers. "Have to get ready for work."

Cami follows you into the bathroom, watches you soap away the evidence of this morning's bedroom adventure. "What time do you think you'll be home?"

"Not too late. Today's just some light framing. Chuck gave me the extra hours I asked for. Everyone else is taking today and tomorrow off."

"But you're home tomorrow, right?"

"Yeah. Why?"

"I was thinking about spending a little time with Noelle, and was hoping you'd babysit. It's hard to talk with Waylon running around, getting into everything. My parents' house isn't exactly what you'd call toddler-proofed."

"Is your sister okay?"

"Sure. We just don't get to hang out much anymore."

"Okay. No problem."

But it kind of is. Cami, at least, has her playgroup friends to do stuff with. Your old buddies don't even ask to include you anymore. Not that you can blame them, really. It's not like they're partnered for life, or doing the daddy thing. Their topics of conversation revolve around basketball and Hooters, not Nickelodeon and Little People.

Besides, even if you still kept in touch with them, you have no spare time at all. Classes. Work. Home. Classes. Work. Home. Once in a while, the odd night out, like on Friday. And look how that ended.

Plot an escape,
or at least a diversion.
You deserve it.

"Oh. I am going to stop by my dad's on the way home. See if he'll front a few dollars to make up for what we lost yesterday." Way to make that plural.

"Your dad's skiing, remember?"

"Oh. Right. Okay, then, tomorrow, when he gets home."

"Are you sure?"

"Uh-huh. PB and J gets old after a day or two."

"As long as you can handle it today. It's all we've got for your lunch." Off she goes to slather Jif.

Maybe you'll stop by your dad's house later anyway. Grace is there, alone with Daniel. It would be good to check up on her. You don't know the guy very well, and while he seemed okay Friday night, something about him bothered you, some indefinable undercurrent that made you uncomfortable.

Even more uncomfortable than the Cami-Grace tiff, and that was pretty bad. Both girls are quite vocal when it comes to their opinions. Sometimes it's better to keep one's thoughts to oneself.

You get dressed, then join Cami in the kitchen, where you pour yourself a big old bowl of Froot Loops.

"I've been thinking. Not sure how we'll work it out, but once the semester is over, we should take a couple of days and go some-where."

"You mean, like a vacation?"

"Yep. Maybe take Waylon to the Grand Canyon or something."

Her face lights up. "Maybe Disneyland?"

"Um . . . That's an expensive trip, Cami. I don't think we could afford it."

She deflates, and you hate how that makes you feel. "I know. Maybe I could get a part-time job or something."

"Cami, we've talked about that. Child care would eat every penny."

"But maybe Noelle . . ."

When her voice trails off, you notice you've been shaking your head *no*. It's okay if Noelle babysits once in a blue damn moon. But every day? No way can you take that chance. Besides, it wouldn't be fair not to compensate her.

You take your half-eaten cereal to the sink, leave it drowning in food-colored milk, pull Cami into your halfhearted embrace.

"Let's find a way to do Disneyland."

The part you leave off is "someday."

If she intuits the unvoiced addendum, she keeps it to herself. Still, the tone of her voice betrays upset. "Okay. It will be our goal." She pushes you away. "Go to work."

The planet tips sideways, throws you off balance. Cami's disappointment is a stinging indictment. One day, you vow, you'll be able to vacation anywhere you please. Disneyland. Disney World. Hawaii. Alaska. Farther. Europe. China. Yeah, sure. How will you do that? Ever?

Dig down deep, Rand. Labor hard. Save up. If others can do it, so can you. But, damn it all, you'd give your right nut to be worry-free for a while. Imagine, being a regular nineteen-year-old kid, living with your parents, all expenses paid, while you finished school.

Too late for that.
Your life is a giant shit pile of worry.

Thermos of coffee in one hand, brown-bag lunch in the other, you start toward the door, only to be stopped by a sleepy voice at your back. "Daddy?"

When you turn, Waylon bounds into your arms, and despite your hands being occupied, your gentle squeeze promises you love him. Just like that, your world rights itself.

"Okay, killer, gotta go. See you later."

It's a twenty-minute drive to the apartment complex you helped construct a while back. Today's job is building frames for the walkways, to be filled with concrete in the coming week. It isn't difficult work, rather mindless, in fact.

The problem with that is it lets your mind wander, and you can't help but travel back to the last time you were here, when you happened to catch sight of Dean. As you wield your level and hammer, you keep glancing around, half hoping, half dreading you might see him again. Though you know he's real, and lives in this neighborhood, he seems more apparition than flesh-and-blood.

Wouldn't it be awesome to turn him into an actual ghost, if such things exist? To excise his evil spirit from his vile body and strand it where it could only *lust* after little boys, lacking the requisite ability to follow through? To make it wander through eternity, hungering to the point of starvation, its appetite whetted every time it passed a playground (or campground)?

Honestly, deliberating about the prick is becoming an obsession. Maybe—no, likely—it's part of the reason you begged Chuck to let you handle this job today. Beyond needing the hours, and the cash that comes along with them, a very big piece of you craved the excuse to be here, scouting the street and sidewalks.

You want to see him, track
his movements, trail him
like the criminal he is.

You need to see where he lives,
know where he hangs out,
what kind of car he drives.
You will find a way
to cause him great pain.

Revenge on the scale you have in mind takes planning. You can't risk witnesses. Prison time would negate everything you've worked so hard to accomplish. Ultimately, Dean would win, regardless of how much you made him suffer. There'd be no police academy, no badge at the far end. Your family would be lost to you, likely forever. No more McDonald's. No more Little People. No more morning sex. No chance at Disneyland and the world beyond.

No, you'll have to be very careful. But you can't wait too long, or who knows how many kids he might get hold of in the meantime. Once you finish your work here, you'll spend a little time cruising the area, and when you have all the information you need, you'll formulate a strategy.

Logic, you remind yourself, must trump emotion. That will likely be the hardest part because it requires patience. And at this moment in time the one goal you keep circling back to is forcing him down on his knees and making him beg for mercy.

It's interesting, really. You're a good guy. Excellent dad. Decent husband, despite the occasional fantasy about some girl other than your wife. But that one episode has carved out a vital piece of your soul.

Exacting vengeance
will make you whole again.
He deserves a slow, terrible death
for what he did to you.

But do you have the balls to do it?

You've asked yourself that question dozens of times over the years. All you have to do is revisit that night and your answer materializes, the same every time.

Absolutely.

Fade Out

DEAREST READER

Have you ever stopped
to consider your personal
limitations? Do you suppose
you own a certain sense
of inviolable morality?

I propose this to you,
that given the moment
in time when you had to push
beyond that sacrosanct line
as a means of sheer survival,

when face-to-face
with the beast, weapon
in hand, there would be
no second thought,
but simply reaction.

If forced into that corner,
no way to fall back
or detour around,
how far would you go?

Now hang on to that answer.
Consider the driving force
is not self-preservation
but rather bone-deep hatred.
Could you not react
with similar conviction?

SHEER VISCERAL HATRED

Is a worm chewing burrows
into the decaying earth
of the human brain.

Blind to the light,
seeking the cool relief
of shadowed sanctuary,

writhing life, driven
by the thrumming pulse
buried beneath blood

sucker skin and time
gnawed bone. It's a breath
taking thing to memorialize.

It's said that wolves,
big cats, and killer whales
rank highest on the food chain.

But invertebrate hate
cannot be underestimated,
especially when weaponized.

IT'S A PHENOMENAL THING

This spineless loathing.
Recognizes no age, no gender,
no race or religion
or single country of origin.

Suitable for any identity.

Like a Death Valley seed,
it can lie dormant for years,
heat-shriveled but living,
hiding in plain view.

Awaiting the thunderstorm.

And when the rain comes
beneath obsidian clouds
arisen in an electric sky,
the bloom is immediate.

Bold and brilliant and raging.

In a single solitary blink
it puts the lock and load
into the silent leviathan
biding time on the bookshelf.

Fade In:
SLIP BACK INTO SILAS'S SKIN

The annoying buzz of your cell phone's alarm slaps you out of an excellent dream. There you were, Silas, lying on a thick bed of jungle leaves, with a redhead on either side. Grace kissed you sweetly while Ashlyn went down on you, and there was nothing sweet about that. It was downright nasty. The kind of nasty that would keep any guy going back for more.

The girl is that kind of nasty for real, and you'll definitely go back for more. Today, in fact. After work. Work. Putrid. Why does it always have to get in the way of fun?

You dig through your laundry basket in search of the requisite khaki pants they make you wear. The pair you find is wrinkled, but not too dirty. No one will be the wiser. Your mom insists you wash your own clothes, "to teach you responsibility." Imagine how she'd feel if she knew irresponsible you has avoided it for two weeks.

Speaking of your mom, you haven't actually seen her in a couple of days. A stranger looking through the windows probably couldn't tell both of you live in a single house, considering your comings and goings. If her car hadn't been parked in the driveway when you got home last night, you wouldn't have known she was here because she was already in bed. But you'll have a few minutes to say hi before work. She's always up ahead of you.

When you open your bedroom door, you can hear her crashing around in the kitchen, and as you start down the hall, it becomes crystal clear she's not alone in there.

"Thank God you've got a mixer. These things aren't impossible to do with a whisk, but they don't turn out near as well." The voice belongs to Len.

Which means when you passed your mom's closed bedroom door last night, he was on the other side. In her bed. And you know what that means. Picturing it makes your gut churn.

If your mom wasn't here,
you'd grab him by the throat,
slowly, slowly tighten the vise.

But she is here.

"Oh," she says, when you reach the kitchen. "You're home. I thought you were spending the night at your dad's."

"I was going to, but I had a friend along. She had to get home."

Len turns away from whatever he's doing on the counter. "She, huh? You have a new girl?" When he smiles, his perfectly straight teeth actually gleam.

You'd really like to punch him
right in his smarmy face.

"Guess I do." Not that it's any of his fucking business.

"That's great, son. Want to tell us about her?"

"No. And I'm not your son." That was a dare, if a small one. You don't want to make your mom unhappy, even if she couldn't care less about your happiness.

The wuss performs as expected. "Sorry. Well, how about some blintzes? They'll be ready in just a few minutes."

"Blintzes? What's that? Jew food?"

"Silas!" counters your mom.

"It's okay," says Len. "Actually, they are. At least, this recipe. It's my grandmother's. Have you ever tried blintzes? They're like thin, sweet pancakes."

Sounds kind of good, not that you'll say so. "What's wrong with regular pancakes?"

What you really want to ask is what the hell he's doing here, sleeping with your mother.

"Regular pancakes are too fat to fold. See, I'm making a cream-cheese filling, which will get rolled inside, along with . . ."

You quit listening. It's no big deal if your mom wants to stuff herself with old-fashioned Jew recipes in your house, in your kitchen. But you're sure as hell not going along for the ride. Screw that. It's still your table, and he does not have your permission to share it.

"Thanks, but I'm running late. I'll get something later."

"You have lunch money?" asks your mom.

No, but I still have a little weed is probably not what she wants to hear. So you stick with, "Actually, no. I'm broke."

"Here," says Len, reaching into his pocket for his wallet. "Reimburse me when you can." He offers you a twenty.

If you were truly proud, you'd say no thanks. But pride is for losers. Ask any billionaire. You accept the bill. "Thanks."

> *There's no need to reimburse him.*
> *You owe him nothing.*

You're out the door before it hits you that most of the words you and your mom exchanged were heated. Not what you wanted.

> *It's all Len's fault.*

The aura of anger intensifies, and when you notice Lolita, it flares. You left her parked on the street, and between last night and this morning, someone keyed her fender. The scratch is long and thick and deep.

You pivot your head, right-left-right-left, looking for the perp. Down the block there's a kid on a bike, and he's laughing. You sprint down the sidewalk after him, bellowing, "Stop, you little fuck! Stop!"

He looks back and, seeing you in pursuit, whips into a driveway, brakes to a halt. As you get closer, you see he's maybe twelve or thirteen, and brown-skinned.

> *He is going to pay.*
> *You will make him pay.*

"What you want?" he calls as you near.

You don't stop until you're hovering over him, fists knotting. "I want to know what you did to my truck."

"What you talking about? What truck?"

"That one right there." You point down the street. "You scarred her, you punk."

"Nah, man. I didn't touch it."

"Who the hell *did*, then?" Your voice cracks as it hits its peak.

The kid smiles at that. "How should I know? You oughta take better care of your things, dude. You *are* a dude, yeah?"

> *You know how to answer that.*

But it occurs to you that you might've painted yourself into a corner. You can't prove he did it, and what are you supposed to do, anyway? Go off on a middle schooler?

The door to the house the driveway belongs to slams, and out come a couple of older guys. Mexicans, too. One who's built like a bulldozer says, "What's up, hermano? This vato bothering you?"

"He said I messed with his truck." Now, bolstered by his bodyguards, he grows bolder. "Stupid shit should take better care of it, no?"

Three on one, you'll get your ass kicked. If only you'd come to this party armed, you'd have Stand Your Ground on your side. At the moment, however, you are not carrying. Something nibbles at you, an emotion you're only vaguely acquainted with. Fear.

> Screw that.
> You can take these guys.
> No one says you have to fight fair.

But you backpedal. "Look. I parked my truck right there sometime after midnight. Between then and now, someone ruined a twelve-hundred-dollar paint job. He was the only person I saw, so I figured it had to be him. If not, no harm, no foul." You take a step backward.

"You gonna tell my brother you're sorry?"

Lie. Find him when he's alone.

"Sorry." That hurt. But with luck you'll escape intact.

You turn on one heel and go, keeping an eye over your shoulder. This is why whites need to remain vigilant, not to mention armed. You don't remember when Mexicans moved into the neighborhood.

"Did you screw up his truck?" you hear Bulldozer ask.

"Maybe yes, maybe no. Who's to say?"

Now the kid's just punking you. Well, two can play that game. You happen to know a TradYouth cop. Cadet, anyway, but he's got friends in the PD. You really should file a police report.

When there's plenty of distance between you and them, you yell, "Hope your papers are in order. Y'all are legal, right?" That was like throwing pebbles at scorpions, but it makes you feel marginally better.

Before you start Lolita, you take pics of the damage and where she's parked, and then you put in a call to your friend, ask for a reference. This doesn't need to be an official report. More like a backdoor inquiry, and a possible off-the-books investigation.

Here in Arizona, there is little to stop cops from random ID checks and other harassment, especially now that

Immigration and Customs Enforcement has so substantially come on board. ICE raids have become common. Easy enough for a local cop to manufacture a reason for a stop-and-frisk, and if a suspect gets roughed up a little? Not a problem.

You start Lolita and as she warms up, Len exits the house, carrying a bag of trash to the can outside the garage. Simpering bitch. That small nugget of domesticity reminds you of what's soon to be and makes you want to heave.

Len glances at you quizzically, waves for you to open the window. "Everything okay?"

"Not really. Someone put a huge scratch in my fender."

He comes over for a look, shakes his head. "That's terrible. Who would do such a thing?"

All you can do is shrug. "No clue."

He actually winks. "You sure it wasn't you?"

Your skin prickles.

"Dude, I baby this truck." Mostly true. You do stop to think for a minute, though. You've had her out in the desert a lot lately. Could you have scraped her against something? No, you'd remember, and surely you'd have noticed it before this morning. Unless . . . last night?

"Okay, sorry. Well, how about insurance?"

"I'm eighteen and work part-time at a convenience store. I can barely afford liability. So, none that will cover this."

He considers. "You know, I've got a friend who owns a body shop. I'm sure he'd give you a good deal."

One of the most vexing things in the entire universe is when someone you can't stand tries to be nice to you. If only you could just explode! But if he can help you work out a deal for the repair, you'll let him. Maybe he'll even loan you the money. "Thanks. Would you see when I could drop by for an estimate?"

"He'll be closed until Tuesday, I'm sure. But I'll give him a call then. And I'm truly sorry about Lolita. Great name, by the way."

No response necessary, you head toward work, stewing. Between yesterday's disappointing outcome and your run-ins with Len today, you're building up pressure like Old Faithful. Figure in Lolita and your new neighbors, the need to jet like that geyser is becoming unbearable.

You stuff it inside, where it stays bottled up until you arrive at QuikTrip, ten minutes late for your shift. The guy you're relieving is pissed, you can tell, but he takes one look at your body language and silently goes to clock out. You slip the requisite red company shirt over your tee and grit your teeth at the necessity of playing nice with customers.

Early on, there are plenty, with people loading coolers and filling gas tanks for Sunday outings. While such distraction might normally quell your ire, every small annoyance only serves to heighten it.

That's okay, Silas. Stay pissed.

As morning segues to early afternoon, things quiet down, but now it's your coworkers exacerbating your irritation. "Oh, no," complains Myra, a not-adorable pixie type. "I broke a nail."

Yeah, because polished claws are perfect for working the register. They're attractive enough on models and such, but do nothing special for Myra except make her gripe. To shut her up, you offer, "Look. It's slow. I'll watch your register. Take a break. Use a nail file or something."

A guy comes in, asks for a pack of Marlboros, pays for them with a fifty. When you open the register to make change, you notice it's stuffed with cash from the morning's abundant haul. Some of that should go in the safe. Tad, the weekend assistant manager, has been remiss. It's not uncommon.

You call his office. Well, it's actually the storeroom in back where he hides out, playing video games. "Dude. You need to come empty the drawers."

It takes a couple of minutes for him to climb off his ass, grab a money bag, and make his way up front. Just as he opens the first register, two guys bust through the door, wearing hoodies and surgical masks.

The one holding the gun says, "I'll take what's inside it. And open the other one, too. And you . . ." He points to you. "Don't even think about moving."

You freeze. These must be the jerk-offs who've been terrorizing Tucson. The ones you saw on the news at your dad's last night. They actually shot a couple of people in a Denny's. That knowledge keeps you frozen. Your gut clenches and unclenches, the earlier nibble of fear nothing compared to this snarl of terror.

Tad hands a wad of cash to the unarmed man, but you can tell he does it reluctantly. His eyes dart back and forth between the two robbers, like he's making mental notes.

"Hurry up," commands the gunslinger.

They've probably been here only a couple of minutes, but it feels like a whole lot longer. When Tad seems to delay, for whatever reason, you urge, "Do what he says. He means it."

"Goddamn straight!"

As soon as the other register pops open, Sidekick reaches across the counter and scoops out the money. He stuffs it in his pocket and both men head toward the door. Before they reach it, Tad dashes around behind them, grasping for something hidden under his manager's smock. He's armed!

"Stop right there!" he yells, whipping out his pistol, which looks like a toy. "Silas, call 911!"

When the men keep moving, Tad decides to play good guy with a gun, firing a shot in their direction. The bullet goes wild, hitting a Coke display near the door. The bad guy with the gun rotates, just as Myra comes running out of the bathroom, screaming, "What's going on?"

Bad guy and good guy decide to duel. Each takes two shots. Somehow, they miss each other, but Myra is caught in the crossfire. You witness all this in the thirty seconds it takes to duck behind the counter, reaching for the phone. By the time you manage to dial 911, the shooting has stopped. You really don't want to see the results.

When at last you work up the courage, the robbers have made good their escape. Tad is sitting on the floor, unscathed but in shock. And Myra? Jesus.

It takes several protracted minutes for the cavalry to arrive. By then you're pretty sure she's gone, and you have learned two valuable lessons.

One: If you're ever in a convenience store bathroom and hear shots, stay where you are.

Two: If you want to play good guy with a gun, your aim had better be excellent.

Which means you'd better practice.

Fade Out

THE DAYS OF DUELS

Have mostly passed,
pressed into the pages
of history books, but how
they linger in memory!

Two men, reputations
mutually compromised,
meet to prove their valor
on the field of honor.

With great ceremony,
their seconds present
the pistols, oiled and gleaming
deadliness in the wavering light.

The rivals take their places
and, beloved guns in hand,
they stand back-to-back,
gathering courage.

Eight paces in opposite
directions, at the signal, turn,
take aim, praying it's straight,
that your sight remains plumb.

Fire.

TO BE SURE

Some purposely aimed high,
or fired into the ground,
satisfaction realized
by the perception of heroism alone.

Not everyone wanted to kill.
Not everyone wanted to die.

It's said some serial duelists
possessed assorted pistols,
each with a different degree
of accuracy and strength
required for trigger pull.
Opponents were measured
for motive and skill,
weapon chosen accordingly.

Was the goal retaliation?
Was the goal to impress a lady?

Each man allowed a single shot,
such deliberation was crucial,
as was personal rationale.

Was he there to save face?
Or was he there to murder?

Fade In:
SLIP BACK INTO DANIEL'S SKIN

Sunday morning, Grace wakes you early, with a surprise. Not *that* kind of surprise. That isn't what she wants at all, not that she hasn't been generous the past couple of days. How easily you've grown accustomed to making love first thing in the morning, and again last thing before sleep.

Don't ever give her a choice, Daniel.
If she says no, take it.

But she hasn't said no yet, and there are other things to love her for, even if that's one of the best.

She's already showered and dressed in a pretty mauve-colored skirt and flowery top. "Get up. Come on, or we'll be late for church."

You haven't been to church since the last mass you attended with your mother, who was a devout Catholic. You didn't understand everything the priest said, but you kind of enjoyed the theatrics—the music and mantras and ceremony. You weren't even sure you believed in a higher power, but your mom surely did.

"Celebramos a Dios, que nos da la vida," she used to say. "We celebrate God, who gives us life."

Thinking about it—and her—drops you down on your figurative knees, and that has nothing to do with genuflecting.

"You go to church?" Lame question, dude.

She nods. "Regularly, since my dad died. You'll come with me, right?"

It sounds like a question, but it's probably not. She'd think less of you if you said no. In fact, she might get angry. It occurs to you, as a passing notion, that maybe she doesn't trust you to stay here alone in her house.

> *Key words: she doesn't trust you.*
> *So maybe you can't trust her, either.*

Regardless, you agree and hurry to get ready. It would suck if something as little as this turned out to be the chink that caused a rift between you. There have been a couple of times in the last few days where she seemed ready to create the split. Maybe the more undivided time people spend together, the more uncertainties are able to intrude.

Yesterday, for example, she went to visit her friend Noelle, and left you to fend for yourself at the mall much longer than expected. Malls are good for people watching, but not much else when you have to save your meager money for food and the Laundromat. By the time she picked you up, you were fuming. And rightly so.

"Thought you got lost."

"Sorry," she said. "Noelle and I got to planning and time just slipped away."

"Planning?"

"Yes. Get this! She invited me to go to Hawaii with her family over spring break. Isn't that awesome?"

Hawaii. That's a long way from Tucson. "How long will you be gone?"

"Assuming my parents sign off on the trip, a week. Seven days in paradise, all expenses paid except for the new bikini."

Oh, how that sunburned your face—way beyond pink, quickly past scarlet, all the way to charred. Bad enough you had to consider a whole week sans seeing your Grace, without thinking about all those beach bums ogling her in a bikini.

Your feelings mean nothing to her.

But you said, "Wow. That's cool. Have you ever been there?" Her parents are flush. Surely they've made that trip before.

"Of course. But not mostly lacking parental supervision. I mean, her mom and dad will oversee, but it won't be the same as being a kid, hauled along to luaus and whale-watching excursions."

Both of which sounded pretty damn wonderful to you.

"Maybe I'll even learn to surf!"

In her new bikini. In front of hundreds of strangers on the beach.

Oh, and she'd need an instructor. One of those buff, tan surfer dudes.

No, that is not going to happen.

You'll think of something to thwart the possibility. But right now you have to get through church.

This morning Grace does the driving, claiming she should because she knows the way to her Methodist church. Sensible, considering you're bumping right up against the usual start time. Despite having left the Catholic Church in your dust, you fret most of the drive. You haven't given confession in years. There's been lots of sinning in the meantime.

The two of you hurry inside and take seats in the very back pew, just as the opening hymn is sung. You don't even try to join in, but Grace knows the song by heart. Her voice rises, a sweet trilling soprano, and love for your angel swells.

As if recognizing the voice in back, a girl sitting a few rows up turns and waves. The person beside her shifts in her seat before shooting a curious glance over her shoulder.

You give Grace a nudge. "Who's that?"

Grace pauses her singing long enough to answer, "The blonde is Noelle. I'm not sure who the other one is."

Maybe it was all the talk of bikinis, but you didn't expect Noelle to be so heavy. The wheels between your ears get to click-clacking. The noise is almost enough to drown out the announcements, delivered by a pastor with a crooked nose and white frost hair. Something about a rally tomorrow at the university.

You refocus and catch the scripture readings and most of his sermon about regular recommitment to Christ. After a few minutes, you settle into the immersive experience. The pageantry is soothing, and the service less intimidating than mass. You even take communion, tossing out a few random Hail Marys before the wafers and wine reach you.

The service has wound all the way down to the pastor walking up the aisle for the requisite foyer handshaking when your cell buzzes. You reach into your pocket and Grace whispers, "What is it?"

"The hospital. Someone called in sick and they need me to come in and work swing."

You'll say no to work if she's disappointed. You'd just as soon do that anyway. What would they do, fire you? Not like it's exactly a dream job. In fact, you have a coworker or two you wouldn't mind never seeing again. The concept of workplace violence? You get it.

"Oh. Well, that's okay."

She'd rather spend the rest
of the day without you.
Maybe even with someone else.

"You sure?"

"Of course. I know you can use the hours. You took Friday off."

That much is true. But some little voice inside your head keeps insisting her motive is to get away from you.

The sanctuary has almost emptied. Grace tugs you to your feet as Noelle and her friend stop to say hello. "It's good to finally meet you, Daniel."

"Uh, yeah, you, too. Grace has told me a lot about you."

"Really?" She actually *beams*.

Kind of pathetic. And so is the way she looks at Grace. She idolizes her. Sort of the way you do. The girl beside her clears her throat.

"Oh," says Noelle. "This is Gabriella. We've been helping Pastor Lozano with the last-minute rally details." She directs her follow-up question toward Grace. "You'll be there, right?"

"At the rally? I don't think so?"

"After all the work you've done on it? Why not?"

Grace glances at you, and it's really all the answer Noelle needs. "Something came up. Why? Are you going?"

"I've been thinking about it. I know it's going to be totally crazy, but that could be kind of fun. Besides, this is something I care about."

Fun? It could be dangerous. You want Grace to stay with you instead, so you interrupt. "Unfortunately, we have other plans for tomorrow."

Grace flicks a *what are you talking about* look in your direction.

Disappointed, Noelle turns her back on you and says to Grace, "Well, if you change your mind, let me know. We could go together. I'd better run. My mom's picking me up and she's probably waiting. Call me. Oh, did you forward those pics you promised to send me?"

"Slipped my mind. But I'll do that right away. Sorry."

"It's okay."

The hug she offers Grace lingers. There's something there. Something off-putting.

Once she's out the door and beyond earshot, Grace says, "Please don't speak for me again. I don't appreciate it."

"Sorry. But we do have plans, don't we?"

"Not really," she huffs. "Let's go." When you file out past the minister, she stops to say hello. "Pastor Lozano, this is my friend Daniel."

Emphasis on "friend."

Up close, you can see the man is Latino beneath that silver cloud of hair. Interesting. Most Latinos you know practice Catholicism. Perhaps that's changing.

"Good to meet you, Daniel. Nice biblical name. I hope you enjoyed the service."

You command yourself to be polite. "Yes. Very much, thank you."

"Aren't you originally from Honduras?" Grace asks Pastor Lozano.

"Yes, though my family immigrated to the States when I was about your age," he answers.

"Daniel's mother lives in Honduras."

"Is that so? Where?"

> *Your mother abandoned you, Daniel.*
> *Don't talk about her.*

"Last I heard, La Lima. But we haven't communicated in a while, so I'm not sure."

"That's too bad. A man should know how to get in touch with his mother."

> *At least he called you a man.*

"Yeah, well, my living situation is a little tenuous, so it's hard for her to catch up with me."

Just how tenuous is none of his business. You plant your feet and cross your arms, daring him to further intrude.

But he doesn't prod. "I see. Well, I have relatives in the Cortés region. They might be able to help find her, if you're ever so inclined. Just let me know."

Such unsolicited kindness makes you nervous. The good pastor wants something from you.

"Thank you. I'll keep it in mind."

"Oh, Daniel. You should let him help!" chimes in Grace.

Truthfully, the offer is tempting, but you cherish your privacy. Opening up your past, letting a stranger sink a shovel into the clay? Tough to embrace.

"You're welcome to join us tomorrow at the rally. It's pro-immigration. Maybe we can accomplish a way for your mom to return to the States."

"Let me sleep on it."

"Of course." Pastor Lozano extends a hand.

You accept it, shake weakly. All the gesture means is *appreciate the offer*.

Grace says goodbye to the minister, stomps off toward the parking lot, firing a shot: "Why were you so rude?"

You hurry behind, catch her just this side of her car, halt her with a tender hand. "Hold on."

She pauses at your touch, turns sharply toward you. "What?"

"Don't be angry. I said I'd think about his offer. And I don't believe I was rude."

Her posture softens. Slightly. "I just don't get you. Don't you *want* to reconnect with your mom?"

A sigh seeps out in the form of a whispered whistle, if there is such a thing. "First of all, there's no promise of that."

"I know. But if you could find out where she is, you'd want the ability to communicate, right?"

"I'm not sure. Look, Grace. She left me here eight years ago, and while she might have believed that was what was best for me, I'm not so sure. Life is a struggle. I have to fight depression every single day. If not for you . . ."

You clamp your mouth shut. That was a major faux pas. The depression isn't something you should admit, not even if it's becoming more and more obvious that it's something you might need professional help for.

Beneath a thick fringe of lashes, her eyes flip from angry to compassionate. "I know it's hard, Daniel. But that's not your mom's fault. She knew you'd have more opportunities here."

Logic is a burr in your butt.

> *She's not even trying to understand you.*

"I get that." The blame game suits nobody well. "Look. I don't have to be at work until noon. Let's get something to eat. The smell of the cafeteria makes me queasy on an empty stomach."

Ironic, but true. You can eat the food there when the need arises, and it has in the past. Many times. But it pays to arrive with something already taking up room in the pit.

Grace's favorite Panera isn't too far away, so she opts to go there. It's sort of pricey for your wallet, but she orders a chicken panini to split, pays with her own credit card. Must be nice to have parents with bottomless pockets.

> *Must be nice to have parents.*

Rather than feeling heartened by the pastor's offer to help, your hollowed soul aches. You long ago gave up on the notion of a happy reunion with your mami. Her letters used to arrive regularly, maybe once a month. When your dad was alive, he'd leave them on your pillow for you to find. Remember how you'd open them so, so carefully, the idea of ripping even a single word unbearable? Once you devoured them, you hid them in your pillowcase, safe beneath the comfort of eiderdown.

Mami wrote of La Lima, a city divided by a river, which at a certain time of year quite often overflowed its banks. The flooding, she insisted, was cleansing, and once everything dried out again it felt resurrected.

She talked about the plantain plantations, the trains that transported the bananas. Of Mayan ruins few people knew existed. Of the desire to dance, amid the despair of poverty. Of home. There. Here. And how no place could really be home without you in it.

Her descriptions were beautiful. She could have been a writer. Maybe she is, and you inherited her poet's soul. But you wouldn't know. The letters began to come further apart. After your father died, your pillow went wanting. You'd search the mailbox, the stack of envelopes on the hall table, the trash. Nothing.

Part of you understands Shailene and Tim were likely responsible. But if they threw her letters away, there would've been evidence of that. You wrote your mami to let her know your dad passed, mailed it to the last address you had for her. It never came back, returned. But neither was it answered. You checked every day for quite a while.

Your dear, sweet mami stopped
worrying about you.
Stopped loving you.
Like everyone.

Everyone, except Grace.

The past couple of days were the closest you've been to belonging, to something approaching normalcy, since your mother was sent away. And they're fast dwindling.

Drop.

Plunge.

Dive.

The murky depths await.

Grace senses your distress. "You okay?"

You shake your head. "I'm missing you."

"But I'm sitting right here."

Her smile paints a halo around her head. Halo. Angel. Yes, that's right. Heaven would be blessed by her presence.

Easy enough to provide
her with a one-way ticket.

"This morning. Now. But tomorrow we go back to borrowed hours."

And you will be back to sleeping on beds of park turf when you can't manage to bum a couch or cot. Imagine being homeless in Minnesota or Maine! People freeze to death in places like that.

She leans toward you, eyes seeking yours. "We can't be together all the time, Daniel. That isn't realistic. This weekend was an exception. It can't be the rule."

She's breaking up with you.
You knew it would come to this.
All she needed was an excuse.

Fury seizes you. Shakes hard. "Why not?"

The rage in your voice propels her backward. "Why are you so angry?" she squeaks. "Because my parents will be home tomorrow. Because school starts again the next day. Because you've got a job and I've got friends. Because no couple can be together every minute of every day."

Way to go. Now she's afraid of you. Her timid tone swears it. Dial it back. Hurry!

"Grace, I'm so sorry. I understand what you're saying. It's just the last couple of days have been like a dream. Waking up will be a painful reminder of how very much I love you."

"Why is that painful?"

"Because I'm afraid I'm losing you."

There. You said it. You've thought it. Alluded to it. And now you've given voice to it.

Something your mami once told you pops into your brain. "If you give fear a voice, it will curse you."

Now that you've uttered the words, will they come back to haunt you?

> You won't let her desert you.
> You'll never let her go.

Fade Out

GIVE VOICE

To any emotion, you empower
it at incalculable risk.

Sadness is the soul-chilling wail
of a child lost in the wilderness,
clutching the final crust
of yesterday's meager sandwich.
Listen, and you will know hunger.

Delight is the nervous chatter
of roller-coaster jockeys,
climbing that vertical ascent
toward the precipitous apex.
Listen, and prepare to fall.

Wrath is the belligerent bellow
of a charging rhinoceros, head
bowed in surprising tribute
to the bull's-eye in clear sight.
Listen, and await the goring.

Fear is the whimper swelling
into a scream, the chant
of necromancers, gathered
around the smoking cauldron.
Listen, and succumb to their spell.

THERE'S AN OLD SONG

Written decades ago,
and covered many times
in a number of ways
because the lyrics resonate
with the human heart.

It goes, "I put a spell on you
because you're mine."

The implication being,
no matter what you want,
you can't escape
because I refuse to let you go.

And I will resort to witchcraft
if I must to remain in control.

What if casting a curse
does not require sentiency?
What if enchantment
does not belong exclusively
to air-breathing beings?

What if the simple reality
of my owning you
has put you under my spell?

Fade In:
SLIP BACK INTO NOELLE'S SKIN

You hardly slept at all last night, caught up in the excitement of the rally tomorrow, not to mention the prospect of traveling to Hawaii with your best friend. This trip will make Grace understand that you need her in your life. Maybe even that you love her. Seeing her at church this morning only made you that much more determined to spend as much time together as possible.

> *Not with Daniel attached, though, Noelle.*
> *Something about him makes your skin crawl.*
> *He just might have tainted her.*

Regardless, you're on a mission. Perhaps even a two-pronged mission: resurrecting an old friendship and cultivating a new one. You hate to elevate your hopes too high about either, but seriously, you don't have much to lose by trying. Plus there is now the tantalizing prospect of romance.

Gabriella invited you over after church to hang out for a little while, the first time anyone has extended such an invitation in a very long time. She lives in a tidy apartment with her sister, Lucinda, who's five years older and just about ready to graduate college.

"Where are your parents?" you asked, and were immediately sorry you did.

"We're not sure. They were afraid to be deported, so they left for California. We hope to hear from them soon."

"How long ago was that?"

"Right before school started."

They left Gabriella with her sister so she would have a safe place to stay. But they didn't realize Lucinda would be in danger of deportation, too. She's a Dreamer—undocumented, but allowed to live in the US as long as she follows certain guidelines. She's adhered to every rule. But the law is changing and her status is in danger.

Which is why Gabriella, who was born in the United States and is a citizen, has been so actively involved with immigration issues, including the rally tomorrow. It was her passion that inspired your own interest. But you never would've guessed she might be attracted to you.

> *Don't be ridiculous.*
> *Who's the "dreamer" now?*

It's a wild notion, you understand that, and you're probably just imagining the way she scooted a little closer when the two of you sat on her sofa, or how the brown suede of her arm brushed your pallid skin more than once as you lettered signs for the rally. And surely her intense gaze when her eyes locked with yours didn't mean a thing.

All those things add up to exactly zero promise of anything more, and are open to interpretation. So you counsel yourself to take it easy and see where, if anywhere, your friendship with Gabriella leads. But between her and beach time with Grace, you've been inspired to reinvest in yourself, something you never would've believed possible only Friday.

But yesterday you took a decent walk around the neighborhood, the first real exercise you've managed in a very long time. While most athletes would probably find that laughable, you're sore today, leg muscles achy with the effort of transporting 215 pounds for forty minutes. You should take pride in that pain. Own it.

Only problem is, you're finding it hard to get off your butt and do it again today. It will be easier once you've shed some pounds, so you go to your computer and research *rapid weight loss*.

There's plenty of information out there. Too much, in fact—one site disputing the "facts" you find on another. Most of them agree on some things: eliminate sugar, especially the sweet stuff found in soda, juice, and alcohol; ditto simple carbs like bread and rice; beef up the protein (or fish or chicken it up); eighty-six salt, drink tons of water.

But some say eat fruit; others, never. Some insist on whole grains; others, not so fast. Fat is good; fat is bad. Caffeine either boosts your metabolism or makes it crash. Exercise early in the day. Or right before dinner. Weight training or aerobic workouts? Yoga or Pilates? It's confusing. Anyway, you're hungry.

Wait. On a hunch, you search *weight loss and epilepsy*. Sure enough, there it is. A whole lot of anecdotal evidence that the drug you're taking to control your seizures is linked to the inability to lose pounds, despite controlled diet and exercise.

Great. One step forward, three steps back. You should talk to your doctor, get her advice. "Consult your physician before starting any weight-loss program." You quote the common disclaimer out loud.

You really are hungry, so head to the kitchen in search of protein, no carbs, except maybe a vegetable, which is the right kind of carb. Probably.

The house is quiet. Your dad is playing golf today, and your mom is having coffee with a friend. "Unless you don't want me to?" she asked when she dropped you off at Gabriella's after church. "We can have a girls' lunch together if you'd rather." Her ever-present worry.

You opt for a can of tuna (protein), minimal mayo (fat), no bread. Plus a cup of instant coffee (caffeine), chased by a huge glass of water. Oh, you're supposed to drink the water *before* you eat. Fool your tummy into thinking you've put more in it than you have. Next time. You groan. Is there a right way to diet? Or exercise?

Might as well try to make the latter fun. You grab your phone and earbuds, head outside, turn on your music, and walk to the beat, mirroring the tempo of each song. Faster rhythm, quicker pace. Before too very long, you're hoping for ballads.

Halfway around the first block, your mom texts: EVERYTHING GOOD?

You reply: PERFECT. DON'T HURRY. I'M WALKING.

Despite your slight discomfort, you find yourself enjoying the activity, especially when you lose track of the effort as your thoughts turn to Hawaii, and Grace. Yesterday was amazing. You thought she'd hurry off, scurry back to Daniel, but she actually stayed for a decent amount of time.

Together you created bucket lists, including things you can maybe check off after your trip to the islands. "I've always wanted to go horseback riding on the beach," she suggested.

"That would be awesome." You agreed, even though your first thought was they'd have to put you on a Budweiser Clydesdale or something so you wouldn't make the poor horse go all swayback.

At that point you were investigating tourist sites. Bad idea. Everything Grace came up with sounded great. For someone her size.

"Zip-lining?" she asked.

"You've got to be kidding me."

Anxiety struck, considering the logistics of strapping yourself into a harness (if they even make one big enough to fit you), then stepping off an insanely high platform (if you could manage to climb the stairs up to it), and rocketing down a wire, praying the brake would work at the far end. Or, alternately, getting stuck halfway so someone would have to come rescue you. You blushed embarrassment, but Grace didn't notice.

"You're not afraid of heights, are you?"

"No. I'm afraid of the cable breaking."

"Don't be silly. They're made out of steel." Her smile was like the first star in the evening sky—familiar, yet something you're never quite prepared for. "Okay, then what about paragliding?"

"Looks fun."

It does. But parachute lines are flimsier than steel cables. And you'd probably need buckle extenders for the life jacket. Quad rides? Maybe, if you can stretch your thighs across one of those big seats. Surfing? Ha ha ha ha. Good one. Bodysurfing, maybe. You're pretty good at floating.

Quit lying to yourself.

You'll never do any of those things.
You'd choke before you even tried.

By the time your lists were completed your brain was exhausted, just thinking about such physicality. Leave it up to you, you'd spend the week reading on a recliner overlooking the ocean. You don't need to *do* stuff with Grace. You just need to *be* with her.

Because, oh, was it thrilling, sitting in such close proximity to Grace all that time.

Inhaling the melon scent of her lotion.

Brushed by the sweep of her long auburn hair.

Every now and again, touching her paper-smooth skin.

Joking. Laughing. Dreaming. Planning.

More than once, you had to stop yourself from throwing all caution to the wind and declaring your feelings.

More than once you leaned toward her, thinking about kissing her, and not on the cheek.

More than once you silently scolded yourself for almost blowing the best chance you'll likely ever have of convincing her to love you the way you love her.

She'll never love you like that.
And neither will Gabriella.
The first time she watches you seize,
she'll run, run away, as fast as she can.

Right before Grace left, she took selfies with you, the first ever. Back when your friendship was going full throttle, neither of you owned cells, at least not high-tech enough to have cameras. In fact, the last picture you have of the two of you is the one with Santa. The one . . . You had to clean free of blood.

Breathing is currently difficult. Lost in thought, pacing yourself with the music in your ears, you've walked faster than you might have otherwise. You pause, draw in narrow pulls of air like sucking it through a straw. This will get easier, right? Sure. Sure it will.

Every scintilla of happiness vanishes, swept into the trash heap by despair. So many times you've stood, toes at the end of the high dive, hoping a gust of courage would push you over the edge. You always chickened out, but the option has remained within reach.

Go on. Take the plunge.

The house is still parent-empty when you get home, which is fine by you. Last thing you want to do right now is talk to your mom. You pop an ibuprofen to fight the tenderness in your legs and prep a bath.

You run the water über-hot, add bath oil beads, and the steam that rises to fill the bathroom smells like cinnamon and apples. It's been a while since you've enjoyed the luxury of a tub. Generally you shower, and you tend to go quickly, as looking at your body tends to be an exercise in self-loathing.

Indeed, now as you start to relax, you can't help but notice how your oversize breasts float barely above two belly rolls. You close your eyes so you don't have to look. There's no reason to beat yourself up when you've made the decision to change, however long that takes. So you go ahead and soak. Absorb the heat. Bask in oily water, perfumed by hints of apple.

Sleep eluded you last night. It tries to claim you now. Your head tips to one side, toward dozing, and in that dreamy state a memory you've tried hard to erase finds you here in the bathtub.

You weren't even as heavy then as you are now, though you'd been gaining weight steadily for maybe a year. A reliable size medium in the past, you'd ballooned into an extra-large, and filled it to the max. Today you're in plus sizes.

But that day you had a dentist appointment and had just finished up. Gums still numb and face swollen, you squeezed into the elevator, which was already crowded. Maybe it was thoughtless, and looking back you guess it kind of was, but all you were thinking about at that point was fleeing the torture chamber.

"Seriously?" groaned a girl in back. "You've got to be kidding me. How much weight can an elevator hold, anyway?"

Most people were polite enough to stay silent, but there was a burst of laughter, too. You kept your eyes tuned on your feet, as much of them as you could see, anyway.

"At least if we fall it's only three floors," added the girl, initiating another round of guffaws.

You were also grateful the ride would be short, and when you got off on the ground floor without causing an elevator crash, you hurried out of the air-conditioned comfort behind the glass doors into the crushing heat of an Arizona summer. The sudden temperature change sent your head spinning.

The blood rushed from your face, and feeling it go cold white, you plopped down hard on the sidewalk, rather than chance a fall. You sat there beneath a cloud of humiliation, internalizing every drop, alternating between rage and ruin. When the sneering girl walked by, you decided you'd show her and went home, where you took revenge by downing a hot fudge sundae.

> *Killing yourself with comfort food.*
> *You've been doing that for years.*
> *There are faster ways, you know.*
> *You just have to decide it's time to go.*

By the time the water cools you've managed to stow that recollection again. Once you towel off, brush through your hair, and get dressed, the need for a nap hits you square. You go to text your mom to let her know you're resting and notice Grace has forwarded the selfies she took yesterday.

Like that day at the dentist, your face frosts over. You thought you looked better in that dress. Well, at least your eyes are pretty, thanks to the makeup you rarely bother with. But you wanted to look especially nice for Grace. You wanted the afternoon to change everything back like it was before. Surely it meant something.

You turn on your computer, dive into social media, scroll through Grace's pages to see if she cared enough to post one of the selfies, because that's what a friend would do. You find pics of Daniel: at the club with Cami and Rand; riding bikes on the same trail you and Grace used to travel together; stopped at your favorite overlook.

There are lots of selfies of the two of them.

But not a single one of you.

Suddenly the air around you goes electric with a static sizzle, signaling the onset of a seizure. Exhaustion plus anxiety, whipped up by a bad case of resentment, are a bad combination. Toss in too much time on-screen, you were asking for trouble.

You lie on the floor, where you can't fall. Grab the pillow on your bed to put under your head as you tumble toward oblivion, hit by the smell of burnt oil and this sentiment:

> *One afternoon can't change everything.*
> *Not even close.*

Fade Out

ONE AFTERNOON

Can't change years
of planning a death.
            Yours.

                  Another's.

It becomes a preoccupation,
considering the method.
            The scheduling.
                  The outcome.

A pleasant experience
might alter the timeline.
            Postpone it.
                  Hasten it.

But eventually the desire
overwhelms caution.
            Judgment.
                  Cowardice.

And once the plan is put
into motion, it's invariable.
            Unalterable.
                  Unstoppable.

SEE, THE THING IS

The human brain
is malleable.
Easily
swayable.

If logic
was the true measure,
emotion divorceable,
body counts worldwide
would plummet.

But hominid
creatures lack mental
stability, rely
on internal drivelines
that are easily stimulated
by circumstance,

manipulated
by momentary
lapses of reason.

Fade In:
SLIP BACK INTO CAMI'S SKIN

Yesterday was a shit storm, start to finish. Seems the best-laid plans always get waylaid, and sometimes hijacked completely. A simple wrong-place, wrong-time scenario sent you reeling. And what's super messed up? You have no one you can commiserate with.

> *What you really hate, Cami,*
> *is how helpless you were under that table.*
> *You can't always be forewarned,*
> *but you can see to it you're forearmed,*
> *or at least armed.*

Some people would say you got lucky. That Waylon and you escaped injury, and all those evil creeps stole from you yesterday was money. Not your phone. Not a stash. No credit cards or jewelry or weapons. The only one of those things in your purse was your cell, so maybe you were fortunate, but it seemed like all they were after was cash.

Rand knows you lost a couple hundred dollars in the robbery, but he has no clue that you're really out more. Not only that, but now you're in debt to one of Tucson's most connected marijuana traffickers, something you have to work your way out of today.

Everything yesterday got pushed back late, so you had to reschedule some of your deliveries. People weren't pleased, or even understanding, despite your legit excuse. The way of drug deals.

This morning, at least, was nice. You woke to Rand's request for lovemaking, and after the hot-hot-hot dream he pulled you from, you were happy to oblige. At nineteen, your sex drive is maturing, changing from passive acceptance to true desire. You've read that hunger will continue to grow, maybe all the way into your thirties.

But sometimes you worry that Rand can't keep pace. He's pretty damn vanilla. If he had his way, it would mostly be straightforward missionary. Experimentation? Depends on the day. For sure he dislikes when you play the aggressor. Sometimes he even recoils. You asked him about it once, when he jerked away from your indelicate touch.

"Hey. What did I do?"

"I don't want to feel like I don't have a choice," he said.

"It's just a game. Some guys like them."

"Some guys are stupid."

Can't argue with that. But you wouldn't mind more variety, no matter who initiates it. Which is why you got clever this morning, simply offering yourself in unusual ways, assuming positions and allowing him to say yea or nay. He didn't disagree even once. So maybe there's hope for the two of you.

If not, you've got options.

Your husband's a hard worker, that's for sure. Took extra hours today to keep your small family afloat. And he agreed to save for a trip to Disneyland. You want to go while Waylon is little, while his imagination is vivid and pure. It will be expensive. Gas to California. Hotel. Food. Tickets. Tough for a young couple on a tight budget. But now that it's firmly on your mind, you're determined to make it happen.

Rand's mom wouldn't help out if she could, but his dad is generous. Rand's going over tomorrow to ask Jeremy to lend a hand after your monetary loss yesterday. Maybe he'd toss a few bucks into the pot?

Come to think of it, your parents would probably contribute. Your mom confessed that they want to take Noelle to Hawaii for her eighteenth. If they can afford that, perhaps they could send a little in your direction, too. Maybe for Waylon's birthday, which is coming up soon.

You should stop by your parents' on the way to do your run. Ask about the prospect, and see if Noelle can watch Waylon so you don't have to lug him around all afternoon. You told Rand the house isn't toddler-proofed, but that isn't exactly true. Mostly, there's nothing for him to play with there. You can always pack a few toys to take over.

You also kind of lied about visiting with Noelle tomorrow, when what you have to do is take Hector his money. Meet his deadline. Because the last thing you want him to believe is that you stiffed him. The man has ties to a big-time cartel. He'd have no problem at all hurting you.

So you can say hi to your sister today instead. Not to mention schmooze your mom and dad. If you go right now you can chill over there for a few. Play the good daughter.

You really are an ingenious girl.

Waylon's watching cartoons. When you toss his Little People and Play-Doh into his travel bag, along with an emergency change of clothes, he asks, "Where we goin'?"

"To Grandma and Grandpa's so you can play with Noelle. Okay?"

"Yay!"

You call to give them a heads-up, but can't seem to rouse anyone on the house phone, so you try Noelle's cell. It goes to voice mail. Next you try your mom's phone. She, at least, answers.

"Hey. Where's Noelle?"

"She should be home. Why?"

"I can't get hold of her. I was going to drop by and say hi."

She pauses. "Last I heard she was taking a walk. Maybe she isn't back yet." Simple explanation, but there's concern in her voice. "I'm at a friend's. I'll head on home and make sure everything's okay."

"I'll meet you there. See you in a few."

You bundle Waylon, his stuff, and your contraband-laden backpack into your car, and it isn't until you've backed out of the driveway that your mom's words sink all the way in: *she was taking a walk.* As far as you know, Noelle hasn't walked much farther than from curb to front door in years.

It's sad, because your sister used to be active. When the two of you were little, you both played softball and soccer, and she aced you at both, despite being younger. Anything that required running, she outperformed you.

She's always rivaled you.
You despise her when she wins.

You excelled at a couple of things. Archery and target shooting, both accomplished from a stationary position. People might assume it was your dad who taught you to hit bull's-eyes, but it was your mom. She grew up on a ranch in New Mexico, where "rattlesnakes infested the woodpile and coyotes fought over our cats and chickens."

It's hard to believe the slightly built, gentle woman who raised you once fought off critters with bullets, but she did. "A girl should know how to protect herself," she said. And she made damn sure both you and Noelle could load and point a gun, and hit what you aimed at.

You've never had to worry about venomous reptiles or wily canids, but if you had to, you'd take them out in a heartbeat.

Thinking about dropping a live target
gives you the shivers
and you wonder if you could manage it.
You could do it. You could.
Imagine the power.
Imagine the thrill.

The garage is open when you arrive at your parents', but only your mom's car is parked inside. Cradling Waylon in one arm, his stuff in the other, you don't bother to knock. It's still your home, too. "Mom? Noelle?"

"In here," calls your mother. "In Noelle's room."

That sounds ominous.

Turns out, it's only semi-ominous. Apparently Noelle had a seizure. She's recovering now, prone on her bed. Your mom is perched on the edge, assessing.

"What happened?" Dumb question. "I mean, I thought your meds had stabilized things."

"For the most part they have," answers your mom.

Noelle looks toward you with eyes lacking focus. "Not enough sleep last night."

"Noelle needs a nap?" suggests Waylon.

"Good idea," says your mom. "Let's let her catch a few winks. I've got cookies in the kitchen."

Of course, Waylon's amenable. Your mom leads him, chattering, from the room, and you take her spot on Noelle's bed. "Was it a bad one?"

"Pretty bad," she agrees. "Worst I've had in a while. Lack of sleep was only one reason."

"Lifestyle change? Mom said you were out walking today."

"Yeah. I want to drop a few pounds before Ha—"

"Hawaii?" you finish.

"You know?"

"Mom mentioned she and Dad were discussing it, yes."

"Did she tell you Grace is coming, too? At least, she was."

You didn't even realize Grace and Noelle were back in touch. Neither has said a word about it. Now for *sure* you're going to push for Disneyland. It's only fair.

"No. She didn't mention Grace. And what do you mean, 'was'?"

Noelle shrugs. "I'm just not sure she'll be able to tear herself away from Daniel."

"They do seem way too attached, but Grace has a mind of her own." As you well know. "Anyway, who could turn down a trip to Hawaii?"

"I hope you're right. I really want her to go. It would be a lot more fun with a friend along."

"Try not to worry about it."

"Easier said than done. For now, I am going to close my eyes for a few. Gearing up for the rally tomorrow."

"Rally?"

"The immigration rally at U of A. I'm going."

"Seriously?"

"Yeah. Gotta take a stand for what's right at some point."

Noelle has been full of surprises today. Exercise. Grace. And now you hear she's become an activist, which is something you'd never expect, especially not for this particular cause.

You huff. "Since when do you care about illegals?"

"Undocumented, not illegal," she corrects. "And I've cared since I've become deeply aware of the issue."

"Enough to march down the street, carrying a sign?"

"That's right."

> She's brave.
> A whole lot braver than you.

"Noelle, you're a hermit. You realize rallies attract hordes of people?"

"Sometimes. And, yeah, it will be weird to crawl out of my cave, but this is something I believe in. Dreamers, especially, deserve the chance at a better future. They don't know any home but America. They should stay."

"You sound like a pamphlet."

She grins. "I've read quite a few."

You'd hang out and debate, but you've got appointments, and your customers have been waiting since yesterday. In fact, one of them left you a terse text message this morning. "Well, be careful. I hear it's going to be insane."

You give her a hug, grab Waylon's stuff, slip out of the room, and go find your mom and son in the kitchen. Waylon holds up a gnawed cookie, smiles a gooey smile.

"Looks good, baby. Hey, Mom, can Waylon stay and play for a couple of hours? I've got some errands to run, and it would be easier without dragging him along. I brought toys or he could watch TV. I was going to ask Noelle, but . . ."

"Of course. Your father's golfing, so my afternoon is free."

Perfect. You'd like to bring up Disneyland now, but stop yourself. It's better to wait. You've already used up a favor.

Before you start your car, you give Tim a quick call to let him know you're on your way. Unlike some of your customers, he's always got plenty of cash, so he's not a bargain-basement shopper. He always takes a half ounce off your hands, and he's willing to pay whatever you charge. With him, you're fair but not overly generous.

He lives with his mom in a very nice home, in an upscale neighborhood north of the city proper. Nothing like your part of town, where houses are shoved in close together and you have to worry about soft crime—burglaries and car break-ins. Not much gang violence to speak of, and as far as you know, at least as long as you've lived there, nothing like a murder. But enough stuff to be concerned about.

Rand and you have discussed getting a dog. As a kid, he had a mutt he adored and he really thinks Waylon should have one. But a breed with a big enough bark to deter a burglar would cost an arm and a leg to feed. Maybe one day. In the meantime, you've come up with a solution that does not require food or poop scooping.

Every house in Tim's neighborhood probably came equipped with alarm systems and security services. Your Civic looks out of place here, where BMWs and Audis are de rigueur, so you're always a little nervous about delivering your wares to his doorstep, and you really hate bringing Waylon here, where you have to worry about him smudging fancy furniture with grubby fingers. At least that won't be a problem today.

Apparently Tim's mother is absent this afternoon, because he invites you into the living room, rather than up to his bedroom.

"Let's see what you've got."

You offer the premeasured twelve-plus grams. Yeah, it should be fourteen, but you always scam a little for personal stash. Not like he's going to weigh it. "It's awesome sativa."

"Sample?"

"Of course. Here?"

"My mom's gone until dinner, but we can step out in back. Doesn't hurt to be cautious."

He leads the way out onto their patio, an interesting geometric pattern of pretty pavers spilling into the xeriscaped sand of their backyard. You settle into a teak chair and light the joint you brought rolled. Tim always asks for a sample.

It takes only a few tokes to confirm your statement about it being awesome sativa. Just as cotton mouth sets in, Tim asks, "So are Grace and Daniel a regular thing now?"

The dude rarely has much to say beyond the usual client-dealer dialogue, so this comes as a surprise, and an uncomfortable one at that. You struggle to find enough spit to form a single word. "Wha-what?"

"Silas told me he saw them together. Like, *making out together*."

Dry mouth or no, you say, "Silas. You mean the guy who's stalking Grace?"

Tim grins. "Yeah, okay. That's kind of weird."

"So what's wrong with Grace hooking up with Daniel?"

His smile dissolves. "Look. I barely even know Grace. But I do know you're her friend, and I'm well acquainted with Daniel. If Grace is someone you care about, I'd warn her. That's all."

"What do you mean?"

"You know Daniel's my half brother, right?"

This is a major blindside.
What else don't you know?

You were aware Tim was involved with Silas putting Daniel in the hospital, but not that little detail, which seems important. "Actually, no, I didn't. I've only met Daniel a couple of times. He's never discussed his personal life. All he talks about is Grace."

As you finish the joint, he relates a story about his father's long-term affair with an illegal Honduran immigrant, the by-product of which turned out to be Daniel. When she was deported, Daniel came to live here, in this very house, with his dad's legitimate family.

"Daniel idolized our dad. I mean, I loved him, but Daniel was like a puppy, following him around, licking his feet. Any time Dad would pay attention to Mom or me, you could see how pissed that made Daniel. He'd do stuff for attention, or to hurt us. Like, he messed up my bike a couple of times, and he started my closet on fire. Dad forgave everything, but once he was gone, things got worse.

"Dad's death hit all of us hard, but Daniel totally flipped out. He'd go on regular rampages, breaking things he knew were important to Mom, like her favorite crystal wineglasses—the ones she loved because they were wedding gifts. Sometimes he'd come to the table and instead of eating he'd just sit there, like daring Mom to say something. Sometimes the food tasted funny, and on one memorable occasion, there was pee on my plate. Eventually, Mom made him eat in the kitchen and fix his own meals."

"Wow. That's crazy."

"Exactly. We got so we didn't feel safe in the house, but Mom had promised Dad she'd take care of Daniel."

"What do you mean, you didn't feel safe?"

"Okay, like, once she woke up and he was standing at the foot of the bed, holding a screwdriver, just staring at her and tapping that damn thing against the palm of his hand. It was two in the morning. After that, she put a dead bolt on his bedroom door and locked him in at night."

Unbelievable. You definitely should say something to Grace. But would she believe you?

"Eventually, he split out the window. That's why he's on the street."

That part you knew. The rest . . .

"After he left, there were break-ins here. Things disappeared, like a high-end camera, a lot of my mom's expensive jewelry, a couple of firearms. We couldn't prove it was him, but it must have been, because after Mom changed the locks it quit happening. Well, that and because Silas and I beat the fuck out of him and told him it better stop."

And so, the plot thickens. It generally does.

"Did you ever get your stuff back?"

"Nah. The cops said they'd check the pawnshops, but I doubt they tried very hard. They said nothing turned up, that the perp had probably sold it cheap or traded it for drugs."

Sounds about right.

"So, you think Grace could be in danger?"

"Only if she gets on his bad side. But that isn't hard to do."

You finish your deal, collect a bill, and take off for your other stops, thinking about Daniel, who's all mild-mannered nerd on the outside, while under the skin lurks a whole different person. Could he turn violent? Of course he could. Because the thing is, he isn't so different from most people.

Including you.

Fade Out

THERE'S A MYTH

That among the ranks
of venomous snakes
the young ones carry
more powerful poisons.
But this is a campfire tale.

Science maintains serpent
venom peaks with aging,
reaching max virulence
in adulthood, and as for
sheer force of delivery,
Daddy can pump ten times
the dosage that Junior can.

As for danger, however,
a grown rattler understands
the folly of overkill. Time
is required to restock
its precious supply,
and so rarely does one
completely empty its reserves.

A youngster, however,
is driven by instincts it does
not comprehend, and therein
lies the peril—lack of self-control.

YOUNG HUMANS

Often react in similar fashion—
thoughtless reaction to an action.

This provides an endless stream
of opportunities for mayhem.

Fields of discontent might lie
fallow, but when cultivated

by sharpened tines of resentment,
fertilized with envy, and sown

with seeds of hate, thorny weeds
will take root, sprouting and vining

and choking off the sustenance
of hopefulness and faith in love.

But this prolonged process can take
decades to bring to fruition.

Better the impulsivity of youth,
when one black storm cloud

pours ambition onto the muddied
soil of momentary madness.

Fade In:
SLIP BACK INTO ASHLYN'S SKIN

One day, by God, you'll have a car. Not that you know how to drive. But how hard can it be? Hit the gas to go, the brake to stop. Turn the steering wheel right to go right; left to go left. You don't want a beater, though.

> *Bartering for a decent ride*
> *will take forethought and a lot of work,*
> *Ashlyn, some of it distasteful.*
> *But you're a clever girl.*
> *You'll know just what to do*
> *when the time comes.*

Public transportation is a pain. It takes you forever to get anywhere with all the stops, people getting on and off, sometimes struggling to find the right change. Babies crying. Old dudes farting. Couples arguing. Or making out. Okay, that can be interesting to watch. Built-in entertainment.

It's not as bad if you're just trying to get around the city, but today you're headed into a northern neighborhood, and once you get close to your destination you'll have to do the last leg on foot.

You could've waited for Silas to pick you up, but he had to work until four, and then he called to let you know he'd probably be late because the QuikTrip had been robbed. One of the employees was shot, the second woman in two days. The other was at Denny's, and the cops think it was the same two guys. There's a citywide manhunt underway for those crazy fucks.

As you exit the bus, a question flashes. What if those guys turned up at the rally tomorrow? Okay, that would be stupid, considering the whole of Tucson law enforcement is currently searching for them. But other dudes with itchy trigger fingers might very well be there. You're pretty sure there will be plenty of guns in evidence. A state-sanctioned open-carry show of force.

> *Don't worry about the risk.*
> *Feed on it.*

Truthfully, you might even attract danger. It seems to find you, so what's the point of working too hard to avoid it? As if to prove the theory, you dive straight into a sketchy part of town, which is between you and the decent neighborhood that is your destination. Can't get there any other way, however, so off you go. On the map it looked like maybe a half mile. Not so far.

The matchbox houses boast sagging fences and faded paint, and the people relaxing outside sit on flat cement rectangles, rather than porches. Heads turn and strange eyes assess you, obviously not a regular here.

"Woot. Hey, mami!" calls some random man, chugging beer with a buddy.

You ignore him, refuse to engage.

"Got some crystal," offers a scraggly guy standing on a quiet street corner.

You try really hard not to look in his direction, but you must pass by him to cross, and you have to wait for a slow-moving car to clear the intersection.

"Try a little taste. You'll like it."

The way he leers makes you wonder if he's talking about the meth or himself. You suspect the latter.

"Gave it up for Lent," you try.

His grin reveals teeth in dire need of repair, not to mention brushing. "Huh. You don't look like the religious type."

Suddenly, you're aware of his smell—sweat, soaked with whatever chemicals the crystal was cooked with. Kind of sweet. Kind of rancid. Luckily, you can chance the crosswalk now. You veer wide around him, step off the curb.

"Hey," he calls after you. "Where you goin'?"

Halfway across, you become aware of footsteps behind you. A glance over your shoulder confirms it's Meth Mouth. Scanning the landscape, you can see other people, but they're not close, and anyway there's no guarantee that they would come to your aid if this guy gets out of line.

He's right behind you.
Challenge him.

"Are you following me?" you yell, your voice sharp and loud.

He slows but doesn't pause. "Just watching out for you. This is a rough hood."

"Stop right there. Do not come any closer. Thanks for your offer of help, but I'm fine on my own."

You reach into your bag, hoping he'll take the hint. The first thing your hand closes around is your phone. Dialing 911 might be prudent, but unless a cop is cruising real close, no way could he get here in time. No, you'll have to deal with this by yourself.

The guy hesitates. "Whatcha got in there? Money?"

Hurt him.

"Dude, if I had any money I wouldn't be walking. See? I'd be a shit customer anyway."

He takes a step forward. "Let me look."

Fucking dopers. More balls than brains, at least what brains they've got left.

"Take one more step and you'll wish you never laid eyes on me."

The guy, who's three or four inches taller, and despite his drug-wasted frame still outweighs you, lunges. You sidestep and momentum carries him into the curb, tripping him forward. He catches himself before face-planting, but as he attempts to recover, you extract a couple of self-defense mechanisms from your bag.

"Fuck off or I will cut you." You flash the switchblade, now open, in your right hand.

"I ain't scared of you."

The thing about meth is it's like rocket fuel for the kind of rage that defeats any semblance of logic. The dude jumps to his feet, comes straight at you. If he manages to bulldoze into you, things could get ugly.

Hold your ground.

You grit your teeth, and when he's close enough so you know you can't miss, you dose him with enough pepper spray to drop him back down on his knees. "Fucking bitch! You blinded me."

Suddenly, you're aware of people moving toward you on the sidewalk, and a car not so far down the block. Time to make a hasty retreat. As you hurry away, you understand that the whole scene probably took less than three minutes. Good thing you never leave home unprepared for situations exactly like that.

You should have stabbed him.
He earned the knife.

Adrenaline pumping, you jog for a while, not that you're worried about the meth head, but rather as a way to alleviate the desire to turn around and demonstrate the proper way to use a switchblade against a deserving reprobate. You've done it before, and would have no problem with a repeat performance.

Fact is, you're a tough girl, and that has as much to do with your innate personality as it does with the circumstances of your childhood. Some kids faced with similar situations would simply fold up and check on out. Not you. You're a fighter. That could very well be a trait you inherited from your bastard father, so maybe it's one thing you can thank him for.

A knife might not be a gun, but it can be a valuable weapon. And unfortunately, there will always be the random man who believes it's his right to take a woman by force. You decided early on that would not happen to you.

It wasn't a switchblade that time. It was a critically sharp boning knife you borrowed from Aunt Lou's kitchen. She never missed it. Her idea of meat is Spam. You can cut that with a fork.

You were a high school sophomore, and you'd gone to a post-football-game party. The guy who was supposed to take you home—you couldn't rightfully call him your boyfriend, more like an acquaintance with a car—wasn't ready to call it a night.

Despite your protest, he drove to a construction site, of course deserted at that time.

"Take me home, please," you tried.

"Sure. After we have some fun."

"Look, I don't give sex away, and you've got nothing I need."

"I've got this."

He unzipped his pants, freeing his erection, then pushed you down on the seat, forcing himself between your legs. You were wearing a skirt, putting nothing between him and you but thin panties. Your purse, however, was in reach on the floor, and you knew exactly where to find the aptly named boning knife. Him, you didn't warn. In one swift motion, you brought the blade down into his shoulder at the same time your foot caught his groin. Neither his arm nor his dick was going to work very well for a while.

The power you exhaled in that moment!
Resurrect it whenever you can.

He jumped off like you were on fire, giving you the chance to escape his car. You ran, but he didn't follow. And when he saw you at school on Monday, he never said a word, at least not to you. A few of the guys looked at you differently after that. There was a titillating blend of fear and respect in their eyes, and that was okay by you. They had nothing you needed, either.

You've been to Tim's house a couple of times, so you recognize it when you turn down his street. It's big and handsome, nothing like the one you live in. His mom must have married well. Her side of the family—your side—does not come from money.

As you start up the walk, a girl comes out the door and hustles over to her Honda Civic, scoots in and drives away. She shoots you a curious look as she passes. Probably not a whole lot of females visit Tim.

Tim, who's still at the door, stands back to let you in. He reeks of weed and his eyes are bloodshot. Bet you can guess what he and that girl were just smoking. "Smells like good shit."

"It is."

He does not offer to share, and that's fine. That's not why you're here. You get straight down to business.

"How are things shaping up?"

"It's been a couple of hours since I last checked in. Let's go to my room."

Okay, that's vaguely discomfiting.

"Is your mom home?"

"Not yet. I expect her around dinnertime."

"Does she know about tomorrow?"

"Only what she's seeing in the news." He leads the way up a long flight of stairs and down the hall to his bedroom. "Shut the door, okay?" He goes over to his desk, fires up his computer, a fancy desktop Mac. Then he pulls up a web page detailing tomorrow's rally.

There's a list of organizations planning to show a united front against illegal immigrants flooding into the country. That's especially important here, in a state bordering Mexico. Together, you and Tim peruse the list.

"Check it out," he says. "Oath Keepers *and* Three Percenters will be there, so we'll have militia backup."

"A heavy open-carry presence, you mean."

"Oh, yeah. Those dudes will come armed to the teeth."

Your skin tingles.

"What about us? Are we arming?"

Tim turns away from the computer, eyes you suspiciously. "Some of us might be. Why? Do you own a firearm?"

"Maybe." No use giving away all your secrets.

"Long gun? Because those are much more impressive."

"No. Not a long gun."

"Can you shoot one accurately? Even under extreme pressure?"

"Absolutely."

Again he stares, not quite able to believe you. "Where did you learn to shoot?"

"ROTC."

"You mean Junior ROTC, right?" He snorts.

"I'm still in high school, so yeah, that would be it."

"They shoot air rifles."

"True. Same general marksmanship principles, however. And I happen to be good."

Damn straight you are. Competition-level good. Not only that, but you ace your matches.

"You joining up?"

"Thinking about it, yeah. First I thought army, but now I'm considering the air force. The big decision is whether to let them send me to college. I don't have a military commitment with JROTC, but I would if I join ROTC."

"I don't know, man. The world is a crazy place. If you do it, don't go army. Too big a chance of boots on the ground."

You've considered that. "I'm not afraid to fight. I'd rather die with honor than spend my whole life working at a shit job. At least I'd join as an officer. Better pay. Better opportunities."

"Personally, I'd rather not die at all, but when I do, I doubt it will be honorable."

As tough guys go, he's kind of a wuss. Maybe you should start a female-centric alt-right organization. White Women Unite, or something. An all-girl armed militia would be an amazing sight.

"So, are you going to carry tomorrow?" Why is it you doubt it?

But he surprises you. "Of course. Taking an AR-15."

"Seriously?"

"Yeah. I'll show you."

You follow him down the hall to a small bedroom, now used as an office. A big bookcase hogs an entire wall. Tim trips a switch hidden behind an encyclopedia and a panel swings out, revealing a chamber stockpiled with guns. It's a huge collection, everything from antique pistols to semiautomatic rifles.

"Holy shit. You expecting the apocalypse?"

He laughs. "Nah. My dad was a collector. Some people would call him a gun nut, I guess. He loved the damn things. Interestingly, though, I can only remember him actually shooting any a few times. He just wanted to own them."

And you just want to caress them. Probably should ask. "Can I touch?"

"Yeah. They're not loaded. We keep the protection pieces where we can reach them quickly if we need them."

The antiques are in display cases. You examine them from behind the glass. But the ones you're most drawn to are housed in simple locked racks attached to the walls. These are military models or knockoffs. M16s. AK-47s. AR-15s. Even at rest, they're intimidating. Powerful. Deadly.

> *So much potential sleeping*
> *within them. Go on.*
> *Touch them.*
> *Stroke them.*
> *Honor them.*

"Beautiful. Which one are you taking tomorrow?"

He walks over, unlocks the bar holding the guns in place, picks up one of the assault rifles. "This one." He strokes the barrel like he might a lover's arm. "Here. See how she feels."

Tease.

You heft the proffered gun, a Bushmaster AR-15. "It's lighter than I thought it would be."

"Yeah. They replaced aluminum and steel with some space-age polymer. Keeps it from corroding, too. Hey, check out this one."

He takes the rifle, replaces it with another. They look almost the same, except this one is more compact. "What is it?"

"Bushmaster Carbon 15 pistol. Awesome, yeah?"

"It's brilliant." What if? Nah, he wouldn't. Would he? "Don't suppose you'd let me carry this one tomorrow?"

That stops him. You can actually see the wheels turning. Finally, he asks, "What's in it for me?"

Pig.

Make him squeal.

Fade Out

IT MIGHT NOT SEEM POSSIBLE

For someone inhabiting
this earth for less
than two decades
to point a gun
at another human being
and pull the trigger.

But it's not unfeasible.
Not even highly unlikely.
Age is not an accurate measure
of temperance.

The desire to kill
is a living thing,
inhaling every slight,
ingesting each rejection.

And all it takes is a hiccup
to bring it crawling
out from under
a rock pile of restraint

into a momentary lapse
of reason.

ONE MOMENT

Is all it takes.

One moment
of weakness.

One moment
of strength.

Tipping points
are not age
dependent.

Stability
is sandstone
awaiting
the tide.

Fade In:
SLIP BACK INTO RAND'S SKIN

There he is. Flaunting moral corruption on social media. You knew him as Dean Halverson, but today he goes by Dean Green, and his blog is the Green Screed. Apparently he's morphed his perversions into white nationalistic hate mongering. And the fucker will be a featured speaker at a protest in Tucson today.

> *This could be your moment, Rand.*
> *The instant you even that score*
> *once and for all.*

There've been rumblings about the rally for a while. Some guys on the construction crew are planning to march on the pro-immigration side. You've heard them talking, and they expect maybe ten thousand path-to-citizenship supporters to swell the streets surrounding the U of A campus. So, of course, a bunch of white-power pricks feel the need to flex their muscles.

This being open-carry-crazy Arizona, you know that "patriots" will dress up in camos and exhibit assault rifles and parade around shouting racist slogans. And Dean fucking "Green Screed" Halverson will climb out of his hole and lead the charge, yelling into a megaphone.

> *A stray bullet could come from anywhere,*
> *and shut him up forever.*

You wouldn't be privy to this information at all if not for an odd conversation you had with Cami last night, and *that* might not have happened if not for Waylon.

When you arrived home from work, Cami's car was absent. About the time you slipped out of your boots and went to wash up, she came in, Waylon in tow. "Where've you been?"

Innocent question, and an innocent answered it. "At Gramma's."

Cami blushed peeled-beet red, the approximate shade of guilt. But her excuse seemed valid. "I called to talk to Noelle and couldn't get hold of her, so I tried Mom, who was having coffee with a friend. When neither of us could rouse Noelle, we both went to see what was wrong. She'd had a seizure and was just coming around."

You tossed up your arms in disgust. "I thought you said her new meds had everything under control."

"I guess she didn't sleep much last night. Exhaustion is a trigger."

You've heard it before. "Uh, yeah." That was pretty much all you had on that. "So then you hung out?"

"For a little while. But she needed to sleep, so I let her nap."

"Me and Gramma took a nap," said Waylon.

"Go play," urged Cami, herding him toward his toy box before turning back to you. "He was really cranky, so Mom offered to lie down with him while I talked to Noelle. Before I knew it, everyone was asleep, so I ran a couple of errands."

Errands. Déjà vu. For someone with very little to do, she sure comes up with a lot she has to do. "Like what?"

"Okay," she confessed. "That wasn't exactly true. I took in a movie."

Last time you went to a theater was almost a year ago, on your anniversary. Your bullshit alarm initiated a hot creep of suspicion. "You went by yourself? What did you see?"

Cami rattled off the name of something current, or maybe not so. You have no way of knowing, anyway.

And then, changing the subject, she mentioned, "Oh, I ran into Daniel's half brother, Tim."

"You mean the guy who helped Silas beat Daniel to a pulp?"

"Yeah. But, listen . . ."

She offered up a woeful tale, the upshot of which was that hooking up with Daniel might very well mean Grace is in danger. Truthfully, there *is* something *off* about the guy. But he dotes on her. And, anyway, Silas is her actual stalker.

Nothing she said made sense in the context of what you know. Something was definitely wrong. And things kept getting stranger.

"So, you visited with Noelle today, you won't need me to watch Waylon tomorrow?"

"Actually, I do. There's a big rally downtown and I promised I'd take Noelle."

"The immigration rally?"

"Yeah. She's all into it. I figure anything that gets her out of the house . . ."

"Cami, that's going to be crazy! They're expecting, like, ten thousand people or something."

"I know. Could you help me figure out a good place to park?"

So, you went online to find out exactly where the rally is supposed to be held, and your research carried you to the planned protest, including their list of rabble-rousing speakers. A couple you've heard of, through your criminal justice classes. But you never expected to see Dean among them.

There will be militia presence, too. Things could get dicey, and as Cami gets ready to leave this morning, you try to talk her out of it. "Sweetheart, I really don't think you should go. What if the demonstration turns violent? You could get hurt."

"The whole point is a peaceful rally. There will be church congregations there. We'll stay where it's safe, and if it looks like that's changing, I promise we'll leave ASAP."

"But you don't care about immigration."

"Noelle does, and I care about her."

"Maybe I should come with you."

"No!"

The force of her response is surprising. "Why not?"

"Because I need you to watch Waylon. There's no time to find a sitter now. Look. I told Noelle I'd take her, and I'm going to. Won't hurt you to spend a couple of hours with your son, you know."

You wince at her excellent button pushing.

"How can you even say that?"

As usual when she knows she'll get her way, she pretends humility, comes over for a kiss. "Sorry. Didn't mean it. Maybe you could take him to the park? You know how he loves the slides."

The sting of defeat nicks your pride and you deflate.

"Maybe I will. Be sure to put his seat in the truck."

"I'm going to sneak out before Waylon gets up. Love you."

"I love you, too."

You do, but as you watch her leave, you think maybe the emotion has tempered. The sex is still good, and you still think she's hot, but after three years together, the fiery passion has cooled to embers. Yes, they can still be stoked, but it takes more work than it used to.

She has changed. Either that, or you've just opened your eyes to the kind of girl she really is.

The selfish kind, you mean.

Not like you can't work with that, and maybe she'll mature into a different woman. But it can be hard to live with someone who always insists on having things her way.

Besides, you value stability, and want that for your kid. Your own childhood was volatile. You never felt secure, even before the thing with Dean. After, it was like walking a tightrope over a pit of self-doubt. Your mom made you believe it was *your* fault, even though she had no clue what had happened. She did that by calling you weak, gullible, unworthy of love.

Waylon will always know he can count on you.

And, maybe, once you settle up
with Dean you'll feel strong,
discerning,
valuable.

The clock informs you it's a little before nine. Unusual for Waylon to sleep in so late. A welfare check confirms he's still snoozing, so you go to the kitchen, make coffee, and turn on your laptop to find streaming coverage of the crowds gathering for the rally. It's going to be huge.

Insane. Too bad you can't go. It would be good cover. You can see the headline: RANDOM BULLET KILLS NEO-NAZI. POLICE SEARCHING FOR SHOOTER.

Then again, there will be cameras there. Lots of them. Thousands of people shooting video on their phones, not to mention reporters with newsroom equipment.

> *You must go to that rally.*
> *Find a way.*

Then again, then again, when you take Dean out, you want it to be personal. Just him and you, so there's no doubt in his mind why he's going to die. You've crafted the scene in your mind many times:

Fade In: Secluded desert location. Old pervert, wearing a Boy Scout uniform, crawls across the sand, begging for mercy.

"Take off your pants," you order, and when he's slow to respond, you put a bullet into the ground next to him.

Coward sheds his trousers.

"Now your skivvies."

*Off come the tighty whities. The sight of his pale pimply ass makes
you cringe.*

"Turn around and face me."

On his knees below you, he turns up his watering eyes. "No. Please?"

*"Once upon a time, I said those exact two words to you, and all
you did was rape me. Do you remember my name? Do you know
who I am?"*

"No. I'm sorry."

*You could let him go. He doesn't know who you are. But that, in
itself, is a problem. You want him to know. "The name is Rand
Bingham. You pretended to be my friend, and then you hurt me,
in the most humiliating way possible. I know I'm not the only one,
but I will be the lucky one who gets revenge for us all."*

And then, a single shot, right between the eyes . . .

"Daddy?"

You jump at the sound of Waylon's small voice, but immediately
fall back into the present. He grounds you.

"Morning, little man. Want some breakfast?"

He sprints across the room, leaps into your arms. "Pancakes?"

"You're going to turn into a pancake."

"Nuh-uh. *You* are."

And so it goes. You dive into the day, keeping half an eye on the news about the rally. Seems the cops are doing a decent job of keeping the two sides separated, though there are sporadic incidents, and some protesters have been arrested.

You've washed the post-pancake dishes and are getting Waylon ready for a trip to the park when your phone rings. It's an unfamiliar number, but something tells you to go ahead and pick up. You're glad that you did, because it's Cami.

"Rand? I'm in jail. Can you please come down here and see about bail?"

"What?"

"I've been arrested."

"Because of the protest?"

"No. Long story. Please come, and bring money. They might let me out OR, but the booking cop didn't think so."

You exhale loudly. "Have any idea how much?"

"No clue."

"Okay. It might take a while."

"Rand? Please don't tell my parents. I love you."

You have to get someone to watch the kid. He's not going to see his mother in jail. What the fuck did she do, if it wasn't something to do with the rally? Was Noelle involved?

To spring Cami quickly will probably require a bail bondsman, so you do an online search and find one willing to come out on a holiday. He was aware his services might be needed, considering that many protests lead to arrests. "I'll check into it and get back to you."

You've got two hundred bucks in the bank, and that has to last until Friday, and you need a babysitter. Your parents are out of town. Who else? Grace! Hopefully, she's around.

You call; she's home. But when you explain you require bail money and someone to watch Waylon, Daniel is apparently reluctant to let her come. You can hear him raise his voice in the background, and after the things Cami mentioned earlier, your brotherly defense mechanism kicks into gear.

> *If that bastard lays a hand on her,*
> *you will make him regret it.*

But Grace remains calm and assertive. "I'll stop by the ATM and should be there in twenty minutes."

"You're okay, right?"

"Of course. Why?"

"Your boyfriend sounds upset."

"He'll get over it. He has to leave soon anyway. I'll see you ASAP."

If she isn't here in a half hour, you're going over to make sure he's gone and she's safe.

The bail bondsman calls back. "They've got her on a misdemeanor marijuana charge. Twenty-five hundred bail, so I'll need three hundred seventy-five in cash. That's fifteen percent, plus my fee. And how about a car title? I need to protect my investment."

Marijuana? There's no damn way! Cami doesn't do marijuana. It's not possible. You'd know. This has to be a mistake.

While you wait for Grace, you dig out the title to the Civic. You've folded it neatly in your wallet when Waylon finally asks, "Park, Daddy?"

You scoop him up, kiss his forehead. "Later, okay? Auntie Grace is coming over to play."

"Where you goin'? Work?"

"No. I've got to go get your mama."

"Where Mama's car?"

Shit. Shit. Shit. You have no idea. Was it a traffic stop? Did they impound it? It would be nice to have some information.

"The engine quit. I've got to fix it if I can, so we can get Mama home."

You set Waylon down and start to pace, realizing you just lied to your son. But you had no other choice, and it pisses you off. Cami has some major explaining to do. If she's convicted, it could very well ruin your chance at a job on the force. You slam your fist against the wall.

"Daddy mad?"

You rein it in. "Sorry, little dude. Everything's okay." Oh, man, another lie.

It takes almost forty minutes for Grace to arrive, and by the time she gets there, you've resumed your pacing. Worried for her. Worried for Cami. Worried for your family.

Waylon greets her. "Gracie!"

"There's that boy. Come give me a hug, then go turn on the TV." Once he's out of range, she says, "Sorry it took so long. I had to drop Daniel off."

"You sure everything's okay with that guy?"

"As okay as things get. Why?"

"Just something Cami said made me think there's something not very nice there."

"Like what? She hardly even knows Daniel."

Apparently, neither does Grace. Which reminds you. "She said his brother told her some stuff. How would she know this Tim guy, anyway?"

"I really don't know. But I do know Tim is a thug."

It dawns on you: marijuana. Maybe she gets it from Tim the thug. "Question. Did you know Cami smokes weed?"

Her jaw actually, physically drops. "What?"

"She got arrested on a marijuana charge."

"No way. Not around me, at least. Not ever."

"Well, that's what the bail bondsman said. She was holding an ounce."

"Oh. Bail." Grace reaches into her purse, pulls out four hundred dollars. "That's all I could get."

"It's plenty. I'll pay you back as soon as I can. Thank you. For everything."

"No worries. I know you're good for it. Go on. We'll be fine. It's been a while since I've had any Waylon snuggle time."

As you leave, you feel a small sense of relief. Grace is safe. Waylon's safe. Cami's safe, because jail is secure.

And yet, with or without your plan for revenge, everything you've worked so hard for is currently at risk.

How could that selfish bitch
do this to you?

Fade Out

RISK

Is omnipresent.
It isn't always in obvious view,
and you can't always hear
it drawing closer.

But it's never far away.

It is driving down
the freeway, motoring
along a deserted avenue,
or fishtailing on a gravel road.

Descending the staircase.

It loiters on the playground,
in classrooms, lunchrooms,
the church parking lot.
It lingers in your living room,
kitchen, backyard.

Everywhere people gather.

It coils in the pit
of your belly, throbs
with each beat of your heart.
It is the song of breathing,
the scream within every cell.

The price tag on living.

YOU MIGHT CHOOSE

To cloister
yourself within
the safe confines
of familiar walls.

Never venture
beyond
certainty
into the realm
of chance.

Rarely seek
variety,
or dream
of existence
beyond acrylic
windowpanes.

But the end
result
for every living
creature
is the same.

And the air
outside
is sweeter.
Dare to breathe
it in.

Fade In:
SLIP BACK INTO SILAS'S SKIN

Hard to believe it's possible for a day to be crazier than yesterday, but today's shaping up to be absolutely bonkers. In a good way, unlike the nastiness in QuikTrip. That was just plain ugly.

Witnessing a homicide
is tough, Silas, especially
when it's someone you know.
Much easier when it's a stranger.
Easier still when it's you
pulling the trigger.

Myra didn't make it. Watching her go down like that, crumpling in on herself as she fell to the floor, struck a nerve you didn't realize you possessed. Death usually creeps up on a person. For it to strike cobra-fast, straight out of nowhere, well, that is sobering. Only after the fact, when the bad guys were gone, did it hit that it could've been you, and that left you shaking.

You put on a good show afterward, erected a steel veneer. A guy has to act tough, like nothing can touch you. But inside you're marked. Scarred. Not afraid, and in fact, even more determined to never be caught off guard.

The masked lunatics will get caught, of course they will, because they haven't much in the way of intellect. Stealing is one thing. Killing someone is something else, and you'd best have a damn good reason for doing it. Shooting people just to watch blood squirt is fucking stupid. You don't even get the satisfaction of flesh-on-flesh connection.

You'll carry today at the rally, of course, but that weapon is all about a *show* of deadly force. What you're hoping for is more intimate violence—the kind that physical force accomplishes. You want to inflict injury with your fists and feet. Anticipation lifts the hair on your arms.

> *You're hungry for that feeling.*
> *Starving for that incredible flush*
> *of satisfaction.*
> *It's been too long*
> *since you've assuaged that appetite.*

Your mom's home, sans Len, this morning, and up early, which is her normal routine. What's different is you're out of bed by seven on a holiday. So she's surprised when you seek her out on the patio, sipping tea and watching the quail that visit regularly. You plop down in a chair next to her.

"Have plans, I take it?" she asks.

"Yeah. Gonna hang out with some friends."

If she wonders why so early, she doesn't comment. But she does say, "May I ask you something?"

"Sure."

"What is it about Len you don't like? He's smart. Funny. Kind. I'd like you to have a good relationship, and so would he."

This one is a tricky question, so you mull it over. Either make up something totally unbelievable, or inform her that you're an anti-Semite. A third possibility hits you.

"I guess it just bugs me that he's sleeping with you."

"Silas, I'm not even forty. You think I should remain celibate because your father left me?"

Maybe that wasn't the best choice after all. But now you're kind of stuck with it.

"Pretty sure no guy wants to consider his mom having sex. With anyone."

One quail—the scout—hops up on the fence, looks around, and sounds the "all clear" to his covey, which follows him over the railing. It would be nice to have a personal scout who could give you the right answers.

"I don't think that's it, at least not all of it."

"What do you mean?"

"Are you going to that rally today?"

You decide to fess up. "I am."

"Don't suppose you're on the pro-immigrants side?"

"I am not."

She sits thoughtfully for several seconds. "I don't understand. This is not the way I raised you."

"Tough. I get it's hard to understand, but I have a mind of my own, independent of your programming."

The force of your words surprises even you. Your mom looks slightly stunned.

> Don't back down.
> It's way past time she understands
> that you are far beyond
> her ability to control.

"Programming, is it? I would have called it 'example.'" Skip five beats. "So you dislike Len because he's Jewish?"

"He's a Jew, and he's fucking you. . . ."

The f-word is purposeful, for effect. First time you've ever tossed it her way, and it works.

"Silas—"

"That is *not* okay in my book. And as for understanding, did you ever bother to talk to me? Ever ask how I felt about him or his religion? No. Never. Always too busy with work. With *him*. Well, guess what? While you weren't paying attention, I found a cause to believe in."

"White power."

"Exactly."

"What if I told you I'll be at the rally, too? On the other side?"

That is unexpected news. If she means it, it complicates things. "Is that true?"

She nods. "Immigration, and especially a straightforward path to citizenship, is important to me. I work with kids all the time who live in fear of deportation—their own, or a family member's."

She pauses for consideration.

"What are you afraid of, Silas? Why embrace a movement predicated on fear?"

> *Why can't she see*
> *you're not afraid of anything?*

But her quiet logic is difficult to dismantle.

"Look, Mom. The whole point of the TYN is celebrating our white European heritage. We don't want to hurt anyone. We only want to be allowed a society exclusively our own."

She cocks her head sideways, and she measures you with gentle eyes. "And who's stopping you from that? Never mind. You don't have to answer. But, son, you are cutting yourself off from many good people, and eclectic, vibrant cultures. It hurts my heart to know I didn't teach you better."

This is not why you came out here. You didn't want her to ever discover your TradYouth connections, but now that she has, your relationship will change. You were trying to repair it. Has it been irreparably severed?

"Don't blame yourself. You were a great role model. It just didn't fit me."

As she stands, a long sigh escapes her. "Maybe I'll see you at the rally. But I hope I don't."

You follow her inside, and before you head out, you take the time to say, "Hey, Mom? Love ya."

"Right back at you. Be careful out there today."

Bravado crumbles momentarily. Your mommy just made you feel like her little boy, and you miss that. But as quickly as the notion overtook you, it passes on by, and you're a big boy again.

> *Everyone has an Achilles heel.*
> *Don't let your mother be yours.*
> *Now is not the time for weakness.*

It would be awkward to crash a barrier, only to come face-to-face with your mom, waving her little peacenik sign. That's what she'd carry, if anything, marching down the street, singing "This Little Candle" and "Kumbaya."

You, on the other hand, will have a shield and a firearm. Both are stashed at Tim's, which is where you're headed, after a quick stop to pick up your girl.

No way around it. You like her. A lot. She's awesome in the sack, and you can't discount that as a factor. But she's also fearless. You've spent much of this weekend comparing her to Grace, and she might have fallen short. Instead, she's risen in your estimation and actually rates higher than expected because she shares your ideals.

Plus, she's incredible to look at.

She's standing there on the sidewalk, rising up and down on her toes, dressed in butt-hugging black jeans and a long-sleeved camouflage top that's tight enough to show off her well-defined assets. Even her hairstyle is starting to grow on you. She's right. It suits her.

You pull up at the curb, and she bounces in, animated in anticipation of today's activities. "Hey, baby!" She scoots across the seat for a kiss. She tastes of peppermint and honey, an intoxicating combination, and you insist your lips linger against hers. She does not argue, not even when your hand drops to stroke the ample rounds of her breasts.

But finally, she stops you. "Not right now. I don't want to be late."

"Girl, I hauled my ass out of bed at six thirty so we'd have plenty of time. You won't miss a thing."

Her excitement is contagious. By the time you get halfway to Tim's, you're anxious, too. You turn on the radio, blare fashwave out Lolita's open windows. People standing on the sidewalk turn to stare. Some smile, supportive. Others flash filthy looks, but that's okay. Fuck 'em. They ain't seen nothing yet.

Ashlyn nudges you. "Check it out."

Several school buses, loaded to the max, head in the opposite direction, toward the university. You can see signs, but most you can't read. One, however, is right at a window. DREAMERS UNITE.

"I don't think we're on the same side."

Ashlyn laughs, but even though you made it, the joke falls flat for you. Your mom is on their side, and unbelievably, your dad is, too. You turned on the news last night to see if you made it on TV. There was a crew at QuikTrip after the robbery, and this goofy chick interviewed you.

If the segment aired, you missed it, but you happened to catch a story about the rally. That news team went down to Nogales to talk to border patrol agents about their views on immigration. One of them was your dad, who actually said he thought it should be easier for Mexicans to get work visas.

"This labor force is at the heart of American agriculture," he said. "They're a boost to the economy already, and if they could work legally, think of the infusion of tax money. Immigration reform would actually make the border safer because then we could concentrate on the real bad guys. Drug runners and such. It would keep families together, and that isn't such a bad thing."

Like he kept your family together.

You've never really talked to your dad about his views on immigration. His living with Zia told you all you needed to know. But to hear him articulate such a positive message surprised you. Reaching way back into your memory banks, you find a different attitude. Years on the job have softened his stance, or maybe it's just middle age. He is not the same man.

Would he be a better father now?

Perhaps. You don't see him that often, maybe a couple of times a month. But he's easier going, definitely not the same ogre who used to verbally pound the tar out of your mom and you. That guy made you tough. The new one is just confusing.

"Do you think there will be very many other girls there today?" Ashlyn pops you back into the moment.

"At least one."

"Who?"

"My mom. On the other side."

"Wow. That's tweaked. What happens if we clash?"

Obviously, you couldn't hurt her. But could you intervene if she was in danger from one of your compatriots?

"I don't know. Hopefully it won't come to that."

You cringe. That sounded weak.

The last few days have offered up a lot of difficult questions, and a fair amount of personal evolution. But there's no turning back from the game plan at this point. Especially not with Ashlyn attached.

"I really hope it does. I mean, I wouldn't want your mom to be involved. . . ."

The "but" remains unspoken.

And now you pull up in front of Tim's house. Expecting you, he greets you at the door, no bell necessary. "Mom's still asleep," he whispers. "Come on up to my room."

What would Shailene say if she saw the array of protest weaponry currently on display in her son's bedroom?

Improvised shields.

Helmets and goggles.

Clubs and Mace.

Firearms.

"Does your mom have any clue about your plans for today?"

"Are you kidding? No way. In fact, we should be moving all this stuff now. Not that she's an early riser, but she'd toss a fit if she saw me leaving with these guns. They're valuable, you know."

Shailene's bedroom is at the back of the house, on the first floor. You station Ashlyn as a lookout while you transport the gear out to your vehicles. Yesterday, in your planning meeting, you decided to take both trucks and park in different locations in case one gets cut off and you need to leave quickly.

Most of the stuff can load into the beds, but the guns go under the seats. For whatever reason, Tim gave Ashlyn permission to carry the Bushmaster pistol. It's definitely a lot more showy than the piece you'll sport, but that's okay. It'll look damn good on her.

She isn't officially old enough to carry. Too young by a few months. But she will be marching with everyone else, and no one's going to notice or ask for her ID. The cops will be way too busy just trying to maintain the peace.

They will be shaking in their jackboots.

Law enforcement will be afraid of you. The thought shoots chills up your spine. As long as they don't start lobbing stun grenades and tear gas.

"Let's do this!" Finished with spy duty, Ashlyn starts down the walk. Her chin is tipped up, her shoulders thrown back, the posture of a warrior.

So why do you feel this sudden need to protect her? Not that she wants you to.

You're really no match for that girl.

Fade Out

WHO'S TO SAY

Why some people embrace
ideals others find repugnant?

It might be upbringing,
a reflection of parental philosophy.

But children often develop
dissenting viewpoints.

Perhaps it's one brittle instant,
augmented in memory by time,

a shadowed glimpse of heartbreak
blown into total eclipse.

Or a random whim of nature
implanted in egg or spore.

Regardless of how one psyche
throws in with the dark side,

if you believe your stand is right,
you'll fight with conviction.

IF YOU SPEAK

With conviction, shade
your words with certainty,
allow no room for argument,
no space for dissent,

if your message is a promise
that every sentence
you communicate
is undiluted truth,

you will be listened to.

If you act
with conviction, no hint
of turning back,
no whisper of retreat,

if you storm the barricades,
no pause before
the busting through, sheer
force of will your propulsion,

no one will stand in your way.

Fade In:
SLIP BACK INTO DANIEL'S SKIN

Your whole world is imploding, and only three days ago, you thought you were on your way. You should've had another whole day, playing house with Grace. But now, not only are you back living homeless, but you're pretty damn sure your tarnished angel has unfolded her wings and flown away.

> *Angels are nothing more*
> *than glorified birds, Daniel,*
> *easily picked off*
> *when at last they land.*
> *Especially with the right*
> *weapon in your hand.*

How could it have gone so wrong so fast?

You could feel her growing impatience with your borderline obsession. But you backed off when her annoyance became obvious. At least, until she went all wild-eyed excited about the prospect of leaving you here in Arizona while she vacations in Hawaii.

Last night after work you were beat. It had been a long, busy shift, the cafeteria abuzz with staff, discussing possible outcomes of the protest at U of A today. Gearing up for the likelihood of injuries should peaceful First Amendment celebrations go wrong and turn violent.

Just as things started to quiet down, everything blew up again when they brought in a cop who was wounded in a gunfire exchange with the two guys who've been robbing Tucson eateries and convenience stores. One of the robbers was killed. The other is in custody. The policeman was in critical condition but is expected to live. Dangerous job, law enforcement. Definitely not a career goal.

You're more of a sneak-in-the-back-door kind of guy than a storm-down-the-street, guns-blazing type. You prefer the odds to be on your side.

Unfortunately, your odds seem to have taken a turn in the wrong direction.

When Grace picked you up, your brain was struggling to turn off the static hum created by the day's activity. All you wanted to do was go back to her house, shower off the hospital germs, and climb into her big, soft bed for a little "stress relief."

But she wanted to talk. Not about anything vital. The whole drive home, she kept on about school. Grades. Extracurricular pursuits. College next year. Like any of that means a damn thing to you, except to remind you of how crazy busy her schedule is. It will be hard to fit in time with you.

Maybe ten minutes in, you closed your eyes, tuned her out. Her chatter became background noise and the droning in your cranium blossomed into a full-blown throb.

"Right?" she asked at some point very close to her driveway.

"What?" It came out a bellow.

You didn't mean it, and that's what you said, but she sniffed at the apology. "Never mind."

When she parked the car, she stomped up to the front step without waiting for you to follow. You hurried after her, caught her arm. Too hard, and she screeched.

"It was an accident. I didn't mean to."

She jerked away. "What is wrong with you?"

If she only knew. If she only knew.

"I'm sorry, Grace. I've got an awful headache. Forgive me?"

"That is no excuse to bruise me," she complained. But she softened, opened the door and let you inside. "There's ibuprofen in the bathroom."

You availed yourself of both painkillers and hot water, hoping when you emerged from the shower, all would be well in the other room. What you found, despite the late hour, was Grace on the phone with Noelle.

The headache was gone, but you were exhausted, and in no mood to sit listening to girls yapping like little dogs. You could only hear Grace's end of the conversation, of course, but that was more than enough. Finally, you slid your finger across your throat, telling her to wind it up.

Grace scowled, and for the first time she didn't look beautiful to you. "Apparently I should go," she told Noelle. "My *boyfriend* says so."

The scornful way she said "boyfriend" made you feel like anything but.

> *That is unacceptable.*
> *She should treat you with respect.*

"No, I'm okay," Grace said to Noelle. "Really. I promise." After a moment, she held out her phone. "She wants to talk to you."

You should've known better. Obviously, she didn't want to talk about the weather. But curiosity got the better of you, and besides, there was no good way to say no.

"Hi, Noelle. What's up?"

Her tone was saccharine. "I just wanted to let you know that I will not let you hurt Grace."

"Hurt her? I love her. I'd never hurt her." Your temperature soared.

"Listen to me. Word's getting around about you. You're one crazy bastard."

And . . . you exploded. "No one calls me a bastard!"

You could almost hear her smile. "I just did. That is all. Now let me talk to Grace."

What did she mean, *word's getting around* . . . ? You had no clue, but handed over the phone and sat there, a decent quota of rage and dread churning in your gut, watching Grace's reaction to their short conversation. Once, her eyes traveled over you, hairline to shoes, and your skin seriously prickled at the intensity of her gaze.

> *She looked at you as if she thought*
> *you just might be a crazy bastard.*

Noelle did most of the talking and Grace ended the conversation with, "Tomorrow, okay?"

"What did she say?" It came off as more demand than question.

Grace didn't answer right away. Finally, "She said she wanted to talk to me, maybe after the rally, unless I change my mind and decide to come."

"That's it?" There had to be more.

"Pretty much."

"You haven't changed your mind about the rally, have you?"

"I'm not sure. I'm still thinking it over."

It was impossible to gauge where she stood in that moment, as far as the rally, or you.

But then she said, "I think maybe you need professional help. Anger management or something."

That stung, but in the way of a wasp you've harassed—deserved. You knew you had to turn things around, so you pretended contrition.

"You're probably right, but I can't afford it."

Even if you could, the notion of confession, whether to therapist or priest, makes you queasy.

"Apply for aid. I'm sure you qualify."

Yeah, but even if you were willing to try, you're back to that paperwork problem. "I wouldn't know where to start. Would you help me?"

That had the desired effect. She melted into your arms. "Of course."

Testing her resolve, you bent down for a kiss, and she did not refuse, though it was not the kind you'd hoped for—more friends kissing than lovers.

She turned on the TV, tuned into a favorite cable show you've never heard of because you rarely get to watch television, except streaming on your phone. When you reached for her hand, you half expected her to resist. But she didn't.

In fact, she seemed to relax. And when you went to bed, she made love to you, though perhaps with a bit less enthusiasm than the night before.

When you wake up this morning, she's right there beside you, asleep, one slender arm across your chest. All is well.

You believe. For about sixty seconds.

Because when she stirs, you try to persuade her into your arms, and when she opens her eyes, sees your face so close to hers, she visibly tenses.

"What's wrong?"

"Nothing. Sorry. I'm not used to waking up to someone in my bed. What time is it?"

You glance at the clock. "A little after nine." You trail a finger gently down her torso. "I love you, you know."

Her muscles relax a little and she sighs. "Love you, too."

Better. But not totally convincing.

"Wanna do it?"

She rolls away, sits up on the edge of the mattress. "Don't you ever get enough?"

Give it one more try.
Push harder.

You move closer, rest your hand on the protrusion of her hip. "I can never get enough of you, Grace."

"I'm not sure what time my parents will be home. Better get dressed."

And . . . she's up and gone.

You lie back against the pillow, drift in a sea of confusion. She says one thing. Does something else. Changes her tone. Disappears. This is not what you expected. Not how you want things to be. Something hammered a wedge between you. Or maybe someone.

Noelle.

If that proves to be the case, you will make that bitch regret it. You have the means, and plenty of practice, to make someone's life hell. You maintain a couple of anonymous social media accounts and use them when the need for revenge arises.

Could be you once doxxed a particularly obnoxious teacher who displayed obvious favoritism toward his white students. And, once or twice, you might have harassed girls who openly snubbed you. It's even possible you circulated obscene pics with

Tim's face superimposed. It would not be difficult to create a similar campaign for Noelle. In fact, it would be fun.

> *No one. NO ONE will take Grace*
> *away from you.*

For now you force yourself to reel that rage back in, or you'll drive your girl away all under your own power.

It's back to the old routine tomorrow. Taking advantage of what's left of today, you follow Grace's path to the bathroom, join her in the shower, revel in the scents of soap and shampoo, the luscious feel of lather against her beautiful body.

"Can I kiss you?"

You ask to make her understand you want it to be a gift, not something taken. You ask to make her unchange her mind. You ask to rend her heart just a little. When she agrees, lifting her chin so your lips meet, the heartbreak is mutual.

As you're toweling off, the home phone rings. Grace lets it go to the answering machine. It's her mom, informing her they'll be home around three. Good. Plenty of time. The morning is steeped in domesticity. Grace fixes breakfast. You wash one last load of clothes, so you'll leave with your entire wardrobe clean.

You're folding them into your duffel bag when Grace's cell buzzes. This call, she answers.

"What . . . Are you serious . . . For what . . . Sure, I can come right over. . . . No, it's okay. I'm not doing anything important."

She doesn't think you're important.

"You're here with me! That's important!" You didn't mean to yell, but you did.

Grace shoots you a nasty look, says into the phone, "I'll stop by the ATM and should be there in twenty minutes. . . . Of course. Why? . . . He'll get over it. He has to leave soon anyway. I'll see you ASAP."

All the anger you stuffed earlier is released again, in a big mushroom cloud. "Who the fuck was that? Noelle?"

"No. It was Rand. He needs me to come babysit Waylon."

"Right this minute?"

"Yes. You're about finished there, right? Please hurry. I'll grab my purse."

With no further explanation, she hustles you out to her car. "Where should I drop you?"

"Can't I come with you?"

She shakes her head. "Better not."

As she backs out of the driveway, you ask, "Will you please tell me what's going on?"

"Sorry. It's a private matter."

She doesn't trust you.
But she's the one hiding things.
What isn't she telling you?

"Grace, we can't keep secrets from each other."

"Daniel, this has nothing to do with you, okay? When I know what's going on for sure myself, I'll let you know. Now tell me where to take you."

You have only a couple of choices. "Main library, I guess." It's around the corner from the park where you and other homeless people hang out when there's nowhere else to go.

This episode has ended so abruptly, it's upset the entire sense of balance you've so recently discovered. You're listing. Sideways. Back toward where you came from. The question is, can you right yourself?

Grace detours a couple of times, doing her best to miss the mess around the university. The rally's going full swing, and some roads have been closed to through traffic, so it takes longer than usual to turn onto Stone Avenue, where the library is located.

As you approach the front entrance, the question that you've been forming over and over in your head for probably the last twelve hours blurts out of your mouth. "Will I see you again?"

She pulls to the curb to let you out. "Why wouldn't you?"

"Because it feels like you're dumping me."

"Daniel, I'm just dropping you off."

"I hope so." You lean over for a kiss. "I love you."

"You, too."

That's what she says before driving away. *You, too.* That's not nearly good enough.

You heft your duffel bag, carry it to the front door. Shit. Library's closed for the holiday. Of course it is. Good thing your phone is charged. You've got some research to do.

You perch on a big planter and look up Rand's address. You've ferreted out more common names in order to dox the people attached to them.

Maybe a surprise visit is called for. A little drop-in, to make sure Grace is on the up-and-up.

One thing's certain. You'd better not find Grace with him, or any other guy, because that would get real ugly.

Real ugly, real easily.
At this point, you don't have a lot
left to lose.

Fade Out

THE END

Of your tether is a thrilling
place to reach, slipping
far, far beyond
external aid, nothing
but personal fortitude
to keep you hanging on
by the tips of your fingernails.

Oh, what a ride,
children,
oh, what a slide.

And then, the letting go,
nothing to stop you,
no chains to brake
the plummet into heaven.

What's that, you say?
You believed paradise
exists in the clouds?

No, no, my hesitant ones,
the key to the kingdom
lies in the fall.

Fade In:
SLIP BACK INTO NOELLE'S SKIN

Yesterday was an emotional thrill ride—zip to the apex, plunge into the abyss, loop-the-loop, hang upside down, and turn right side up again. Anytime you see Grace, you skyrocket. Confronting Daniel dropped you through the floor. A seizure is a sideways merry-go-round. Participating in the rally today will be a giant step toward the future.

> *Don't count yourself mended yet, Noelle.*
> *You've got a long way to go,*
> *and there's no guarantee you'll get there.*

Your heart is still the same—overflowing love for your family and Grace, contempt for that SOB Daniel, and compassion for the people you're going to throw your support toward at the university today. No. Your heart hasn't changed. Your head has.

It's fascinating how a single dose of optimism can lift you up, make you feel worthy of the self-care you've disdained for years. And now Gabriella, your new friend who might become more, has given you yet another reason to buckle down and stop struggling with your weight.

Truthfully, though, "struggle" is the wrong verb. You haven't been fighting your poundage gain at all. "Accepted" isn't accurate, either. "Embraced," yeah, or even "encouraged." It's like you've been challenging the people closest to you to take you as is or walk away. They're still there, so the game was pointless. Now the trick is to balance heart, brain, and body, in a bid to grow into the woman you want to become.

Step one: prove to everyone, especially yourself, that you're capable of handling not only the jostle, but also the intrinsic dangers of a huge crowd of highly polarized people. Your parents don't know you're going. As long as you don't chicken out before you get there, you'll tell them after the fact, once there's no reason to worry.

It would be better if Grace were marching next to you, which is what you originally envisioned. She was one of the first to volunteer to help Pastor Lozano, coordinating social media outreach and helping with the posters your congregation plastered all over town.

She also encouraged your own participation. "It will give you something positive to focus on," she claimed. And it has—a real issue to throw your energy toward. (Not to mention, Gabriella.)

Unfortunately, as this weekend neared, Daniel attached himself to Grace more and more firmly. He's like a remora, suctioned to her in a death grip, nothing but a parasite who won't let go until she's drained dry. It's obvious to anyone with open eyes.

Despite that, you expected her to be there at U of A today, with you and the majority of your church members, plus several other congregations, strength in sheer numbers. If you can yank your semi-agoraphobic self out from the confines of your house into tepid February sunlight, to stand elbow-to-elbow in the name of the cause, why can't she?

She might show up anyway; when you last spoke, she still wasn't sure, though with Daniel holding her reins, you seriously doubt it. Either way, you asked to meet up with her later and she said okay. That's important because you've got information about Daniel that she really needs to know, and obviously you can't impart it with him listening in.

It was Cami who brought you that news when she came by yesterday evening to pick up Waylon and stopped in to check on your post-seizure recovery.

"I hope you got your nap," she said. "How are you doing?"

"I slept like a baby, and I'm rock solid now, thanks."

"Sandstone or marble?" It was an old joke, not funny, but relevant.

"Fool's gold." It's your standard reply.

"Oh, hey. Wait till you hear this!"

Cami was dying to tell you what she'd just found out about Daniel. How she knows his half brother, Tim, remains her secret. Before you could ask, she swamped you with stories about their childhood relationship. Now you get why Daniel freaked out when you called him a bastard. He totally is one. It's sad about his mother being deported and all, but boy, was his father a player.

It makes sense, you guess, that a boy could grow up not quite right in the head with a background like that. But the stuff about poisoned food and midnight creeping, screwdriver in hand . . . No wonder his brother and stepmom didn't care when Daniel chose to live on the street.

All you or Cami had ever been privy to was Daniel's take, and even then it came filtered through Grace. Hearing his brother's side warped that perspective entirely. Daniel is, at least, a well-practiced manipulator. But seems he might also be a full-fledged sociopath. He's dangerous. But so are you, because you know the truth of who he is, and you will make damn sure Grace knows, too.

It's hard to say how she'll react when you tell her. As Cami said, she has a mind of her own, and she was not happy about how he tried to exert control. And the way he freaked out at you on the phone? If she's seen signs of such behavior before or since, surely she's had second thoughts about him.

Put that kind of rage behind the wheel of a car . . .

> *Tell her that. See what it gets you.*
> *Probably not what you want.*

You were surprised that Grace took Daniel to church, which has been her private harbor since her dad died. Even though you followed her to that Methodist church and she was your impetus to keep attending services there, you've respected her need for isolation within the comfort of larger communion and never insisted on close proximity in the pews.

Sometimes she'd sit next to you, but it was like she lowered a force field around herself, and you never tried to lift it. Before her recent rally volunteer work, once the ceremonies finished, she never stuck around very long, and only on rare occasions did she invite your company after.

It took you some time to understand the meaning of Christianity. Well, one definition, anyway. As far as you can tell, there is more than one, and while the designation is supposed to be centered around one Jesus Christ, there seem to be a number of ways to interpret his teachings. It's confusing.

You weren't raised with religion, and as for faith, you're still not certain you've found it. You hear it will find you, if you open your mind to the possibility of something much bigger, something inexplicable unless it *does* come looking for you.

What you have discovered is a sense of purpose, thanks to Pastor Lozano and his undying support for the Latino community. Citizens. Undocumented. Migrant workers. Dreamers. He harbors no prejudices. As he's fond of saying, "God will never ask for your papers. He loves all his children equally."

Before the minister's call to dispel bigotry, you never gave it a whole lot of thought. Tucson is a diverse city. You went to school with people of color until you finally quit going to school. Ethnicity was never a concern for you. Kids were kids were kids. Nice, mean, athletic, sedentary, smart, not so. Those traits were independent of skin shade. Yes, there was always the gang faction, but criminals and druggies come in Caucasian, too.

Daniel happens to be Latino. But that isn't why you hate him.

Now, considering your own disability, something that over and over again sets you apart in way too many eyes, the concept of "different versus mainstream" has become personal. Like anyone, you want to be accepted and respected for who you are inside, not how you look or because your brain doesn't always function correctly.

You dress for the day's occasion—in a peasant blouse and long gauzy skirt, which will mostly disguise your comfortable walking shoes. Not only will you be on your feet most of the day, but your feet will be around thousands of other feet. No use getting your toes stomped on.

Breakfast is a necessity, as you might miss lunch altogether, so you head to the kitchen, where your parents are finishing their own bacon and eggs. There's a decent portion on a plate for you. When your dad sees you all dressed up, he asks, "Where are you off to?"

No way could you have told them you planned to take part in the rally. Your mom's heart would probably collapse. "I've got a church thing."

"On a Monday?" Your mom sounds suspicious.

"It's a holiday, remember? We're planning an Easter pageant and egg hunt. You guys should come."

Your dad laughs. "Pretty sure the Easter Bunny doesn't appreciate old farts stealing goodies from the kids."

"To the pageant. Not the egg hunt. Jeez, Dad."

"It's nice you're getting involved," says your mom.

"Yeah. I get to help direct. Which basically means herding kids around." The lie slides easily from your mouth, and you only feel a little guilty. Is that good or bad?

"Sounds fun," comments your dad. "Your mom and I were going to go do a big shop. Costco. Whole Foods. The carnicería. We can drop you off."

"That's okay. I'll take Lyft."

"It might be hard to find one. There's the big protest downtown today. You'd better steer wide of that. It will be dangerous," says your mom.

"Oh, right. I forgot about that. I'm going to eat and run, and hope for the best."

You gulp it before they ask any more questions, and then

summon a car. Pastor Lozano said Lyft or Uber would be the best way to go to the rally anyway, though depending on the courage of your driver, you might have to walk a bit.

Walk a bit.

And then walk more.

> *You can't do this. It's too much for you.*
> *Retreat while you still can.*

Before you can change your mind, your Lyft arrives. Your driver is Manuel Ramirez.

"Okay if I sit up front?" It always feels weird, sitting in back, like you're being chauffeured. But today that seems especially wrong.

He gives you a quick once-over. "You going to the stadium?"

That's where the pro-immigration activities will occur— speakers, music, dancing, fund-raising. The protesters, most of whom will swing way alt-right, according to the hype, will not be allowed inside. That's the plan, anyway. Local law enforcement is nervous.

"That's correct."

"To the rally?"

"Uh-huh."

"Not to the demonstration?"

Is it possible you look more *protest* than *rally*, dressed like this? How many protesters, does he suppose, will be there wearing skirts? Give him your most winning smile. Go on.

"Hey, Manuel? I'm on *your* side." You open the front passenger door, and supposing he gets your drift, you settle into the seat.

"How you know what side *I'm* on?" he asks.

That stops you. But now he chuckles.

You laugh, too. "So, okay. We're cool then?"

"I will get you as close to the gates as possible, señorita."

He's kind of cute. For a guy.

"You don't have a sister, do you?"

You can't believe you made a lesbian joke.

It falls flat on Manuel. "No hermanas, solo tres hermanos. Only three brothers."

That's okay. You recognize your humor, and that's what counts. This is what "normal" feels like, or at least close to normal, and it's been a long time coming (back to).

Manuel knows the city well, maneuvering a maze of side streets to avoid traffic, which grows heavier and heavier approaching the university. It isn't just cars. People drop off the jam-packed sidewalks, into the streets, and it's a slog. This is only the edge of the crowd, and as you reach the stadium, your breathing falls shallow and fast, signaling a possible panic attack.

> *This was a stupid idea. Turn around.*
> *Your voice is meaningless.*

Today there are two voices in your head. The one you're used to, that always insists you can't, that you're not good enough and never will be. And a whisper that's telling you this is your chance to change the way others perceive you, the way you look at yourself. It's urging you to prove you can do it. Prove you're more than just talk. You decide to listen to that one.

Do not give in to fear.

Swallow it.

You've got this.

A couple of blocks away from the entrance, Manuel pulls over. "I have to drop you here. It's okay?"

Looking down the avenue toward the stadium, you understand. Sixth Street is blocked by barricades and phalanxes of men in riot gear. Hopefully, they're the good guys.

You thank Manuel, exit the car, and dive into the tide of humanity, most of it brown-skinned where you are. No one pays attention to you, despite your pale hue. There's too much going on beyond the barricades, where protesters are threatening to shut down, or at least shout down, the rally inside the stadium.

Pastor Lozano expected a minimum of five thousand on the pro side. Math is not your best subject, but you guess there must be three times that many, working to get through the entrances. This is insane! All you can do is fall in behind the people falling in behind other people. It's a one-way flow. You couldn't change your mind now if you wanted to.

At this point you've become one tiny part of a giant machine. You got your required wristband at church yesterday. Security checking for those and searching bags at the gates is overwhelmed. No way could they find every piece of contraband. Don't worry about that. What's the point? What will be will be.

There's a stage at one end of the football field, at least you think there is. It's hard to see over the gigantic human flock. But that's where the sound is originating from—an entreaty for a peaceful demonstration of unified purpose.

The view will be better higher up, and you'll feel less claustrophobic, so you climb the nearest stairs into the bleachers. You're already puffing with the effort of making it this far, so you take your time, assessing the situation below. Everything in here seems fine.

Organized. Prioritized. At least semi-secure.

Outside, however, there is shouting. Protest met by counterprotest. It wouldn't take much to instigate panic.

A firecracker. A backfire. A bullet.

As if reading your mind, the current speaker reminds the crowd, "Everyone please look around and locate the nearest exit. We don't anticipate trouble, but should a problem arise, please be mindful of your neighbors."

This is unbelievable. Not just the event itself, but the fact that you're here, immersed in it, or at least perched above it. Participating nonetheless.

It's exhilarating.

It's dizzying.

It's terrifying.

You really believe you've got this?

Fade Out

IMAGINE

If your dream catcher
would set your nightmares free,
standing street level
at ground zero,
a willing witness, aware
of the imminent destruction
that will any second storm
down on you from above.

Do you pull your children closer
and soothe them with lies,
fates intertwined, no way
to alter the outcome,
knowing they will succumb
in the shelter of your arms?

Or do you offer the narrowest
chance at escape, scream
run, run, don't stare at the sun,
it will blind you forever?

Do you summon your lover,
demand one last lingering kiss,
seeking recollection
of the first, that moment
among billions
when you positively knew

no one else could ever be half of you?

Or do you fall to the ground,
pull your paramour down
and assuage the need, rising
to demand for final physicality,
body-to-body connection
a tempestuous ride
upon a violent sea,
ultimate destination infinity?

Do you embark on the voyage
alone, no one to still
your heart's trembling
insistence that you could
have accomplished more,
but damn it, you never expected
your earthly days
would be so short?

Or do you look up, confidently
blinking against the silver sky,
eyes fixed upon the promise
of deliverance, praying
to catch a glimpse
of the fist of God?

Fade In:
SLIP BACK INTO CAMI'S SKIN

You, Camilla Renee Whittington Bingham, are a freaking idiot. To have wound up here in a holding cell in the Pima County Jail, surrounded by strange women, some no more than protesters caught up in a swirl of pre-rally violence, others pretending innocence for crimes so much worse than your own.

> *Ah, but give it time, Cami.*
> *You have both the ability*
> *and the means, and all it takes*
> *is circumstance to move beyond*
> *petty crime into the felony realm.*

Somewhere in your brain you must've known this outcome was a distinct possibility. You've been associating with a heavyweight drug trafficker, for God's sake. But you're just one little fish in a very large school of his dealers. It was as much bad luck and crappy timing as lack of caution that put you here.

Maybe karma had something to do with it, too. To escape the house this morning, you made up a totally false story about taking Noelle to the rally. You wonder if she actually went and how it would be the height of irony if she wound up here, too.

Rand asked you not to go. "What if the demonstration turns violent? You could get hurt."

But you owed Hector that money, promised it to him this morning, and he is not someone you want to mess with. So you made your husband feel guilty.

"Won't hurt you to spend a couple of hours with your son, you know."

Karma. If you manipulate others, especially people who love you, it often nips you in the ass. This time it excised a chunk.

You got to Hector's a little after nine. In your purse was the money you owed him, plus a decent profit, and the whole way over, you'd been arguing with yourself. After the robbery, your bank account is terribly low, and the extra cash you earned yesterday could go toward groceries or bills. But then you wouldn't have enough to score again for quite a while, and since Rand said he'd ask his dad for some extra. . . .

As usual, you parked on the street. Still immersed in the internal debate, you never noticed the dark sedans. Had you recognized them for what they were, you wouldn't have exited your car, or started up the cracked sidewalk, avoiding the toys littering it.

When you knocked, Hector's Akita announced your arrival and Melinda was called to put him outside. Routine. Inside, you could hear kids making noise in the kitchen as you settled up with Hector and made the decision. "Could I get an o.z.? I've got the cash."

An ounce would have to do. You didn't want to be in debt to him again. You figured you'd off it quickly, maybe borrow a little from whatever Rand could get from his dad and be back for a couple more before the end of the week.

As Hector reached into the cabinet for the weed, the Akita started freaking out in the backyard. "What the hell? Melinda. What the fuck's up with that damn dog?"

He tossed you the ounce, and you put it in your purse as he went to the sliding glass door. At the same time, someone banged on the front door.

Melinda came running in. "Hay policías en el traspatio."

There were police in the backyard. And also out front. Several of them. Ignoring you, Hector tried to escape down the hallway and out his bedroom window. There was a cop there, too. The one at the front door had a search warrant.

It all happened so fast, you never thought to eighty-six the dope, which was still in your purse when Officer Cardoza took it from you. "Any weapons in here?" she asked.

You were quite relieved to say, "No, ma'am." And even more relieved that you weren't in possession of any when she patted you down, not that there were a lot of hiding places in the shorts and cropped tee you were wearing.

She escorted you outside. "Is that your car?"

There wasn't much use lying. They'd witnessed your arrival. In fact, it was a good thing you said yes, because when they ran your license plates, no negative information came back. No wants, no warrants, not even a ticket. Which made your claim of just being a customer there to purchase a personal stash seem valid.

That is one of the few good things that happened today. You've never been in trouble with the law before (also good), but they've got you dead to rights on a possession charge. Fortunately, the ounce was in a single bag. Had it been divvied up, they could have gone for intent to sell. And thank God Waylon wasn't with you, or he would've wound up in protective custody, along with Hector's brood.

You've been handcuffed, stuffed into the backseat of a patrol car. Hustled inside the jail to be searched, probed, fingerprinted, photographed, and questioned. Booked on a misdemeanor marijuana charge. Allowed the phone call that will, hopefully, secure your release today, if Rand is successful in posting bail.

And then the real fun will begin.

It takes several hours, and during that time the holding cells swell with protesters and counterprotesters. Here on the women's side, it's mostly the latter. Apparently white supremacy skews male. There's plenty of drama to entertain you, and as the morning drags into afternoon, the stories become more and more steeped in viciousness.

Some of the women come in, bruised and bloodied, they say, by clubs and flags and even fists, wielded by men flaunting their white power as the two sides went at each other.

Windows have been smashed.

Cars have been torched.

Shots have been fired randomly into the crowd, people hit and hurt, maybe worse. Who can say, when you're running away?

Law enforcement has been coerced into action, lobbing tear gas and firing rubber bullets.

You could be there instead of here.
Imagine the rush!

As far as you can tell, this is all outside the stadium, site of the peaceful rally in favor of immigration, none of it the fault of those gathered inside, though leaving makes them targets.

Again you wonder if your sister has been caught up in the violence. Worrying about Noelle takes your mind off your own troubles. At least, until a cop calls, "Camilla Bingham?"

Rand has managed to arrange bail. It takes a while to complete the paperwork and get your stuff back. Well, everything but the o.z., which is now evidence. More money you can't afford to lose down the drain, along with three hundred seventy-five dollars to the bail bondsman. It's been an expensive few days, with nothing to show for it but a huge net loss.

When you finally see Rand, you flush with happiness, but that blush vanishes immediately. He's pissed. He *should* be, you get that. But you need his support now more than ever, and the first words out of your mouth are, "I love you."

When you reach for his hand, he shakes you off. "Damn funny way of showing it. Let's get out of here."

Instinct tells you to toss a joke at him, but you refrain. Inappropriate humor would not be appreciated. Instead you aim a question at his back. "Where's Waylon?"

"Not here."

Rand keeps walking, but you hesitate, anger puffing up at his curtness.

You're the injured party here.
He could offer a little sympathy.

He turns. "Can we go?"

You follow him to the truck, climb up into the cab, where you have to move Waylon's car seat out of the way to take your place on the passenger side. You touch it gently. "Who's taking care of him?"

"Grace, as if you care."

"Of course I care."

"Really. Then why are we here?"

"Because I'm stupid. Rand, I'm sorry."

He rolls down the windows, unwilling to go anywhere just yet, and you can actually witness confusion behind his creased forehead.

"How long have you been smoking weed?"

"Since the eighth grade. I used to get high every day, but not anymore. Now it's just once in a while."

He digests that for a minute. "How much was in your possession?"

You've got some decisions to make, and you'd better make them quickly. You must decide how much to tell him, and how honest you're willing to be. Your marriage could disintegrate right here unless you fight for it.

"Can we get out of here, please?" This is not where you want to give your confession.

"We have to go pick up your car. Thank God they didn't impound it."

"Okay, but first can we go somewhere and talk?"

His sigh is heavy-duty, but he starts the truck. Both of you stay silent, mired in thought, as he motors to a park between the jail and Hector's neighborhood. When he stops, he stares out the window.

You've decided to confess almost everything. "Would you please look at me?"

Take a deep breath.

"I had an ounce in my purse."

His cheeks puff scarlet. "That's an awful lot for smoking once in a while."

"You're right. I've been dealing a little. Not much, just to a select few, and just enough to earn a little extra cash."

"What the hell? How could you take a chance like that? I don't get it. We're doing okay."

"No, we're not. I mean, we're getting by, but there's never any extra. It's not your fault. I know how hard you work." You pause to consider. There's more he should know. "Okay, I want to be honest. I'm tired of keeping secrets. Tired of feeling like I can't talk to you because you won't care about what I've got to say."

Now he turns and looks at you. "Cami, you can always talk to me."

"Yeah. About what's for dinner. Can I please go to the bank? Did I pay the phone bill today? Never about what's bothering me, or what's bothering *you*, for that matter. I hear you're tired, and I understand why that is. But you never mention what's making you happy. *If* you're ever happy. Or what you're angry about. Sad about. Afraid of."

He doesn't respond. Is any of this sinking in?

"I'm only nineteen, Rand. Sometimes I feel overwhelmed with trying to be a good wife and mother. I know it was a choice I made, but once in a while I really wish I'd have made a different decision."

"What are you saying? You want a divorce, and that's why you're selling dope?"

He can be dense.

"Seriously?"

"*Do* you want a divorce?"

"No. I love you. And Waylon needs both of us. I don't want to be a part-time parent, and I know you feel the same way. But I also want to have fun, or at least not be bored all the time. Can't we figure out a way to do that together? Or maybe *you* want the divorce."

Again, he contemplates quietly. Finally, "You've changed."

"I'm older. People change as they grow older."

"But usually for the better. You're more self-centered. That isn't better."

"And you're needier. More withdrawn. A lot of times I look at you, and you're a billion miles away. I feel like you're keeping secrets. Are you?"

Now that you've said the words, you realize you mean them. You've never articulated that sentiment before. Truthfully, if you look hard at your relationship, you're not the only one who's been driving the two of you apart.

But Rand's not ready to admit it if he is. "I'll tell you this. I haven't lied to you, but you've been so untruthful to me, it's hard to understand. I wondered about all those phone calls, not to mention the 'errands.' Duh. They're bullshit. Taking Noelle to the rally this morning. More bullshit. I have no clue where you've been going or who you've been hanging out with. How am I supposed to believe anything you say from here on out?"

He's got you there.

"I'm finished with the lying, Rand. I get that it will take time to prove that to you, but I'll try. That's the best I can do."

He stews for a short while. "Why can't you be like other girls and babysit or dog walk for extra money?"

"Do you think I'll have to go to jail?"

"Doubtful. First offense, possession of such a small amount, you'll get a fine and maybe community service. Plus you'll have to do regular pee tests for a while. We can't afford an attorney, so when you're arraigned, ask for a public defender."

"When will that be?"

"Sometime this week."

"Will I have to testify against Hector?"

"Hec . . . ? Oh, your supplier? Jesus. I can't believe I just used that word in relationship to you. Cami, how could you hide this from me for so long?"

"You weren't looking."

"I never guessed I had to." A long sigh escapes him. "Ready to get your car?"

"If you are."

Do not let it go. Don't.

"Hey, Rand? What is it about *you* I should be looking for?"

No reply.

Following your directions, Rand threads through Tucson's eclectic neighborhoods. When you pass Denny's, he's reminded, "Oh, they caught the guys who robbed you. One dead, the other in jail. Also a cop in the hospital."

"Don't blame me for that."

"What? I wasn't. Where did that come from?"

"I don't know."

Is this the way you're going to be from now on? Is this kind of relationship survivable? Even if it is, is it worth the effort of trying to repair something shattered by deceit? Maybe it would be better to admit defeat and start over.

Huge questions looking for answers, when all you really want to do is pick up your car, drive it home, and hug your kid.

Rand turns up Hector's street. Most of the houses look very much like his.

In need of repair.

Crumbling.

Crashing down on their foundations. Literally. But mostly figuratively.

"You brought Waylon *here?*"

"Hector has kids, too, you know."

Did, anyway. Once again, you realize you could have lost your son today, disappeared into the system until you could fight to get him out.

"I'm talking about *my* kid. You had no right."

You need to acknowledge the truth of that statement.

"I know." And, again, "I'm so, so sorry."

Approaching Hector's house, it's apparent someone recognized the significance of the Honda Civic, parked in front. Your staid little family car now sports spray-painted graffiti. It isn't gorgeous art, nothing like the incredible murals you see downtown. Just squiggles and several unintelligible words.

But the message, front and center on the windshield, is easy enough to interpret.

Shut the Fuck Up Bitch. I Know Where You Live

> *He knows where you live.*
> *And where Waylon lives, too.*

Fade Out

IF YOU KNEW

Your time would be through
in a matter of seconds,

say staring down the barrel
of a gun, certain the person

attached to the trigger
was determined to squeeze

it, if you were positive
you couldn't talk your way

out, that it was impossible
to duck behind cover or flee

fast enough to avoid the inevitable
outcome, would you stand

right with the world, owing
not a single apology, or would

you heave a final sigh
coughing up regret?

Fade In:
SLIP BACK INTO ASHLYN'S SKIN

What an extraordinary moment in time and here you are, sunk right down into the middle of it. For once in your life, you are part of something so much bigger than yourself it boggles the mind. And, for once, you are sharing such a moment with a guy who believes exactly the same way you do.

> *For once you are powerful, Ashlyn,*
> *and you carry yourself that way.*
> *For once other people take one look*
> *and hurry out of your path.*

You and Silas are like Bonnie and Clyde, a pair of misfits representing a chapter of history that can never be rewritten. Those two went on a cross-country crime spree, and at the time were feared or revered, depending on what side of the bank counter you were on. Later, they became folk heroes, and that's what you are, or assume yourself to be.

Hopefully today won't end the same way for you and Silas, though. You'd much prefer not being mowed down by a hail of bullets.

Here you are, on your way to the University of Arizona mall, along with hundreds of like-minded people. You've been to that grassy strip before, for the annual Tucson Book Festival. Reading is your secret pleasure, and the chance to meet some of your favorite authors at a free event was almost as exciting as this. Almost.

But the festivities today have nothing to do with writers or publishers hawking their wares. The reading materials floating around will be calls to action and invitations to join one cause or another.

> *You're already part of a movement.*
> *Prepare to flaunt it.*

Ever since Friday night, when you learned about the protest from Silas, your excitement has built steadily. You've barely slept or eaten. Well, you ate plenty of tacos in Nogales on Saturday evening. Enough to fuel you for a couple of days, and that's a very good thing considering the relative lack of edibles at Aunt Lou's.

On the ride over from Tim's, you start feeling a little shaky, however. "Any chance we could drive-through somewhere? I'm not sure I can make it all day without something."

Silas looks at you, notices the way your hands, resting on your legs, quiver. "When was the last time you ate?"

"I had some cereal yesterday before I went to Tim's."

"Not cool, Ashlyn. You have to eat." The concern in his voice is genuine. "You're not, like, dieting, are you?"

That elicits an actual giggle. Weird. You don't giggle. Ever.

"Dude, the only dieting I do is the kind forced on me by a parental figure who goes grocery shopping twice a month.

If it wasn't for the free lunch program, I'd never eat anything 'fresh,' or at least as fresh as that gets."

"I'll buy you breakfast."

Fast-food sandwich, cheap fuel, which is fine by you. He buys it with change. All quarters.

"You have a mint in your bedroom?"

"Nope. Just a stash I sometimes tap into."

You eat on the move, and are picking the crumbs out of your teeth when Silas parks on a quiet neighborhood street several blocks from U of A. There are lots of ways in, and the one he's chosen is a direct route to the mall, the heart of the campus.

As he extracts the guns from beneath the seat, he looks at you curiously. "How did you talk Tim into loaning you the Bushmaster?"

"I told him when you dump me he could be next in line."

Not exactly the truth, but you're not anxious to confess that you gave Tim a hand job, with the promise of something more in the future, right there in that secret chamber behind the encyclopedia. Whether or not you'll fulfill that vow is debatable, but getting to carry this crazy-cool pistol was worth dealing with a palmful of semen.

More than worth it. You'll see.

Silas tugs you into his arms, kisses you like he really, really means it. "He'll have to wait. In fact, he'd have to fight me. I plan to keep you around for quite a while. That is, if you want me to."

You do, and that's exactly what you tell him before strapping the Bushmaster into its underarm holster, which actually rests on your rib cage. Someday you want to fire it. *That* would be a trip. But for now it's all about the show, and this Carbon 15 is hot to look at, and you look even hotter with it attached to you.

Unlike Silas, whose much less obvious pistol rides on his hip, you choose not to carry a club. They're nothing more than hefty sticks, and your minimal upper-body strength would render one pretty much useless. You do accept the offer of a helmet and goggles, however. Head and eye protection is a very good idea.

The mall is a long corridor, with sod in the middle and sidewalks on either side. The stadium, where the rally itself is taking place, is at the far end. It's fenced, and getting inside required preregistration. Participants must produce wristbands to make it beyond the barricades. Of course, a few rabble-rousers will have acquired the green, white, and red passes, but no weapons are allowed, and security is checking bags.

"See your mom anywhere?" you ask Silas, who's squinting in that direction.

"No. But she's there somewhere."

There might be a lot more people gathered in the stadium, a strong show of support for immigrants, legal or not, but your crowd is ten times more passionate about its own agenda—white lives matter. That passion is evident, loud, and definitely armed.

A line of cops in riot gear is stationed mid-grass. Unreasonably, the alt-right has been moved to the left. Actually, considering the stadium is on the right, it makes perfect sense that counterprotesters, the so-called antifascists, are positioned on that sidewalk.

Government and history are fascinations of yours, so you find some recent terminologies—antifascist, for instance—interesting. You consider yourself a nationalist, someone who believes in a strong national identity. But fascism? Living under a dictator's rule is definitely not your idea of a good time.

You also welcome the term "alternative right", the ultra-conservative umbrella for organizations gathered on the protest side here today. Some skew way libertarian, others push closer to the Ku Klux Klan or even the Nazism that you eschew, but all agree their white European heritage is in danger. You're not sure you agree one hundred percent, but that hardly matters. You're part of something big. Huge. Important.

It's easy enough to hook up with Tim and the TradYouth people, who seem most comfortable with each other. Same with the other alt-right groups, and trust is most definitely a factor. You need to believe someone's got your back.

Not everyone's armed, but many are. Some hold signs sporting swastikas or crude renderings of Pepe the Frog, a cartoon character pressed into service as a representation of the white supremacist movement, much to the chagrin of his original creator.

The camouflaged militias are the most obvious, patrolling the perimeters of your assigned area and surrounding the raised platform where some guy named Dean Green is currently yelling into a microphone. He's a total tool, and as he raises his squeaky voice to make himself heard over the shouts of counterprotesters, the noise level becomes earsplitting.

As expected, there aren't many women on this side. Perhaps surprisingly, there are a lot more among the counterprotesters, and some of those antifascist whores are openly carrying. Somehow that seems wrong, but you can't really say why.

You've watched videos of similar protests, but can't remember this many people with firearms. Of course, not every state has the same kind of lax gun laws Arizona does. People strap them on for trips to the grocery store. Shoe store. Toy store, even.

Arizona is where you belong.

After several minutes of listening to Dean screaming his ranting message, you signal to Silas that you want to back off a little, and he nods. When you're far enough from the loudspeakers to be heard, you tell him, "All this weaponry reminds me of a war zone."

"Yeah, only lacking airpower."

Inside the stadium, a huge cheer goes up, initiating a negative response from the left side of the mall, in turn drawing a raucous round from the right.

Left: *Build that wall!*

Right: *We'll tear it down!*

Left: *Blood and soil!*

Right: *Nazis suck!*

Left: *Fuck you!*

Right: *Fuck you!*

The shouts crescendo.

Both sides begin to move.

So do the cops, who call for order.

Someone lobs a water bottle.

Water bottles begin to rain, left to right, right to left.

This is brilliant!
Embrace the moment.
Step into the affray.

"Come on!" orders Silas. "Stay behind me, you hear?"

At first you're afraid he's going to try and take you away. Instead, he moves straight into the brawl, and when the clubs start swinging, his is among them. You don't have one, but you did bring your pepper spray, and when some antifa bitch breaks through from the right, you let her have it, straight in the face. She howls and backs away, then crumples to the ground.

Go after her!

Eyes streaming tears, skin blistering, she's no match for you, and you're fired up, high on the scent of victory. So close. All it takes is a few forceful cuffs to her face and out she goes.

That was phenomenal!
You were made for this!

Everything around you is now in motion.

People coming at you.

People running away.

People circling, throwing punches.

People ducking, falling to their knees.

Up on the dais, someone yells into the microphone, "White America is the only America!"

The fighting heats up.

Sometimes law enforcement stands idly by, allowing protesters and counterprotesters to play their war games unimpeded. The Tucson cops have other ideas, moving in both directions, riot shields and batons raised.

"Disperse! Disperse!"

Some heed the order. Others are only enraged by it, surging forward.

For the first time, you notice the guys dressed in black, with face masks and shields emblazoned with *No Hate*.

They close in on the militia dudes, holding the opposite line and refusing to fold, despite the likely outcome.

Suddenly, you're confused.

Go?

Stay?

Run?

Fight?

Fight!

Your mind is made up by an eruption of tear gas. Law enforcement has had enough. Goggles or no, you inhale a whiff, and it threatens your equilibrium.

"Move!" urges Silas, turning away from the melee. He grabs your hand and starts sprinting in the direction of his truck, yanking you behind him.

That's when you hear the shots. Fired from who knows where, but not so far away. The sharp reports cannot be mistaken for backfires or firecrackers.

People scream.

People dart, in random directions.

People drop.

Whether that's because they're hit or instinctively diving for cover you can't tell. But Silas lets go of you and picks up speed.

You try to follow, try to run, but abruptly you're tackled from behind and go down beneath a large pile of weight. "Let me go!"

"Do. Not. Move."

Face against the grass, you struggle to look up, see where Silas is, beg him to help you. But your eyes can only gain purchase on a few inches.

"Silas?"

He's gone, of course. Sometimes there are no heroes. Only survivors, and you're determined to be one of those.

You've still got your pepper spray in your right hand. The moment the guy on top of you moves just enough to allow a small rotation, you reach up and let him have it.

"Goddamn it!" he roars. "I will kick your ass!"

There's a vicious loud *clunk* against the back of your helmet, which you're very grateful to be wearing because it softens the blow that might well have cracked your skull open.

"You are under arrest . . ."

The cop dismounts, allowing you to roll onto your back, staring up through grass-stained goggles at the bright Arizona sky. You are relieved of Tim's Bushmaster. He's going to be pissed.

Your head is spinning. Somersaulting. Catapulting. You flip back over and decorate the grass with a half-digested cheap breakfast sandwich. Paid for with quarters.

Now you're jerked to your feet.

Hands zip-tied together at the wrists.

Marched to a parking lot and fed into a police van, along with enough other people to fill it completely.

Fuck.

Fuck.

Fuck.

You're devoid of ID, which you left behind purposely, never thinking you might need it to prove your identity to a booking officer. You were hoping to avoid anyone knowing who you were.

Still dizzy, eyes burning, you consider your plight all the way to jail, where you'll most probably be booked as an adult. And whom can you call to get you out?

Aunt Lou? She'd just as soon let you rot in a cell.

Silas? He has no legal say, though he could bring your ID, which happens to be in his truck.

Tim? Maybe his mom could talk to Aunt Lou, convince her it would be in her own best interest to have you under her roof. How do foster care payments work if your foster kid is in jail?

Here's an idea. Don't worry about it. One way or another, they'll have to let you out eventually. Talk to the judge.

You attended a protest. That is protected by the First Amendment.

You carried a pistol. Protected by the Second, although your age will present a slight problem.

You pepper-sprayed some random person. Who was coming at you, looking for a fight.

You knocked the bitch out. She would've done the same to you.

You pepper-sprayed a cop. Who you didn't realize was a cop until he arrested you.

That last one will be the most problematic.

At least you'll eat for a couple of days.

And, oh, the battle scenes
you'll relive in your dreams.

Fade Out

MEANWHILE

In a little tract house
in a decent neighborhood
in a desert city called Tucson,

a sweet little boy
wearing a Batman T-shirt
and a soggy Pull-Up under his shorts

wakes up from a nap
on the couch. His babysitter
is in the kitchen. She's fixing

him a sandwich, though
he doesn't know that. All he knows
is he's missing his mommy,

who's off somewhere with Daddy,
who's fixing Mommy's car.
At least, that's what he's been told.

But maybe they're home now.
He should check. So he goes into
their bedroom, where the sun

filters in through the blinds
in low, slanted rays. So pretty.

He rarely comes in here alone.

"Mommy? Daddy?" No answer.
He climbs up on their bed,
takes a few jumps, just because.

On a downstroke, he catches
sight of the drawer
in their nightstand. It's cracked

open a little, and one of those
sunbeams catches something
glittery inside it. Waylon

decides to investigate, and
howdy boy, does he come
across an incredible find!

This one is mostly metal,
and way heavier than his own
plastic model, but he can lift it okay.

Does it work the same way?
He carries it into the kitchen.
"Gracie? Let's play cops

and robbers, okay?" She turns
exactly as he says, "Bang-bang
the bad guy!" And he does.

WAYLON BINGHAM, ALMOST THREE

Found 9, a light, compact,
safety-free Ruger pistol,
in his parents' nightstand.
All it took was a wink.
He didn't mean to kill Auntie Grace.

He loved her, as did everyone
who knew her who didn't hate
her. Funny the games fate plays.
Wait. It gets better. So much
better. Get this. Can you guess
who heard the gunshot?

Who found the girl he might
have eliminated himself?
Say the name out loud
before I tell you or
your guess isn't valid.

I'll give you till the count
of three, or however long
it takes you to turn the page.

DANIEL

That's right. Isn't that delicious?
He found the Binghams' address
on the net and came over
to convince Grace to keep him
in her life or make her wish
she'd decided to.

He never even considered
the child inside the house
until he found Waylon wailing
because he couldn't wake
his bloodied Gracie.
Delectably ironic.

Daniel couldn't leave the kid
like that, so he dialed 911.
Paramedics were on scene
when Rand and Cami arrived,
right before one of the few
city cops not assigned
to patrolling the rally.

They had a whole lot
of explaining to do.

ONE

Or the other of them purchased
9 from Zane, either

as a means of protection
from drug deals gone wrong

or to become an anonymous
instrument of revenge.

One or the other of them
put the gun in that drawer,

within easy reach, never
thinking about the curiosity

of their little boy, who loved
playing cops and robbers.

I could tell you which one,
but why bother?

It doesn't matter *how* the gun
fell into the wrong hands.

It only matters that it did.

TAKE A DEEP BREATH

We're not finished yet.
Oh, no. Not by a long shot.

Get it? See what I did there?

Grace Joy Shatner, age eighteen,
was pronounced deceased
at the scene, the casualty
of an accidental bullet to the heart.
Paramedics tried to resuscitate
her, but she had flown
this world before they arrived.

If you believe in an afterlife,
you can take comfort in the fact
that her spirit joined her father's.

If you don't, then she's just dead.

Both she and her dad were
victims of random gunplay,
and afterward people
would comment that fate
has a cruel sense of humor.

Fade In:
One Last Time
SLIP INTO RAND'S SKIN

Guilt is a terrible thing, especially when it's well-deserved. It steamrolled over the top of you after Grace's death, smashed you flat. Even now, six months later, self-reproach hovers just there, within easy reach. The honed blade of recollection has blunted, but its scars will remain for the rest of your life.

> *If there's an upside, Rand,*
> *you've quit listening to me.*
> *I'll keep trying, though.*
> *You never know*
> *what the future might hold.*

Your entire family has suffered because of a potent act of carelessness. Cami. Waylon. Noelle. Your dad and Grace's mom arrived home from their ski trip two hours after the coroner took possession of Grace's body. It was you who broke the news.

The first few weeks after were crushing. You stumbled through every waking hour, then tumbled into bullet-strewn nightmares. You missed work. Blew off assignments. Luckily, your boss and teachers allowed you time to recover from the initial shock. Eventually you settled into some semblance of a routine.

Grace's blood was easily scrubbed away, but not the stain of that day, so you and Cami moved across town. The new place is freshly painted, every room a different color than in the other house. The fenced yard is easily large enough to accommodate the pup you plan to give Waylon for Christmas. He needs something warm and loving to help him fight his own memories.

Who can say exactly what they are? He knows something bad happened to Grace, but death is an abstract concept for a just-turned-three-year-old. His therapist claims his brain will closet the episode. You pray she's right. On your end, you hold him a little tighter, spend more time playing with him (anything but cops and robbers). Soon you'll teach him guitar.

Right now the two of you are building a Hot Wheels track he got for his birthday. "Okay. It's ready. Let 'er rip!"

While he places his favorite hot rod at the starting line, you turn your attention to the TV, where the ball game has segued into a newscast. Up on the screen pops a mug shot of Dean "Green" Halverson, who has just been sentenced for his nefarious role in last February's Tucson immigration protest.

According to the anchor, "Halverson randomly fired a gun into the crowd, killing one person and wounding two others. He will spend twenty-six years in prison."

> *He'll never kneel in front of you*
> *and scream for mercy.*

That brings a small sense of disappointment. But you take immense satisfaction in a detail not mentioned in the news story.

A rubber projectile fired from a policeman's weapon hit that bastard square in the groin. The damage was consequential.

Cami bounds out of the bedroom, animated and happy. "Okay. All packed. California, here we come!"

School starts again in a couple of weeks, so tomorrow you're taking a vacation. You saved up for months, accepted cash gifts from your dad and Cami's parents.

"Yay!" Waylon jumps up and down. "We're going to Disneyland!"

And I won't be far behind.

Fade Out

Fade In:
One Last Time
SLIP INTO SILAS'S SKIN

Tomorrow's the big occasion. Your mom and Len are tying the knot. Rubbing rock salt into the proverbial gaping wound, the ceremony will be here, at home. Which is why you're packing your bags. As per your agreement with your mother, you're moving out. And you won't be attending the wedding.

> *You're angrier about this*
> *than they suppose, Silas.*
> *If you didn't love your mother*
> *so much, you could make*
> *the evening end badly. Brutally.*
> *The Jew deserves nothing less*
> *for taking her away.*

You did your level best to change your mom's mind. All it did was drive the wedge deeper, widen the rift. In retrospect, however, the protest just might have been the kill shot. That she seriously had no clue about your nationalist proclivity means she wasn't looking, didn't care enough to listen.

Plenty of people listen to you now. Gradually, indisputably, you're becoming a YouTube sensation. You've built your brand on a simple "white is right" philosophy, and it's reached beyond the TradYouth movement, into more mainstream crowds. Well, mainstream on the surface. Beneath, they're anxious for the coming civil war.

You're helping foment that action, creating videos that stir unrest and spark conspiracy theories that go viral. You've discovered a talent for that, and are learning how to monetize it. You didn't even need that high school diploma you struggled to earn.

You check your phone and find a couple of text messages. The first is from your dad. *CAMPSITE'S ALL SET UP. TAKING ZIA FISHING. SEE YOU WHEN YOU GET HERE.*

The second is from Ashlyn. *READY WHEN U R.*

You were surprised she agreed to go camping with you. The two of you have tried to hang on, but you've been slipping apart. She's never quite forgiven you for leaving her behind at the rally, not that you had much of a choice unless you wanted to end up in jail, too.

That morning is branded into your brain, both for the powerful rush of outrunning both cops and bullets, and because it was the day Grace died. That was a damn shame, and an incredible waste of a beautiful girl.

> *When you have a kid,*
> *you'll teach him*
> *to respect firearms,*
> *and beat his butt*
> *for ever touching one*
> *without permission.*

You will have a kid one day, but it won't be with Ashlyn. This campout is a goodbye, to her, and to your dad. When the tents come down, you'll toss your fishing pole and hunting rifle behind the seat, throw your heavily stuffed duffel into Lolita's bed, and drive north. You're heading to Montana, where militias roam freely.

And you're taking me along.

Fade Out

Fade In:
One Last Time
SLIP INTO DANIEL'S SKIN

Tucson swelters in August, so life on the streets stinks, in more ways than one. Not even the monsoonal rains cool things off much. They arrive on the wind, pound superheated pavement, lifting steam into the air. But the mercury still climbs into the one-hundred-degree range during the day. At night, you sweat beneath a blanket of sultry air.

> *The heat only serves to heighten*
> *your foul mood, Daniel.*
> *No one had better mess with you.*
> *It could lead to an ugly end.*

God, how you miss Grace! Your eighteen years on this planet have netted little joy. She was the one hint of bliss you've known since your father died, and now she's gone, too. You've been cursed, gored by the horns of the devil, as your mami—wherever she is—might say.

It's true that you might have had bad intentions when you went over to Cami and Rand's, where Grace was babysitting. Her aloofness that day frustrated you, setting off a chattering inside your head, and you knew nothing but direct confrontation could quiet it.

You were a block away when you heard the gunshot, though you weren't clear that's what it was. Still, it rooted you to the sidewalk until you felt confident a bullet wasn't headed your way. When a second shot wasn't forthcoming, you continued your quest, all the way to the Binghams' front door. Behind it, a child was crying.

The bell, and your subsequent knock, went unanswered, so you chanced the knob, which turned easily. You found Waylon in the kitchen, trying to rouse Grace, who looked like she was floating in a pool of blood. She was beyond help at that point. At peace. That's what you thought as you dialed 911 and waited. And that's how you remember her now.

> *Yes, but she left you here*
> *to struggle on, alone.*
> *And in times of uncertain clarity,*
> *you hate her.*

Mostly, you're still in love with your angel, who took wing and flew home. But in dark moments, shadowed by isolation, you despise the memory of her. This peculiarity made its debut performance at Grace's funeral. You wanted to sit up front, but by the time you arrived, the church was mostly full. So you sat toward the back, stewing.

Pastor Lozano invited those who cared to share memories to come forward. You wanted to recite that poem, the one you'd written inside your head the last time the two of you were together. You had it memorized perfectly, but were toward the end of the line, and each person in front of you kept confusing the order of your words with sentiments of their own.

When you reached the microphone, you stared at those tearstained faces, and your poetry vanished. What came out of your mouth was, "She promised she loved me. She was a liar."

After several stunned seconds, you were "escorted" from the building. Rand bulled his way up to the dais, grabbed you by the collar and belt, and pushed you out the door. He never even let you say goodbye to the girl in the casket. Your girl.

Grace should have been here with you today. Instead, you're celebrating your eighteenth birthday in a homeless camp in the park. Surrounded by the familiar faces of strangers. Each has sob stories to tell. Each is happy to share them.

Better keep yours to yourself.

Fade Out

Fade In:
One Last Time
SLIP INTO NOELLE'S SKIN

It's been a rough climb up steep terrain. Six months and you're still stumbling, though you're mostly over the boulders. Now it's crevices you struggle to avoid. It's not that you can't see them. It's just that circumventing them takes a lot of effort.

> *Think of the fall, Noelle!*
> *Remember how it felt to step over the edge,*
> *plummet toward oblivion.*
> *No fear. No regret.*
> *Just a flight to freedom.*

Six months since Grace died, and only now are there days you don't think of her at all. Your shrink says that's good, that her memory should wane and only rise when you summon it. To forget her completely would be traitorous. But you can't keep rewinding and replaying that day.

It began like a brilliant bolt of light. You woke with new purpose, and a determination you didn't realize you possessed. To go to that rally, fold yourself into a crowd of that size, become a cog, however small, in a giant, turning wheel! It was exhilarating to understand you could fit in anywhere, if you only made the effort.

The violence outside the gates didn't touch you personally. But even from a distance, you could see people clashing, hear the gunfire, feel the primal drive toward savagery, and witnessing such hate firsthand made you even more determined to join the swelling movement to annihilate it.

You escaped the stadium, swept along by a chaotic human sea, but you didn't panic, and somehow your brain maintained control of its synapses. You just kept moving forward. To find a Lyft home, you had to walk a long, long way. No driver wanted to come near the disruption at the university. As you waited for the car, you called Grace, to tell her you were safe, but mostly just to hear her voice.

You'll never hear it again.

Cami came over later that day, unwilling to tell you about Grace any way except in person. You didn't believe her. "Dead? No. I just talked to her. We're going to Hawaii for my birthday. We're going to learn how to surf."

You never made it to Hawaii.

The day of Grace's funeral, you refused to go. "I can't see her like that," you insisted, though your mom thought you needed the closure. You chose a different resolution, swallowing a bottle of your meds. Every last one. All you wanted was sleep. All you wanted was to join Grace. Luckily, your dad intuited your intent and checked up on you with enough time to get you to the hospital. It was a close call.

At first you hated him for saving you. Today, you're grateful he did. You spent twelve weeks in a psych hospital, growing stronger day by day through therapy, the support of your family, and the possibility of love. Gabriella visited you often. Now she's helping you catch up on the schoolwork you missed. It's easy to get distracted. She's a great kisser. When you finally travel to Hawaii, maybe for your next birthday, you hope she'll go with you.

All's well that ends well.
And if that doesn't prove to be the case,
you know where to find me.

Fade Out

Fade In:
One Last Time
SLIP INTO CAMI'S SKIN

Anticipating tomorrow's trip, you can't sit still, so you turn on some music and dance around the house, picking up stray toys as you shimmy. Finally, after way too much time paying penance for your many adult wrongs, you feel free to act like a kid again. Disneyland beckons.

> *Southern California is steeped*
> *in crime, Cami. It would be wise*
> *to take a weapon along.*
> *Be prepared. Stay vigilant.*

This is the first time you've danced since you were at the club on Grace's birthday. It's like a monstrous weight is being lifted from your shoulders. Lifted with a crane. Inch by inch. Whether or not you can slip out from under it completely, you can't say. But you're damn sure going to try. It's time to walk in the sunlight again.

Drifting through the preceding ebony days, you've learned a lot. Perhaps the greatest lessons were the value of truth, and how to ask for help. If only you'd understood the importance of those things earlier. If only . . .

Grace's specter is never far away, and neither is the blame you bear. If you hadn't been arrested, every single thing about that day would've been different. You can't change that now. The past is set in concrete. All you can do is be better.

A better mom.

A better wife.

A better person.

Rand was right. You were all about yourself, and you're determined to change that.

The scariest thing is how close you came to losing Waylon. He could have turned that gun toward himself and pulled the trigger. Losing Grace was heartbreaking. Losing your little boy would have imploded you. You understand that now, realize how very much he means to you.

Rand, too.

You hope you never see the inside of a police station again. Between the possession charge and the investigation of Grace's death, you've experienced enough cop interactions to last a lifetime. Of course, assuming Rand follows through and graduates the academy, you'll live with a cop, and that's all right, you guess.

You can't honestly say you'll never touch marijuana again, but it won't be for a while. The judge let you off with a diversion program, and long as you complete it successfully, the charge will be dropped. That means submitting to drug tests to prove your sobriety. That will not be a problem.

They found no legal culpability with regard to Grace's death. This *is* Arizona, after all. The Ruger was returned, and Rand sold it the next day.

At some point he'll own a service piece, but at home it will be secured in a lockbox, hidden from view. You won't feel any safer, knowing it's there.

> *That's what you think now.*
> *Time will tell.*

Fade Out

Fade In:
One Last Time
SLIP INTO ASHLYN'S SKIN

You never thought you'd like camping (dirt! snakes!), but it's awesome. Being so far away from the city's illumination, it's like you can see every star in the vast nighttime sky, and you understand their light has reached your eyes from eons ago. You are humbled.

> *It doesn't take the Big Bang*
> *to humble a person, Ashlyn.*
> *All it takes is a BANG!*

It is true the protest chastened you. The bravado you felt marching in vanished when the shooting began. For one brief moment, you considered unstrapping that Bushmaster, but when people started dropping, you changed your mind. You were not ready to die for the TradYouth. If you're going to give up your life for a cause, it must be one you absolutely believe in.

Being hauled off to jail was also humiliating, especially the intake. The booking officer seemed to take it personally that you arrived sans ID. "How are we supposed to know who you are?" she spat.

But you've read enough to understand you're not legally required to carry ID. You gave her your full name, told her you were only seventeen and didn't belong in adult lockup.

She laughed. "Prove it."

At least she let you call your aunt Lou, who surprised you by caring enough to bail you out. It took several hours, and you spent that time in a holding cell, listening to women maintain their right to dissent as promised by the First Amendment. Most of them shouldn't have been locked up. It was like the cops picked the easiest targets rather than those who most deserved jail time. The law should be fairly applied.

A log on the campfire crackles, sending a column of sparks toward the moon-drenched sky. Silas pulls you closer, and you lay your head against his shoulder and sigh. "Thanks for bringing me along."

"You can really thank me later."

You smile. "One for the road?"

You know this is goodbye. He told you so, and you're good with that. You've got your own places to go, and they don't include Montana. You'll miss Silas, though he tumbled in your estimation when he left you there on the mall, with a cop on your back. Despite every claim otherwise, he's a coward.

And a coward with a gun
is treacherous.

Fade Out

Fade In:
EPILOGUE

Rand earned his criminal justice degree and graduated from the police academy, giving him the opportunity to chase down plenty of bad guys in Tucson. Cami got a job at a preschool, where she could keep an eye on Waylon while earning small but legit paychecks. Against hard-stacked odds, their marriage survived. Waylon's little sister arrived when he was six years old.

Ashlyn went on to college through the ROTC. She became an attorney, serving her country as an air force JAG (judge advocate general) lawyer. She continued to earn medals in marksmanship and eventually married her shooting instructor.

Silas moved to a compound in the Montana wilds, home to a budding militia movement, and continued to build his white nationalist brand through his YouTube channel. He was arrested, on more than one occasion, for inciting riots, though he never attended them himself. A coward with a gun is still a coward.

His mom was crushed by his decisions, but eventually Len fished her out of her depression. "Now that you're a Jew, please don't buy into the 'long suffering' stereotype, okay? You and I are a celebration." They remained happily married until death by advanced age parted them.

Ditto Silas's dad and Zia, though they never signed papers to make their living arrangement legal. Border Patrol Agent Wells became an advocate for Dreamers—the young immigrants brought to America by their parents through illicit channels.

One of those Dreamers was Gabriella's sister, Lucinda, whose fate even to this day remains uncertain. Noelle came out, loudly and proudly, when she and Gabriella decided to move in together. Her parents weren't nearly as surprised as she expected them to be.

At eighteen, Daniel became eligible for a special program that put him into transitional housing and helped him finish school. He wanted to put his computer skills to work and learn to write code. Unfortunately, he refused the mental health counseling he needed so desperately and, within a couple of years, found himself living on the street again. He was stabbed one night by one of his homeless brethren, who killed him for his sleeping bag.

It was cold that winter.

AND SO YOU UNDERSTAND

It doesn't take a gun
to end someone's life.

Noelle almost snuffed out
her own by swallowing
a bottle of pills.

Daniel went down, down,
all the way down
beneath the blade of a knife.

All it really takes is desire
and a stiff shot of courage.

Another day, Rand might
have enjoyed a personal reckoning
with Dean Halverson.

Another time, a drug deal
or robbery could have forced
Cami to fight for existence.

Another blow to a protester's
face might've put Ashlyn
away for manslaughter.

And Silas? Who can say
whether or not his desert games
caused someone to perish of thirst?

SEE, THE ABSOLUTE TRUTH

Is
people
do
kill
people.

A
gun
just
makes
it
easier.

Even a child can do it.

Fade Out

ACKNOWLEDGMENTS

A huge shout-out to Everytown for Gun Safety, Moms Demand Action, March for Our Lives, Sandy Hook Promise, and others working daily to mitigate gun violence in this country. Their dedication is heartening. These organizations deserve our support financially and on-the-ground. As I write this, yet another school shooting with multiple fatalities occurred just hours ago. It's on every single American to help stanch the carnage.